ALIENATED

··CREATED BY··
DAVID O.
RUSSELL

··WRITTEN BY··
ANDREW
AUSEON

ALADDIN
NEW YORK LONDON TORONTO SYDNEY

This book is a work of fiction. Any references to historical events, real people, or real locales are used fictitiously. Other names, characters, places, and incidents are the product of the author's imagination, and any resemblance to actual events or locales or persons, living or dead, is entirely coincidental.

ALADDIN

An imprint of Simon & Schuster Children's Publishing Division
1230 Avenue of the Americas, New York, NY 10020
First Aladdin paperback edition October 2010
Copyright © 2009 by Alienated, Inc.
All rights reserved, including the right of reproduction in whole or in part in any form.
ALADDIN is a trademark of Simon & Schuster, Inc., and related logo is a registered trademark of Simon & Schuster, Inc.
Also available in an Aladdin hardcover edition.
For information about special discounts for bulk purchases, please contact Simon & Schuster Special Sales at 1-866-506-1949 or business@simonandschuster.com.
The Simon & Schuster Speakers Bureau can bring authors to your live event. For more information or to book an event contact the Simon & Schuster Speakers Bureau at 1-866-248-3049 or visit our website at www.simonspeakers.com.
Designed by Lisa Vega
The text of this book was set in Adobe Garamond.
Manufactured in the United States of America 0810 OFF
10 9 8 7 6 5 4 3 2 1
The Library of Congress has cataloged the hardcover edition as follows:
Russell, David O., 1958–
Alienated / David O. Russell and Andrew Auseon. — 1st ed.
p. cm.
Summary: Santa Rosa, California, junior high school students Gene and Vince try to become famous and popular by publishing a free tabloid about real aliens, but a clash over whether to print a certain story not only damages their friendship, it lands them in the middle of an intergalactic conflict as well.
ISBN 978-1-4169-8298-2 (hc)
[1. Best friends—Fiction. 2. Friendship—Fiction. 3. Extraterrestrial beings—Fiction.
4. Tabloid newspapers—Fiction. 5. Conduct of life—Fiction. 6. Junior high schools—Fiction.
7. Schools—Fiction. 8. Humorous stories.]
I. Auseon, Andrew. II. Title.
PZ7.R915388Ali 2009
[Fic]—dc22
2009008073
ISBN 978-1-4169-8299-9 (pbk)
ISBN 978-1-4169-9686-6 (eBook)

To Matthew Antonio
—D. O. R.

For everyone who's ever felt like an alien, on Earth or elsewhere
—A. A.

ACKNOWLEDGMENTS

First and most I thank my son, Matt, who has guided me for years through all the best books and films in the magic world and inspired me to go into alien territory for young readers; his imagination is as fantastic as his storytelling. I also thank his mom, Janet, for making this journey possible and sharing so much of it. Thanks to Ari Emanuel for introducing me to Ellen Goldsmith-Vein, who oversees a broad swath of enchanted film and literature, who breathed life into the entire project and shepherded it tirelessly till it came into being. She is a truly inspired cornerman and partner in crime, who led me to collaborator Andrew Auseon, a joy to write with, as is the inimitable Craig DiGregorio, co-blazer of our screenplay trail. I'm also grateful to Simon & Schuster, editor Liesa Abrams, Mara Anastas, and secondarily to Mamaroneck cohort Jennifer Klonsky just for being from the place where I grew up. Thanks to Mike Richardson, Lindsay Williams, Michael Prevett, and Chuck Roven, and to Holly Davis for believing and pushing, and to Bruce Ramer, Jeff Mandell, Matt Muzio, Graham Broughton, Ena Frias, and Maria, my mom the writer, and Bernard, my dad the book impresario, who met working at Simon & Schuster when they were eighteen. —D. O. R.

First of all, I'd like to thank David O. Russell, an artist I respected and admired long before this project came about. I'd always suspected he was from another planet, and now I know for sure. I have not laughed so hard in ages.

This novel's journey to the page was at times strange, inspired, and hilarious, but also quite challenging. Two women deserve recognition for helping me emerge from the process with my head still attached. They are my wife, Sarah Zogby, and my editor, Liesa Abrams. Their patience and trust made it possible for me to produce some of what I consider my best work to date, and all without experiencing heart failure. I owe them both a huge debt of gratitude.

I'd also like to thank Ellen Goldsmith-Vein, for having such strong faith in my talent even when I don't, and my agent, Barry Goldblatt, for always keeping me in his sights. Additional thanks to Craig DiGregorio, Eddie Gamarra, Michael Prevett, Kate Angelella, and Lawrence Fells a.k.a. Abobo.

And I'd like to include one last special shout-out to coffee—dear, sweet, sweet coffee, how I adore you and your alchemical powers.   —A. A.

1

IT WAS AN EVENING LIKE ANY OTHER IN THE SMALL TOWN of Santa Rosa, except for the fact that Gene Brennick's fingerprints were falling off. He'd been eating a cinnamon Pop-Tart when the skin on his thumb unrolled like loose string and landed in the kitchen sink. "That's weird," he said, and then popped his earphones into his ears. Weirder stuff had happened to him. Just yesterday he'd been swallowed by a giant plant that lived behind the old water-treatment plant and called itself Eddie.

Gene sat on the steps of his front porch, alone. Even with all the lights on he was easy to miss. His short, thin frame was perfect for squeezing into out-of-the-way spaces, and his helmet of jet-black hair blended into most shadows. The only way to spot him was to look for the ears, two pale white orbs that stuck out from the sides of his head like a pair of raw mushrooms.

Eyes closed, Gene strummed an air guitar as passionately as if it were real. He imagined that he was onstage, jamming in the front of his imaginary band, which he sometimes called Galactic Hammer and sometimes called the Gene Brennick University of Funk. Bobbing his head, he whispered along to the music blasting through his earphones, a song only he could hear.

As Gene's cell phone beeped for 6:00 p.m., a tall figure approached from the sidewalk. It moved slowly up the front walk to the house, long legs sticking slightly out at the sides like a cowboy's. Hair stuck up in sharp spikes from the shadowy head. This was not a hairstyle. It was most likely the result of many nights without sleep and of pulling one's hair in frustration.

Gene didn't notice any of this. He was too busy totally destroying the guitar solo from Sonic Chimp's hit single "Don't Touch Applesauce."

Finishing a riff, Gene opened his eyes. Standing over him was his best friend Vince Haskell.

Gene jolted with surprise, then, popping the earphones out of his ears, he whammed Vince's toes with his fist. "Don't *do* that."

Vince smiled. He had a nice smile, a nice face all around, but he was tall and gawky. His mom had trouble buying clothes for him because his arms and legs were unnaturally long. Whenever he wore pants, the cuffs rode up two or three inches above his socks. "It's kind of hard to resist when you're rocking," he said, scratching his nest of brown curls.

Gene glared at Vince as he put away his iPod and got to his feet. "Let's go. We're late *again*. Because of you."

Vince followed, but a few steps behind. "Well, I do have a geometry test tomorrow," he said. "*We* have a geometry test tomorrow. Do we really have to do this now? Couldn't we do it on a weekend?"

"Listen," said Gene, patting Vince on the back. "You'll do fine on the test. You're a great writer."

Vince raised an eyebrow. "Last time I checked, geometry was mostly numbers. Not so much the writing."

Gene walked to the driveway and picked up his bike. "I'll take your word for it," he said. "I'm failing both geometry *and* English." Pushing off, he coasted down the driveway and into the darkened street. As usual, Vince hurried to keep up.

Gene and Vince wrote articles for a newsletter called the *Globe*, which the two of them had started earlier that year. It was a cheap publication, one they printed themselves on the backs of old science worksheets to save money. They handed it out for free at school and left bundles of it in several other locations around Santa Rosa.

The boys may have been only fourteen years old, but they were the most respected and talented writing team on the newsletter. That was because they were the *only* writing team on the newsletter. Their staff consisted of Gene, Vince, and three other students who just so happened to be their friends. The boys had once put an advertisement in the *Globe* for more reporters, but since no one else in school believed their reporting, no one ever applied.

"Remind me why we do this," asked Vince, puffing as he pedaled. "I haven't slept in, like, three days. I've been up every night writing the San Diego Dwarf story."

"That's an important story!" said Gene. "What we do is a public service. People need to know."

Vince frowned. "Well, sleep definitely helps with grades. Want to know what I got on the last pop quiz?"

"What pop quiz?" Gene asked as he left the road to avoid a puddle of pink goop oozing from a paper cup.

"*Yesterday's* pop quiz," said Vince. "I got a four out of ten. On the question 'Water consists of what two elements?' I said, 'Hydrogen and ranch dressing.'"

"And what are the right answers?" asked Gene.

"I have no idea," said Vince, "and that's my point. I would have known if I'd actually had some time to study."

But Gene had already moved on. "Someday people are going to find out that aliens like Hip-Hop Sasquatch and Wolf Boy are real. And from that day on, my friend, no one will ever make fun of us again."

Vince smiled and shook his head. "I'll believe that when it happens," he said. "I'm pretty sure they're just going to keep treating us like weirdos."

"We are *not* weirdos," said Gene, flashing his friend a stern look. "Now let's go interview Mold Man."

Jumping a speed bump, one after the other, the boys passed the crooked sign for Lodestone State Park, and then turned a sharp left. Above them a low-hanging canopy of trees swayed gently in the evening breeze. It seemed to swallow them up as they rolled down the long, lonely road into the forest. The only sound was the whir of their gears, the scrunch of the tires on the gravelly asphalt.

It was almost completely dark when they reached the parking lot, which lay empty but for a park ranger's dusty old truck. A thick layer of fog floated a few inches above the ground, swirling, twisting, spreading, as if it had a mind of its own. Gene and Vince rode over to the farthest corner of the lot, where the map of the hiking trails stood on posts beside an overstuffed trash barrel. A dirt path wound away into the trees and disappeared. High up on a lamppost, a single lightbulb burned like a star.

"Creepy," said Vince as he came to a stop with a shower of gravel.

"It makes sense that he'd live here," said Gene, pulling alongside. "Only weirdos would ever come all the way out to the state park."

"Exactly," said Vince as he parked his bike.

"Knock it off," said Gene.

Somewhere in the forest, in the fog, something moved loudly through the underbrush. "Are you boys going to talk all night?" said a strange, low voice. "My favorite reality TV show starts in ten minutes."

Out from the shadows stepped an alien, a real live extraterrestrial being from another planet. Of course, it was the third one Gene and Vince had seen that week. So they weren't too impressed.

Mold Man resembled neither mold nor man but rather someone made entirely of bumpy green balloon animals. Stretched over his body was a see-through jumpsuit that seemed to be made out of plastic, like a full-body poncho. This included a helmet and face mask. Inside the upper part of the helmet was a small blue bulb that bathed the man's entire body in an otherworldly light.

"Blue raider," said Gene, using the code word. He raised one hand, something he'd seen people do in movies when they approached an alien they didn't know. It was supposed to mean, "I come in peace," but most of the time the aliens pulled out laser guns and turned a couple of minivans into toast.

Mold Man nodded when he heard the code word and took a step forward. "You know Fred?" he asked. His voice fuzzed through the little metal speaker on the front of his face mask. It made him sound like someone taking your order at a fast-food drive-through window.

"He's my cousin," answered Gene.

"Cousins are nice," said Mold Man. He turned to Vince. "Is he your cousin too?"

"Um, no," said Vince. "But I like him."

"Works for me," said Mold Man.

Looking around suspiciously, the bumpy green guy took a pack of Super Blast chewing gum from a pocket of his jumpsuit. He opened a tiny trapdoor on the side of his helmet and popped in a piece. Then, closing the hatch again, he began to chew. "Did anyone follow you?" he asked.

"No," said Gene. They hadn't seen a single car since they left his house.

"Good," said Mold Man. Then he reconsidered. "Unless it was a cute girl," he added. "I never get to meet any girls."

"What's with the awesome outfit?" asked Vince, pulling out his notebook. "Are you unable to breathe without it? Does it protect you from our sun? Is it comfortable?"

"I have to be in UV light twenty-four/seven," said Mold Man, "or my body starts growing spores from planet Porkus. They itch, and that's not the half of it."

"Whoa," murmured Vince, writing as fast as he could. "So, Mold Man, what do you do for fun?"

Mold Man rolled his big eyes. "Don't call me Mold Man," he said.

Gene hummed, tapping his finger against his chin. "A few of us were actually wondering about that. So is it Mold *Boy* or Mold *Man*?"

"It's Alan, moron," snapped Mold Man. "I have a name just like everyone else."

"Alan Moron is not a name like anyone else," said Gene, writing.

"Do you have any hobbies?" asked Vince.

"I like online poker."

"Is your job mold related?"

"I'm an accountant."

"Does mold feel good, or is it annoying?"

"It's annoying. I can't touch anyone. I have to wear this suit all the time; during the day it's totally see-through, as you can see, so I can't go out much in public. Kissing girls isn't even an option for me."

"It's not an option for me either," Gene said with a sigh as he snapped some photos with his cell phone camera.

"Who are some of your alien friends?" asked Vince, turning a page of his notebook.

Mold Man held up his hands. "Why don't you just slow down, kid?" he said as he blew a big pink bubble and popped it with his tongue. "Don't just ask the obvious questions. What kind of story do you want to write on me? Not something like that fluff piece you wrote about Calamari Girl, I hope. Because that kind of celebrity magazine junk isn't what I'm interested in."

"You saw that article?" asked Gene with a grin.

"Sure I saw it," said Mold Man, blowing another big bubble. "I'm not totally clueless out here." Suddenly the gum bubble burst, coating the inside of his helmet with pink. "Crud," he groaned.

Opening the helmet's small hatch, he tried to stick one

hand inside and scrape away at the big splat of gunk. It didn't work. He managed only to spread it around even more so that the whole inside was streaked pink.

Just then a horn honked far away in the direction of Highway 10, and Gene turned to search the road. He saw nothing. Mold Man froze to listen, his arm bent at a strange angle, his knuckles smearing strawberry-flavored gum into his eyebrows. "Are you sure no one followed you?" he murmured, his voice filled with static.

"Pretty sure," said Vince.

Then a sound became clear. It was a car engine revving, and soon the crush of gravel underneath tires could be heard down the long, lonely road behind them.

Mold Man tried to yank his hand free of his helmet but didn't seem able to do so. The sleeve of his suit had snagged on a screw. So instead of pointing, he jerked his body forward to show Gene where he meant him to look. "If you weren't followed, then who's that?" He wiggled around again, bobbing his head toward a black SUV that pulled into the parking lot with its headlights bouncing.

"Calm down," said Gene. "I bet it's just some kids from Fulton Junior High."

"Don't tell me to calm down!" shouted Mold Man,

backing away into the bushes. "You're not being hunted! It's not your friends who are getting rounded up!"

"Who's getting rounded up?" asked Gene, wide-eyed.

"The San Diego dwarf," said Mold Man.

"I just met her!" gasped Vince.

"Tried calling her lately?" asked Mold Man.

Vince's mouth went dry. "She hasn't called me back."

"They got her, that's why," said Mold Man, nodding knowingly. "Pie Face, Window Brain, they got them too."

"Why?" asked Gene.

"Because *they* want to take us back," said Mold Man in a grim whisper. "And word on the street is they've sent someone from the Salplex Constellation, someone *really* scary."

"What do you mean really scary?" Gene said as he looked up from his pad. Mold Man replied by stepping back farther into the bushes.

Vince closed his notebook. "Maybe we should go," he said to Gene. "I don't want to get him into trouble or anything."

Gene grabbed Vince's hand before he could put the notebook away. "This is good, man. The more people see *him*, the more people believe *us*."

"He said the government's after him, plus the dude from Saucepan," said Vince.

"Salplex," corrected Gene. "Why do I always have to be the one to keep us on the big stories? Don't chicken out!" He slapped the notebook against his friend's chest.

Unfortunately, when the boys turned back around, they found that Mold Man had made his escape. The strange alien was sprinting as fast as he could across the darkened state park, one arm pumping and the other cocked up at a weird angle, the hand trapped an inch from his face.

"Come back!" called Gene, hurrying to catch up. "You're tomorrow's headline!"

"Go away!" barked Mold Man, looking over one shoulder. Then he ran into a drinking fountain. "Ugh!"

It was tough for him to get back to his feet with one arm. But after a few seconds of flailing around like a spider with a few of its legs torn off, he was gone again.

With Mold Man enjoying a good lead, Gene and Vince followed him across the outskirts of the state park. They crossed a tennis court spotted with murky black puddles. They crisscrossed a playground where two teenagers sat on a pair of swings, kissing. They passed the lake and the boathouse, which superstitious kids claimed were haunted by the ghost of a camp counselor who had been eaten by a tortoise. Finally, they cut through a stable full of sleeping horses, avoiding landmines of manure at every turn.

As he neared the information shack at the other end of the park, Mold Man seemed to realize that there was nowhere else to run. He slipped into the public restroom. It was a dead end. Anyone who had ever gone to the bathroom would know this. Apparently, Mold Man didn't get out very often.

Trying the door, Gene found that it was locked. He signaled Vince. Then he pointed at the small rectangular window high up at the corner of the building. It was unlatched, and a bright yellow light poured out.

Gene walked over to Vince and proceeded to push him to his knees on the grass. "Why do I always have to be the footstool?" complained Vince.

"Because you're taller," snapped Gene.

"That doesn't make any sense," said Vince.

Climbing up his friend's back, Gene pushed open the window and reached inside, searching for a handhold. Then, very sloppily, he pulled his body up and through.

He lowered himself down onto a toilet tank in one of the four restroom stalls, and then dropped quietly to the floor. The stall door was covered with scribbled graffiti. Weak fluorescent bulbs buzzed overhead. Pushing open the door, he stepped out of the stall. Above the sinks hung broken mirrors that reflected the sputtering light, throwing strange shadows across the walls.

Out of the corner of his eye, Gene saw a movement in the last stall at the end. Someone was inside. Gene could make him out through the cracks in the closed door.

"He's here!" hissed Gene. "Move it!"

Scrambling up the side of the building, Vince flopped through the window. In his clumsiness, he failed to look where he was going and ended up with a foot in the toilet. There was a splash and a screech. With a twist of his leg, he tried to tug his foot free of the toilet bowl, only to lose his shoe. He fell to the cement floor, his soaked sock making a squishy sound.

"Way to sneak," said Gene, rolling his eyes.

Side by side, the boys crept along the restroom wall toward the last stall. "You're safe in here," called Gene. "It's okay to come out. We don't want to hurt you or anything."

There was no answer.

"Come on," added Vince. "I could be doing anything else on a Wednesday night, but I'm not. I'm here in a bathroom with *Mold Man*."

With a bang, the last stall door flew open and struck the wall. Then the green, bumpy stranger stepped out. He pointed the finger of his free hand at Gene and wagged it. His other hand was still lodged tightly in his helmet. "Let me go, please."

"Tell me about the bad guy from Salplex," said Gene.

Mold Man kept shaking his finger at them. "It's a terrible creature, and it wants to bring us back to where we came from. And it *hates* humans, doesn't trust them, thinks our kind should band together to rid the galaxy of all of them."

"What are you talking about?" asked Gene. "We talk to aliens all the time, and no one has mentioned anyone like that."

"They're afraid," Mold Man said, lowering his voice to a whisper in an attempt to sound spooky. But with a clump of bubble gum hanging from his nose hairs, he didn't exactly come off as scary. "Strange things are happening." Then he shrugged. "Besides, you're just a couple of kids. You have no idea what you're caught up in. How do I know you're not working for the other aliens, working for the bad guy?"

"We're not!" said Gene.

Suddenly, and with a loud grunt, Mold Man freed his hand from his helmet. As he did, there was a metallic crunching sound, and the blue bulb on the inside of his helmet went out. Grinning happily, Mold Man stretched out his arm. He fanned his fingers, flexing them into and out of a fist. "You see that?" he said. "No problem."

That's when Mold Man's green skin grew dark, *very* dark.

"Uh-oh," he mumbled. And he began to change.

With a series of popping sounds, large green warts began rising up across his arms and neck. Where there were already bumps on his skin, new bumps appeared. Each one was as big as a golf ball and covered in very short, very fine hair, like fur. In a matter of seconds his whole face was covered in a lumpy layer of alien spores from the planet Porkus 12.

"What's going on?" asked Vince, writing as fast as he could but also starting to back toward the restroom door.

"My UV light broke," said Mold Man.

"What can we do?" asked Gene. But the ripping sound of Mold Man's jumpsuit drowned out his voice. The transparent plastic split down the front like a banana peel, as it could no longer contain the rapidly swelling spores. By now Mold Man had nearly vanished under the growing green bumps. They grew a foot thick over his entire body, making him look like a giant black-and-green marshmallow.

"I know what we can do," said Vince as he stuck his notebook under one arm and whirled around. "We can *run*!"

But it was too late. Without his special ultraviolet light and jumpsuit, Mold Man was growing at an alarming speed. One second he was normal-size, and the next he was pressing up against the walls of the restroom. Blobs of him began to push out the window and into the empty stalls, stretching, growing, and throbbing green.

"Come on!" Vince shouted.

"Wait!" shouted Gene. "Get next to him so we can see how big he is." He shoved Vince into the growing mound of Mold Man and then snapped a picture.

"Hey!" Vince looked horrified as six-inch-thick mold encased his arm, then his shoulder. "Help!" he shouted. Then his head was gone too.

Within a matter of seconds, Vince was completely absorbed. One wiggling leg stuck out from the mossy gunk like the stick of a lollypop.

"Wow." Gene's jaw dropped as he snapped more photos.

Mold Man continued to grow. He became so big that the restroom building could no longer hold him, and with a crash the whole thing came apart in an avalanche of cinder blocks. As he grew heavier, he began to roll. As he rolled, he began to gather momentum. And of course, it just so happened that the state park sloped downward. This was bad news for Gene, who had tried out for the school track-and-field team twice and been cut both times.

Nearly out of breath, Gene raced down the hill to the lake, the growing boulder of mold spinning behind him. As it rolled, the ball absorbed everything it touched. First it took a picnic table. Then it took a couple of Dumpsters and a trail sign. It grew so huge that when it reached the boathouse, the ball sucked up the haunted old shack like it was nothing. Then it crossed the lake—shore to shore—in a single bounce.

At the last second, Gene dove headfirst into the knee-deep muck along the shore, just as Mold Man soared through the sky like an asteroid. The world went black as a wave of lake water sloshed over him. He looked up again in time to see Mold Man bounce his way toward the Interstate.

Now, something the size of Mold Man's gigantic mold ball cannot last forever. It is bound to encounter something of equal or greater size. When it does, and those two large objects collide, only one of them will be left standing. In the case of the growing orb of spores, the only thing large enough to stop it was the Santa Rosa water tower, which stood just outside the boundary of the state park. Luckily, this is exactly where the mold ball was headed.

With a great bonging noise, Mold Man struck the water tower. The impact shook the ground for a half mile in every direction. People who felt it thought they were experiencing an earthquake. In an explosion of green fuzzy chunks, the mold ball burst. It sent a shower of mushy green goop down into a nearby field, followed by junk that it had picked up along the way—garbage bags, lost shoes, stumps, dogs, and even a rowboat with its oars still attached.

Last was Vince. He somersaulted out of the slimy mess and came to stop in a patch of grass alongside one of the legs of the water tower. Blinking, he took a deep breath and said to himself, "Whoa."

In the silence of the evening, Vince lay staring at the stars. It was a beautiful night. The grass was soft and smelled faintly of onion. The trees rocked, making a wonderful low groaning noise like the purring of a giant cat. Somewhere far away a car engine revved. Everything was peaceful.

As he lay there, Vince heard footsteps. Gene appeared, limping down the hill covered in mud, his wet shoes making splat sounds with every step.

Vince looked up at Gene and angrily threw a clump of spores in his face. "This kind of thing doesn't happen when you're studying geometry," he said. "Tell Mold Man bye for me." Then he got up and limped away toward the far parking lot.

Gene watched him go. Vince was right. They needed to get their bikes and go home. It was seven o'clock. The sun was almost gone. And his mom was expecting him for dinner.

Dusting sticky spores from the front of his pants, Gene looked around. He wanted to check on Mold Man to make sure the strange alien was okay, but he was nowhere to be seen. Gene shrugged, scooped some thick, snotlike mold out of one ear, and followed Vince across the field.

Even if the boys had looked for Mold Man, they wouldn't have found him. That is because he wasn't there. As the boys walked back to their bikes, Mold Man was lying tied up in the backseat of a black SUV. It was the same SUV that Gene and Vince had spotted earlier in the parking lot and the same SUV that was now speeding away from the state park on Highway 10.

2

THE BRENNICK HOME AT 216 CANARY LANE WAS A SMALL one-level ranch house with a giant inflatable Frosty the Snowman sitting on top. The giant snowman hadn't come with the house. In fact, Gene's father had put it up there ten years ago, before he died of a tropical disease that he'd picked up on a business trip. Since both Gene and his mother were afraid of heights and refused to climb up on the roof, Frosty just sat there, droopy. Every so often they started the electric pump and straightened him up, but that was rare. Once, one of their neighbors asked Mrs. Brennick why they didn't just hire someone to take it down. She explained that Gene had asked her not to. It reminded him of his father.

Mr. Brennick had never made a lot of money, and he hadn't owned anything of real value. So Gene thought of the giant inflatable decoration as a family heirloom. It was one of the few things he had left of his father's. He planned to pass it down to his own kids when he himself died of a strange tropical disease. Until then he'd keep it inflated, even if it meant a higher electrical bill.

That night Gene sneaked in through the back door. He trailed glow-in-the-dark green mold like bread crumbs. So it was easy for his mother to find him as he attempted to sneak leftovers from the fridge.

As Gene stuck a finger into the meat loaf, the kitchen light came on. Peeking around the fridge door, he saw his mother sitting at the table, a frown on her tired face. She wore a worn pink bathrobe and slippers with lace straps. Her hair was in curlers, a sure sign that she was about to go to bed. This is what she always did when she waited for him to come home.

"Good evening," she said. "Looking for a late-night snack?"

"Dinner, actually," said Gene, trying to smile. "I forgot to eat."

"Was that before or after you went on the hunt for Larva Guy?" she asked.

Gene shook his head as he shut the refrigerator door. "It's not Larva Guy," he said. "It was Mold Man. Why can't anyone ever get that right? They're two totally different people." He sat down at the kitchen table with a plate of cold meat loaf.

Gene and his mother stared at each other across the table. This was how they spent most nights, arguing over the sugar bowl.

"You're missing the point," she said. "You missed dinner, and I was worried."

"How did you know I was working on the newsletter?" he asked.

"I haven't seen you all evening, that's how," she said with a laugh.

Gene took a bite and talked with his mouth full of meat. "Not that. How did you know that I was talking to Mold Man?"

Pushing back her chair with a scrape, his mother stood and tied the belt of her bathrobe tightly around her waist. She smelled liked fabric softener. "Mrs. Haskell called."

Sighing, Gene slumped back in his chair. "Why does Vince always tell *his mom* everything!" he growled. "He is so dead tomorrow."

Mrs. Brennick leaned against the kitchen counter, arms crossed on her chest. Traces of a mud mask from earlier in the evening still clung to her cheekbones. "People have a habit of watching out for you," she said, "since your dad's not around to do it."

"Yeah, well, then it's their fault I keep getting into trouble," said Gene, pulling off his shirt. Spore blobs fell from the fabric to the kitchen floor.

"What is *that*?" asked his mother.

"Mold!" said Gene. "Weren't you even listening to me?"

He started to walk out of the kitchen, still wrestling with his shirt, when he noticed something odd. A few more of his fingerprints had come off completely. They'd stuck to the insides of his shirt sleeves like dryer lint. "Weird," he said under his breath. Now his fingers had no prints, they were smooth and blank.

As Gene left the kitchen, his mother followed him into the hallway. "No, it's *your* fault you get into trouble," she said, trying to catch up. "It's the same with everything—with school, with the newsletter, even *me*. You never do things the easy way. You always have to do things your own way."

"Funny," said Gene, entering his bedroom. "I always thought being yourself was a good thing. I guess I was wrong."

Reaching his doorway, Mrs. Brennick stopped and stood in the hallway. Despite her deepest wishes to cross over into his personal space, she resisted. "Listen, Gene," she said. "I want you to see the school guidance counselor this week. I want you to go see Mr. Grocer and talk. You need to quit running around town chasing 'aliens.'"

"Fine," said Gene, resting his forehead against the open door. "I'll talk to him, don't I always? It doesn't help."

Taking a deep breath, Mrs. Brennick reached through the doorway, stroked his hair. "I just want you to be happy," she said in a whisper. "That's what your father would have wanted, isn't it?"

Gene smiled weakly and shrugged. "I guess we'll never know, will we?"

He took her hand, kissed it, and then began to close his bedroom door. "Good night, Mom," he said softly as it clicked shut.

Ear to the door, Gene listened. Once he heard his mother turn and walk back to the kitchen, he hurried over to his desk and sat down. He snapped on his lamp and booted up his laptop. In the quiet of his room, he pored over the notes he'd taken during his encounter with Mold Man.

Sure, he had a test at school the next day. When didn't he? But there were more important things in life than grades. Gene was on deadline, and he had an article to write.

The Haskell home—Condor Towers, apartment 301—was nowhere near as peaceful when Vince came in late that night.

"Leave me alone!" shouted his sister Sally, who was seven. She stood in the corner with a pillowcase over her head. "I won't do it! You can't make me take it!"

Another of Vince's sisters, Sharon, stood on the other side of the room, a spoonful of medicine in her hand. Sharon was sixteen, taller than Vince, and gangly, with long arms and legs. "Stop fussing or I'll stuff this medicine so far down your throat you'll burp it up at your wedding!" Sharon shouted at her younger sister.

Vince's third and oldest sister, Susan, sat on the couch in the middle of the room. She was trying to talk on the telephone but was having a difficult time with all the screaming. Her solution to this was to scream too, just louder.

"Everyone just shut up so I can talk to Daryl! He's trying to study for exams and he can't get anything done with all of this noise! And if he fails out of school, then he'll never marry me and we'll never move to Sacramento! *So can everyone just shut up?*"

Vince closed the front door, and then he walked through

the madness unnoticed. When he got to his bedroom, he tossed his backpack and sweatshirt in the corner and then fell face-first on the bed. Groaning, he tried to tune out all the screaming, which should have been easy since he was around it all the time. He tried to imagine that the sound was the crashing of ocean waves or the gentle patter of a summer rain. This didn't work.

"Hello there, Mr. Workaholic," said a voice. It was his mother.

Mrs. Haskell came into Vince's room and stood at the head of the bed gazing down at him. There were dark bags below her eyes. Wrinkles creased her forehead. Curls of her reddish brown hair spiraled out in every direction like an overgrown plant. That was her "look"—*exhausted*. She embraced it. When you have three girls, a boy, and a baby, you don't really have much of a choice to do otherwise.

"So, how was the interview with Mold Man?" she asked in a falsely cheerful voice, as if she was really interested.

"You don't have to pretend, Mom," said Vince.

"Pretend what?" she asked, still jolly.

"Pretend to care," he said. "I know you don't believe aliens exist."

His mother suddenly grew very serious. It was no act. "If it comes from you, I believe it, always," said Mrs.

Haskell. Opening her mouth, she seemed ready to say more but stopped herself.

"What is it?" asked Vince.

Mrs. Haskell sat down at the foot of Vince's bed. She folded her arms over her stained red Berkeley sweatshirt. Her hands were dry and cracked from using too much hand sanitizer. "Well," she began, "I just don't know if spending all your time with Gene is a good idea. I like him, you know that, but he asks you to put all of your time and energy into his newsletter and—"

"It's *our* newsletter," said Vince.

"Fine," she said, shrugging. "I stand corrected. But I think it might be in your best interest to do some things on your own, or maybe with a new friend."

Vince sat up in bed. "I like Gene," he said. "He's my best friend."

"I like him too," said Mrs. Haskell. "But you work on the newsletter because you like to write. And there are opportunities out there to write. Gene won't be able to rely on your talent forever, honey."

As she smiled down at him, Sally began screaming in the other room. *"Get that spoon away from me now! You'll accidentally put it in my eye!"*

"Oh, I'll put it somewhere," shouted Sharon. *"But it*

won't be in your eye and it won't be an accident!"

Taking a deep breath, Mrs. Haskell smiled patiently. Then she opened her mouth and screamed at the top of her lungs. *"Harry, get your butt in here now and peel these girls off each other before I come drag you out of bed myself!"*

There was a series of loud bumping sounds through the wall, and then Vince caught a glimpse of his dad rushing past the doorway in his pajamas.

"Come on," said Mrs. Haskell. "You need to eat dinner."

She led Vince into the kitchen, where he sat on a small stool at the bar and munched on a slice of cold pizza. His entrance was interesting enough to cause a break in the screaming.

Vince's sisters stared at him curiously. This is what they did. Whenever there was a break in their attempts to kill one another, they turned on him, an easy target. Sally took the pillowcase from over her head. Sharon capped the medicine and put away the spoon. Susan put Daryl on hold and set the phone aside. Now they were all about Vince.

"Why did you miss dinner?" asked Sally.

"Maybe he had a date or something?" said Sharon.

"Yeah, a date." Susan laughed from her spot on the couch. "Who would Vince have a date with, Lobster-Face?"

"No, let me guess," piped in Sharon. "Martian Martha."

"Oh, wait," yelped Sally, flapping her hands around wildly. "He went and got ice cream with the Living Sundae."

The girls exploded with giggles.

Munching his cold crust, Vince ignored them. He tried to imagine that the laughter was something else, such as the rolling thunder of a tropical storm or the whoosh of cars passing on the highway. He pushed the sound, and the girls with it, into the background.

This time it worked. Vince smiled.

After a very long day and an even longer night, he was finally able to relax.

3

AT SIX O'CLOCK THE NEXT MORNING, GENE ZOOMED UP
to Santa Rosa Junior High School on his bike, trying to
beat the coming storm. The hood of his black rain slicker
was cinched up so tight it hid his face. Locking his bike to
the rack outside the front doors, he glanced up once as the
first drops began to fall, and then hurried inside. A crack
of thunder split the still, gray sky.

Once inside, Gene tore off his hood and sat on the
lowest step of the stairwell. He was out of breath and tired
and stressed. That's what no sleep did to a person. If not
for the Coke he'd just chugged, he probably would have
drifted off right there on the stairs.

It wasn't just the newsletter deadlines either. Gene
was having nightmares. They were about his dad. His
nightmares were *always* about his dad.

As if those weren't bad enough, he'd woken up in the

middle of the night drenched in a cold sweat. His head had been pounding. The armpits of his T-shirt had turned black with sweat. The weirdest thing of all was that he'd been hungry, starving . . . for tinfoil. He wanted to chew some, so he went to the kitchen and gnawed on it until it made him gag and he had to spit it out. Gene tried to explain away this strange development. Clearly someone who spent as much time hanging out with aliens as he did was bound to start acting like one of them.

Unzipping his backpack, Gene pulled out a printout of his Mold Man article. He wanted to forget all about his nightmares and about his dad. The best way to do that was to get lost in the *Globe*. It was easy to forget about his own problems when he focused on the problems of other people. Silently, he read through what he wrote the night before, keeping an eye out for ways to make the story more exciting. As if a story about a giant mold boulder could ever be considered boring.

Gene was so lost in his article that he didn't notice the captain of the wrestling team enter the building. "Dungeons and dragons and aliens and losers," the big kid shouted as he snatched the papers out of Gene's hands and crumpled them into a ball.

His ears still ringing, Gene watched the big kid disappear into the hallway crowd. His article ended up in the trash.

"Don't let Zach get you down," said a sweet, quiet voice behind him.

Gene turned and found his friend Lucy Herman standing behind him. Her long dark hair was in a braid down her back. It was the color of sugary pancake syrup—the fake kind that doesn't contain a hint of real maple. She wore a pink skirt and a white shirt with a small snake embroidered on it. Below the snake was the word "Hiss."

Both Gene and Vince liked Lucy a lot. They'd felt this way ever since the second grade. Of course, back then they showed their affection by stapling her ponytail to her desk or throwing her bicycle in the school Dumpster. That was just how some boys were in the second grade. By the eighth grade, however, things had changed.

The problem with Lucy Herman was that neither Gene nor Vince could act on their feelings for her because of their friendship. They even made a pact against any romantic involvement with Lucy. This turned out to be tougher than they'd expected, especially after she joined the staff of their newsletter. She was a talented designer and kept track of alien gossip outside Santa Rosa, such as who was dating whom on other planets and which galaxies were "Hot" and which were "Not."

Together, Gene and Lucy stared down the hallway into the growing sea of students. "Alien dorks," said another jerk, laughing and knocking Gene's books from his hands as he passed.

Lucy sighed and crouched down to help Gene collect his stuff. "Just imagine what the Claw or Hip-Hop Sasquatch could do to those creeps," she said. "They wouldn't be laughing then."

Gene smiled, pushing his hair out of his eyes. "Do you ever get tired of being a loser?" he asked.

Lucy elbowed him in the side. "I don't know about you, but I'm not a loser."

"No," Gene persisted. "I mean, like, do you ever wish people just saw you, without all the stuff that's weird?"

Lucy looked at him, puzzled. "I thought you believed in what we do."

"Of course I do," said Gene. "Forget it." He wanted more than anything to be able to bring Hover Boy or Gum Girl to school for real, to show everyone that he and his friends were not crazy, that their alien friends actually existed. But the Ails, as Gene and Vince called them around the office, didn't trust humans that much. They preferred to keep to themselves, to blend in without being noticed. The only reason Gene had any access to the Ails at all was because of his cousin Fred.

Fred, a strange old comic book fanatic, stumbled upon his first alien forty years ago, when he was trout fishing in a remote part of the state park. Ever since then Fred had drummed it into Gene's head how endangered the Ails were, how they must be protected at all costs. Of course, this warning had never stopped Gene from stealing the names of Ails from Fred's old address book.

The office of the *Globe* newsletter was located in room 113, Santa Rosa Junior High School's old audiovisual studio on the first floor. Before it was canceled, the student-run TV show *Coming at You, Santa Rosa!* was filmed in the AV studio. The program aired once a week on the local public-access television station, between two and three o'clock on Sunday mornings. It came right after *That's My Kitten!* and *Vampires: Moonlight Desire*, a show on which women in robes whined about how lonely it was to live forever. After sixth months, the school shut down the AV studio and canceled *Coming at You, Santa Rosa!* That was five years ago.

Since then, 113 had been all but forgotten. Occasionally

a teacher used it for a class project, but mostly it was storage space and a room where upperclassmen went to kiss during lunch. After Gene and Vince had asked numerous times for permission to use an empty room as an office for their new student newsletter, Principal Mahoney had finally given in. As long as they didn't touch any of the equipment, and occasionally cleaned the rat traps, the studio was theirs.

A large black stage stood in the center of the room. Atop it, the old *Coming at You, Santa Rosa!* news desk still sat covered with a layer of dust. The rest of the floor hadn't been vacuumed in years and was stained with oil and covered with crumbs. Thick power cords slithered along the ground, stuck together with duct tape. The TV cameras had been turned off and draped in plastic covers to keep out dust. All around the room, like small moons around a sun, were the desks belonging to the newsletter's staff. They were arranged in no particular pattern except for what kid liked to sit next to what other kid. So, of course, Gene and Vince sat together.

As Gene and Lucy walked into the room that morning, Lucy went directly to Quiet Matt, who had notebooks and files spread around his computer.

Matt was thirteen and spacey, with large, soulful brown eyes and a face that was both friendly and a bit shy. He typed away furiously on his computer, constantly scratching his crooked nose. The kids at school called him Quiet Matt because he only ever spoke in one-sentence bursts.

"What are you guys doing with all this?" asked Gene.

"We're creating a database of all our interviews and articles," said Matt, "so we can cross-reference everything and find information about Ails more easily."

"I'm not sure we have time to create an archive," said Gene. "Tomorrow's stories are what matter most."

"Trust me," said Lucy, winking. "This is going to come in handy. Keep up the good work, Matt."

Matt nodded silently and continued his data entry.

"Gene!" He looked up toward the voice and saw Linus, staff editor and proofreader.

Linus was plain, her short bob of straight red hair ending at her cheekbones, where her freckles started. And she smiled all the time, even when she was saying something harsh. People often wondered if Linus was physically capable of *not* smiling. Gene had tried to look this up in a medical dictionary once after Linus told him, while smiling, that a draft of an article was "woefully overstated and sadly disorganized."

Now she smiled as she called to Gene in a singsong voice, "Come over here, please, I need you."

He walked over. "Yes?"

"Good morning to you too," said Linus. "How did the Mold Man interview go?"

"It was . . . ," Gene said, and then paused to remember the giant ball of mold spinning across the park, crushing small cars and trail signs. "It was spectacular in many ways."

"I heard it was a disaster!" said Linus. "Vince got covered in thick spores, like, encrusted, you might say. Then mold guy hit a water tower. Vince lost his shoe."

"How do you know all that?" Gene asked, dropping his bag on the floor and unzipping a pocket. "My story's on this disk right here and no one's seen it but me." He began to flip through his CDs.

Linus shrugged. "Vince e-mailed us his article last night. It's already laid out for the next issue."

"Slow down!" Gene held up his hands. "I worked all night. *This* is the story."

"You can't always have the front page, Gene," said Linus. "Don't be a glory hog."

"Vince didn't even want to do the story!" said Gene. "He wanted to quit again."

"Glory hogs are not cool," said Linus, looking at her page layout.

"Leave Gene alone," said Quiet Matt from behind his messy desk.

Linus smiled, reclining in her chair. "But it's so much fun," she said. "Gene deserves to be taken down a peg every once in a while. He'll do anything to get his name on the front page."

"That's right," said Gene, feeling a little better. Then he grabbed Linus's chair and shoved her rolling across the room before walking on to his own desk.

Gene's and Vince's desks sat in the far corner of the room, behind a large fake background of New York City. The boys had pushed their desks together to make more workspace. On the wall hung their favorite copies of the *Globe*, like the issues about when they met the Shock Brothers and bowled a game with the Troggs, and the one with the time they fell into that vat of slime while chasing the Plasma Pod. Some people had trophies on their shelves. Gene and Vince had their articles.

Checking his in-box first, Gene found it empty, and then dropped into his chair. He sipped from an open Coke that had been sitting in his desk drawer for who knows how long, and then settled in.

As he waited for Vince, Gene rolled a giant ball of fur back and forth between the palms of his hands. The ball had been a gift to him from Hip-Hop Sasquatch, a teenage alien who wore sports jerseys every day and who grew hair at a rate of five feet per hour.

When Gene needed to think or felt insecure, he often absentmindedly picked up the ball and played with it. It helped him remember to hang tough like Hip-Hop Sasquatch always did, hiding from hunters, slipping into town for a burger even when everyone said, "Nice Chewbacca costume." Gene knew it was gross to play with some dude's fur and that he should stop, but it gave him confidence. He needed that during the hard times. Like today, when he was stuck wondering why his best friend had scooped him.

At about ten minutes before eight o'clock, Vince entered room 113 and rushed to his desk. He said nothing and avoided eye contact.

Gene was the first to speak. "If you try to bail in the middle of Mold Man, you don't deserve the front page," he said.

Neither boy said anything after that. This was because they both knew that Gene hogged the front page even when Vince *did* get the story all on his own.

Gene watched Vince squirm uncomfortably. It made him feel bad, because he knew he really was a glory hog, just like Linus said. It bothered him. Why did he always need the most attention? Why was he so terrified that his best friend was gunning to take the top spot on the *Globe* staff? All the stress caused jitters and shortness of breath, and it made it hard for him to concentrate on anything. It was what drove him to try and get every front page.

Was it simple competitiveness? Maybe, but Gene was starting to wonder if his anxiety was from something else entirely. Like the strange sweating, the cravings, and the nightmares. He knew he couldn't go on like this forever.

Remembering his appointment, Gene hoped the guidance counselor could help. He knew that guidance counselors usually just help students with things like college planning and avoiding gangs, but he had his own problems. And they were big. You didn't know stress until your fingerprints came off.

4

GENE'S FIRST THOUGHT UPON ENTERING THE OFFICE
of the new guidance counselor was, *How did they get a
fireplace in here?* It was a good question. No other office in
Santa Rosa Junior High School had one. Most of the other
teachers didn't even have desks. Mr. Albert, the natural
science teacher, sat on an overturned trash can. He kept
his chalk and grade book on the cardboard box he'd gotten
when he bought a new washing machine.

Recently, Gene had gotten into the habit of visiting the
school guidance counselor once a week. His name was Mr.
Grocer, and he had a friendly smile. The two had spent
quite a bit of time together talking about Gene's dad and
his job at the newspaper and sometimes even about Lucy
or Vince.

Then, last Tuesday, Mr. Grocer quit his job at Santa
Rosa. Well, he didn't exactly quit. He just stopped showing

up for work. No one knew why, exactly. In fact, no one had heard from him since that previous Monday. Eventually someone would get worried and call the police, but no one had yet.

These weren't the kinds of details Gene thought about. Although it might have interested him to know that his old guidance counselor was now on a faraway planet working in a factory and being whipped by ogres with three legs. But since he didn't know about this, he couldn't care about it all that much. He wasn't sure where Mr. Grocer had gone, but he wished him the best.

As Gene waited, he strolled around the office, taking in the sights. A lot had changed in the week since Mr. Grocer had vanished, especially with his office. The fireplace wasn't the only interesting addition. There was the private bathroom, complete with monogrammed hand towels. There was the circular skylight in the ceiling and the large overstuffed chairs with fancy throw pillows. There was the huge oil painting of a bear wrestling a Viking. There was something new and interesting everywhere Gene turned.

Strangest of all was the large bear standing in the corner, claws out, looking as if it was about to attack. True, a lot of schools owned and displayed stuffed mascots. What was strange about this one was that the Santa Rosa Junior

High School mascot was a puffer fish. "Maybe it's hard to stuff fish," Gene wondered as he sat down in one of the large overstuffed chairs. The new guidance counselor was about to be late for their first appointment.

As he waited, Gene got comfortable. Leaning back with his arms behind his head, he took a deep breath and tried to reassure himself. This would be the same as meeting with Mr. Grocer, only there was a fireplace and a wall full of African spears. Other than that, though, it would be just like chatting with old Grocer, who was as bald as a cue ball and had a giant mole on his nose. Nothing had changed. This was a safe place, despite the grizzly bear standing in the corner.

From out in the hallway came a weird zapping sound. A few seconds later, the whole office filled with the smell of burning plastic. Then the office door opened. In walked a woman—the most beautiful woman Gene had ever seen in his entire life. And she was just on time.

Dr. Jinks was unlike anyone Gene had ever seen. She stood unusually tall and wore a classy business suit and skirt. Her hair was long, brown, and lustrous, and rays of light seemed to slide across it like fingers across harp strings. On the end of her nose she wore a pair of wire spectacles that brought out the shiny bronze color of her eyes. The whole office seemed to change when she arrived, become safer, cozier, as if it hadn't been cozy before.

"Good morning, Gene," she said with a smile, "I'm Dr. Pamela Jinks. I'm sorry I was late."

Unbuttoning her jacket, she sat down in the high-backed leather office chair. For the first minute or so she shuffled through a messy stack of papers on her desk-top, and then searched through the drawer for a pen that worked. Gene also noticed that she had a couple of copies of the *Globe* mixed in with her paperwork. This made him feel proud and a little nervous at the same time.

Pen in hand, leather-bound pad ready, Dr. Jinks smiled across the desk at Gene. "Sorry about that," she said. "Things are a little crazy."

"It's okay," said Gene. "You're new here."

She nodded. "Yes, I am." Then she waved the pen like a magic wand and pointed it at him. "So, let's talk," she said.

"About what?" he asked.

"Tell me about school," she said. "How do you like Santa Rosa?"

The question caught him by surprise. Gene had gone to Santa Rosa Junior High for almost a whole year. In that time he'd never really considered what he thought about school. He knew how he felt about certain people, like Cody Waldorf, the football quarterback who once stuffed him into a urinal. Or Dawn Geyser, who called him "pumpkin butt" because of the way he looked in a certain pair of shorts. Or the countless other kids who regarded Gene as an idiot living some alien fantasyland. As for school itself, classes, they were just something he did between issues of the *Globe*.

"It's fine," he said.

"Not 'good'?" asked Dr. Jinks.

"I don't know," said Gene.

"Okay," said Dr. Jinks, starting to scribble notes on her leather pad. "Let's talk about your feelings. What makes you happiest at school?"

Gene shrugged. "Working on my newsletter, I guess. It's not really part of school, though. They just let us use the room because we change the rat traps every month."

This answer brought a smile to Dr. Jinks's pretty face. She plucked one of the issues of the *Globe* off her desk. "Yes, the newsletter," she said. "It's all very, very fascinating. Tell me, Gene. Do you write these articles about aliens to get attention?"

"Not really," he said.

"Do you create these characters because you're lonely?"

"They're not characters," said Gene. "They're real."

Dr. Jinks smiled at him. It was a smile he was used to. It meant someone was being nice to him because they didn't want to hurt his feelings. "Gene, you know that's not true. You know that aliens don't exist."

"Actually, they do," said Gene, shrugging. "Last week I had breakfast with Hip-Hop Sasquatch. That kid can put away like eight sausage-and-egg biscuits."

With a quiet sigh, Dr. Jinks shook her head in disappointment. "Listen, Gene," she said. "You have to stop believing in fantasies. Your classmates will never take you seriously if you continue to lie."

"But it's the truth!" he said. "I can take you to meet one, if you want. That way you can tell other people that I'm not making it up."

Dr. Jinks's eyes flashed, and she no longer seemed disappointed. "I would like that very much," she said. "Tell me more about them. Where do they live? How many are there? What planet do they come from? Is their leader with them? What's his name?"

"They're all different," said Gene, not finding the questions to be a little strange. "Most of them have friends, but only within their small groups. They can't go out in the open. If they did, people would probably laugh at them."

Gene paused. "Actually, I think they're pretty lonely." That's when he stopped talking.

"It sounds like you know how that feels," said Dr. Jinks, "to feel different."

Gene stared out the window at the waves of rain sprinkling the sidewalk. He didn't answer right away, because she was right. He knew what it felt like to have friends but still feel lonely. He knew what it felt like to be laughed at. Calamari Girl, Fish Foot, the San Diego Dwarf—they were all real aliens. But just because Gene wasn't an alien didn't mean he couldn't feel like one.

"Humans treat anyone that's different like they're monsters," said Dr. Jinks, her kind smile turning into a frown. "I often think they should be punished."

Gene said nothing.

"Gene?" Now it was Dr. Jinks's turn to wait.

Taking his time, Gene let his gaze wander. He saw the rain clearing up. He saw the American flag flapping on the flagpole. He saw the clouds drifting lazily through the blueing sky. And he saw Vince standing outside in the bushes with his face pressed against the window, tongue waggling.

Vince mashed his face up against the window again. It was smudgy and there were a few squashed bugs on it, but he couldn't help himself. Taking a deep breath, he inflated his cheeks with a huge farting sound. Vince watched through the glass as, inside the office, Gene lowered his eyes and began to shake his head.

Then Vince saw a woman walk into view. Vince's heart skipped a beat. He jumped away from the window. That whole time he'd thought Gene was alone.

The woman at the window wore a business suit and had small black eyeglasses perched on the tip of her nose that looked as if they might fall off at any second. With the click of a few locks, she opened the window and stared down at Vince with a pair of beautiful brown eyes. She didn't look like any of the other teachers at Santa Rosa Junior High School. First of all, she was young, probably still in her thirties, and she was pretty. Her fingernails were painted a bright fire-engine red, and her hair fell around her shoulders like a waterfall.

"Can I help you?" she asked Vince.

"Uh, no," said Vince. He squirmed. It was bad enough that he was shy around pretty girls, but pretty *women* made him feel even weirder. "I'm just looking for Gene."

"Well, Gene is in here with me," said the woman.

"Okay," said Vince. "I'll wait for him."

The woman looked at him suspiciously.

"I mean I'll go wait for him *somewhere else*," said Vince.

"Thank you," said the woman.

As she was closing the window, Vince raised his voice and said, "Excuse me, ma'am." The woman paused and stared at him again. "Who are you?" he asked.

"I'm the new guidance counselor," she said coldly. Then she closed the window and pulled the curtains.

For a moment, Vince stood in the flower bed, wondering if this was true. The woman was very pretty. She reminded him of women in shampoo commercials or the girl who read the lotto numbers on TV. But who was to say that guidance counselors couldn't be pretty? It's not like they list it in the job description.

Walking away, Vince wondered what Gene was talking to the woman about. What did he have to say that he couldn't tell Vince? It was impossible to tell what Gene was thinking. That's what made him Gene—he was unpredictable. Waiting to hear what he'd say next was often part of the fun, like opening a birthday gift, one that might get you in trouble with your parents. Then, other times, it was like opening a gift that never had your name on it, but just Gene's. Like how Gene's name was always on the front page of the *Globe*—Gene's, Gene's, Gene's, but never Vince's.

Hands in his pockets, Vince walked around to the front of school, and then sat on a low stone wall to eat his bag lunch. By now the rain had completely passed and the sun was peeking through a wall of gray cloud. It was turning out to be a nice day. Vince watched students come and go, saying hi to one another but never saying hi to him. This was just something he'd gotten used to over the last year.

As Vince ate, he became distracted. A high-pitched grinding sound kept repeating from the faculty parking lot around the corner, next to the tennis courts. When the noise didn't stop, he stood, crumpled up his brown paper bag, and hurried over to see what was going on. Anything was better than eating egg salad alone.

In the faculty parking lot, a black SUV was unsuccessfully trying to turn so it could pull into the street. This turned out to be a highly entertaining activity to watch, because the driver of the truck clearly had no idea what he was doing. A crowd of students had gathered on a small hump of grass to watch the progress. They cheered whenever it looked as though the driver was steering in the right direction and moaned when he got confused. The oddest part of it was that the parking lot was completely empty of other cars. Vince leaned against the wall of the school and watched the excitement.

Reversing, the SUV rolled too far backward, bumped up over the curb, and struck a fire hydrant. With a loud hissing sound, water began to splash across the sidewalk. Then, lurching forward again, the SUV drifted to the left and scratched along the batting cages for about ten feet before hitting the statue of school founder James Burnside. The large stone figure fell onto the hood of the truck with a crunch. His head popped off like a bottle cap. It took three of the truck's passengers—men in dark suits and sunglasses—to drag the statue off. Then they tossed old Mr. Burnside into the nearest Dumpster and climbed back into the truck.

After several more minutes of property damage, the SUV finally pulled out of the parking lot. Everyone clapped and whistled as the truck shot down the street like a black bullet. As the SUV sped away, Vince couldn't help feeling like he'd seen it before.

"Wow. That was crazy," said someone next to him.

Vince looked over and found his friend Lucy standing under a sapling. She waved, and then grinned, flashing the cute gap between her front teeth.

"Where's Gene?" she asked.

"He's talking to that new guidance counselor," said Vince.

"What about?" asked Lucy.

"I don't know," he said.

Vince felt wobbly, so he walked over and sat down on the grass. He leaned against the trunk of a little tree. Lack of sleep was getting to him. In geometry class that morning he'd fallen asleep on Rod the Bod, the smelly kid who sat next to him in the third row. And that was in the middle of a test. Every one of his joints ached from running all over town chasing aliens. He couldn't take much more.

"Are you okay?" asked Lucy, folding her dress under her legs and sitting down next to him. The grass was damp but not muddy. She sat on her backpack.

"Yeah," said Vince, "just tired."

Lucy watched him for a few seconds, and then said, "I read your story."

"Gene put his on the front page, not mine," said Vince, looking up.

"I don't mean that story," said Lucy. "I mean your short story, your fiction, the one you made up." She shifted her bottom on her backpack and flipped her braided ponytail to one side.

Ever since he could remember, Vince had wanted to make up fantastical stories. When he wrote, it was as if he could visit places beyond his shabby three-bedroom apartment, his little town, or this whole world. He discovered places no one had ever been to before. It was almost like he had magic powers. Best of all, though, writing made Vince feel special.

That's why he'd helped start the *Globe*. He wanted to tell stories. But all he ended up doing was telling *true* stories about all the Ails they met through Gene's cousin Fred. Still, Vince was the only one of them who could write well. They needed each other. Gene had the connections and Vince had the talent. The newsletter had been a partnership ever since, if not always an equal one.

Vince looked at Lucy, trying not to blush. So she'd finally gotten around to reading his Mexican cyborg novella, *El Robo-Mariachi*.

"Did you like it?" he asked.

"It moved me," Lucy said. "The cat machines destroying the pyramids, all while Shawn ate the tamale that Maria made. It was amazing. He finally trusted her."

"Yes! Exactly!" said Vince. "And then the titanium snowflake, right?"

Lucy wrinkled her brow. "The titanium snowflake, I'm trying to remember that."

"It's near the end," said Vince. "When he's in the Valley of Memory Drives, the snowflake's metallic perfection is a sign that all is ordered and safe under the gaze of the Machinist, with a capital 'M.'"

"I didn't get that," said Lucy.

"Well, thanks for getting the rest of it," said Vince, warming up.

"You should write more novellas," said Lucy.

Vince puffed out his cheeks and exhaled. "I just don't have time," he said. "I spend all of it working on the news-letter."

Leaning in close to him, Lucy winked. "Take a vacation," she whispered.

She was every bit as lovely as people thought. Her wavy brown hair was held in place with a small barrette in the shape of a butterfly, and her face beamed joy even when she wasn't smiling. It was easy to fall for Lucy Herman. That's precisely why Gene and Vince had their pact.

Vince wasn't allowed to like Lucy, not like that. It didn't matter that she smelled like a vanilla milkshake or that she made him feel good about himself. His friendship with Gene was more important.

Gene was glad to get out of Dr. Jinks's office. It was a creepy place to be, and he was pretty sure the school would have frowned upon her pet squid. Just thinking about it lurking in that bowl on the big Oriental rug gave him the willies. His appointment with the guidance counselor had been a very strange half hour. If Gene hadn't known better, he would have taken Dr. Jinks for an alien. However, no one knew better than Gene that aliens did not look like TV news anchors.

Leaving the building, Gene hurried across campus. He wanted to stop by the convenience store two blocks down and buy a couple of bags of Doritos for lunch. When he rounded the corner, he spotted his friends Vince and Lucy sitting under a small tree by the curb. He opened his mouth to shout to them, to call out, "Hey, dorks!" Instead, his throat went as dry as if he'd swallowed a cactus.

There on the damp grass, Lucy and Vince were laughing their heads off like a couple of lovebirds. One thought, and one alone, crossed Gene's mind: Vince had broken the pact.

5

WITH A SIGH, FRED BRENNICK REACHED OVER AND TAPPED the dancing hula girl propped on his dashboard. She swayed back and forth, smiling. Fred opened his car door and stepped out into the dusty drive. Above him towered a giant billboard for Crater Park, the trailer park off Highway 10 where he lived. The "P" in "Park" was a little green space man. He wore a space helmet and flashed a cheerful thumbs-up. Fred was in no mood for smiles, or for thumbs-up. His friends were disappearing.

Thunder rumbled across the sky. Fred was expecting rain and had covered his beaded leather vest and camouflage pants with a tie-dyed poncho. His long ponytail lay on his shoulder like a sleepy gray snake. Thirty years ago Fred had worn the exact same outfit to a rock concert for a band called Pudding Hat. Back then his potbelly had been half the size and the lenses of his glasses had been half as thick.

Sometimes, when the world was quiet, Fred could still hear Pudding Hat's hour-long guitar solos ringing in his ears. But those days were long over.

Sighing again, Fred shuffled up the path to his 1966 Airstream, a rounded silver trailer that might have passed for a UFO. Along the path to the door stood a series of white ceramic lawn ornaments—gnomes, windmills, rabbits, and even a life-size horse with wings sprouting from its back. Fred called them his "kids." Head down, he clomped up the steps to the front door and flipped through his jumble of keys, looking for the right one. Then he unlocked the door and pulled it open with a rattle.

A crack of thunder shook the trailer. At last the darkened skies opened up, and it began to rain. Drops pinged off the Airstream's aluminum sides.

Grumbling about his bad luck, Fred slipped into the trailer before he could get caught in the downpour. He was having probably his worst day in months. Two of his poker buddies hadn't showed up the night before to play their usual Thursday game. His septic tank was on the fritz and beginning to smell. Most of all, though, Fred was worried about his young cousin Gene, who was just a kid, but the kind that got into big trouble. And to top it all off, it was raining cats and dogs outside.

Times were tough, and all Fred wanted to do was take a nap on his futon. Unfortunately, when he walked into his tiny living room, he found three strange men sitting on it.

Now, Fred had grown up in the sixties. Those were wild times, and he had been a little wild too. Once, he'd even marched naked in a Fourth of July parade. So it was safe to say that he knew all about men in dark suits and sunglasses. Guys who dressed like that were either aliens or government agents.

"Good morning, Mr. Brennick," said one of the men, raising a leather wallet. Flipping it open, he revealed a small gold badge with the letters BSSM printed on it. "My name is Agent Park of the Bureau of Strange Security Matters. We need to talk."

Fred sighed one last time. When it rained, it poured.

"Fred!"

It was growing dark fast, and the lights of the trailers dotted the desert like stars in a vast open sky. Gene took a deep breath of the cool, dry air and wrapped his sweatshirt tightly around him. He didn't want to be out in the cold, especially not in Crater Park, which he knew for a fact used to be a military research facility. Sixty years ago, that stretch of sand had been struck by a falling meteorite that leveled the whole area. At least that's the urban legend Gene had heard.

Gene was convinced that the old testing ground was crawling with ghosts. Aliens he could stand, but ghosts were something else altogether. Shivering, Gene made his way toward the Airstream, carefully walking around the huge crater for which the trailer park had been named.

"Fred!"

"Find anything?" asked Vince, who sat on his bike in the shadows at the end of the path.

"Nothing," said Gene. "This is usually when he takes his walks."

"Should we go in?" asked Vince, dismounting.

"Fred doesn't like surprises," said Gene, hopping up the steps of the trailer.

"Well, I'm not standing out here in the dark all night," said Vince. "My mom is going to kill me."

"Relax," said Gene, tipping up a flowerpot and grabbing a worn old key from underneath. "It's only seven thirty. You won't miss your tubby and bedtime."

"Funny," said Vince, smirking.

"It was, wasn't it?" said Gene, pleased with himself. Ever since he'd seen Vince and Lucy together under the tree, Gene had felt uncomfortable, as if he were walking with a stone in his shoe. Teasing Vince made him feel better.

Gene didn't understand how his friends could do this to him, how they could leave him out. Wasn't he already left out of enough? Why did his friends have to start leaving him out of things too? Who would be left, his family? Would his mother start excluding him from dinner? That is, if he ever actually showed up for dinner.

Unlocking the front door, Gene didn't wait and stepped inside the Airstream alone.

All the inside lights were turned off, but the glow of the TV could be seen flickering off the walls at the far end of the unit, behind the kitchenette set. Sounds of the Game Show Network filled the small room. Contestants clapped and cheered while an excited contestant hurriedly tried to remember the ingredients that go into making a deviled egg. Closing the door behind him, Gene walked slowly down the length of the Airstream, ready for whatever awaited him.

When Gene stepped into the blue aura of the TV, he found a man with eight legs flopped on the dirty futon. The mess of knobby white legs sprouted in all different directions from a pair of purple athletic shorts with a hole on the left thigh. Over his upper body the man wore a

Los Angeles Lakers jersey covered with milky lumps of wet breakfast cereal. Eyes glazed over, he stared stupidly at the game show.

When he noticed Gene, the spider-man looked up and nodded. "What's up?"

"Hey, Arachnid Boy," said Gene, giving a small wave. "Is Fred around?"

"He's bummed out," said the spider-man as he flipped stations on the TV by shooting small balls of webbing at the buttons below the screen. "He's out back in his garden."

"Thanks," said Gene.

Burping, Arachnid Boy shot a long stream of web over Gene's shoulder, snagging the half-empty box of Rice Blocks and whipping it back into his open hand. "Here's a warning," he mumbled. "The dude is in a mood."

Out behind the trailer, Gene found his cousin Fred sitting in the place he called his Groovy Garden. It was little more than a series of concentric rings that Fred had arranged on the ground using smooth circular stones. Around him on the scraggly desert trees, crystals dangled from bits of twine. Every prism gave off a fractured light and colored the red sand with rainbows. In the middle of the garden, Fred sat in a saggy green lawn chair, his shirt still unbuttoned from catching rays earlier in the day. The entire garden, including Fred, perched dangerously close to the steep edge of the crater.

"You stole a name from my address book again, didn't you?" said Fred, not opening his eyes.

Gene stayed outside the ring of stones. He was worried that he'd get cursed or something if he stepped over the line. "What address book?"

"Don't play dumb," said Fred.

"Then I guess I'm just dumb," said Gene, lying.

"Well, something you did was picked up by the BSSSS something," continued Fred, standing up and buttoning his shirt.

"BSSM?" asked Gene, pretending he didn't know what Fred was talking about.

"Does it matter?" snapped Fred. "There was a report of a giant boulder rolling through Lodestone State Park two nights ago, and now the government is sniffing around." He whipped off his sunglasses. "They were here, Gene! At my home, asking questions."

"Sounds exciting," said Gene, still acting.

"Well, it's not," said Fred. He stepped over the stone rings and up to Gene. "Don't you remember what happened with Ron?" he said, gesturing to the trailer behind him.

"Who's Ron?" asked Gene.

"Ron!" said Fred, throwing his arms into the air. *"Arachnid Boy!"*

"Remember my name, dude!" came Ron's shout from inside the trailer. "I remember yours!"

Gene suddenly understood. And he remembered very well what had happened with Ron.

About forty years ago, Fred met an alien named Arachnid Boy from the Bulgar Cluster, a galaxy about ten million light years beyond Neptune. At the time, Fred was a struggling artist. One day he had the bright idea to write a comic book about his new friend, who had the power to shoot webs out of his hands and could climb up walls. Fred pitched the idea to several publishing houses. They all turned him down, only for him to wake up one day and find out that the Arachnid Boy idea had been stolen. A big comic book company published the story under the title of Spider Guy or Web Thrower or something like that. And they hadn't even used Arachnid Boy's real powers, like his eight awesome legs or his ability to lay eggs.

Fred hadn't seen a dime. Worse, though, was the irony that the world would gladly accept a pretend freak spider-man, while the real one had to hide for fear of being carted off to a government research lab or being hunted by a mob.

Sitting down on the back step of the trailer, Fred patted the space next to him. Gene hesitated for a second and then he sat too. They watched the heat shimmer over the faraway dunes. The only sound was the creaking of a crooked telephone pole.

"I can't prove that you stole a name out of my address book," said Fred. "But if you did, make sure it's the last time. The aliens listed in there are not to be fooled with. I know they're exciting; I know you want to show off. You've gotten it into your head to be a big shot, to prove to everyone how cool you are. But this is bigger than you, Gene. It's bigger than all of us. You'll figure that out someday."

"How big is it?" scoffed Gene.

"You want to know how big it is?" asked Fred, clucking his tongue. "You know plenty of aliens, Gene, but you've never met any of the *bad* ones. And trust me, boy. There are some real nasty suckers who want to be left alone and will *not* react well if they are bothered, just like the rattlers I showed you in the mountains as a kid." He picked up a small white stone and tossed it far into the next trailer's yard. "You've got to ask yourself if popularity is more important than avoiding bringing a whole universe of hurt down on our heads."

"It doesn't even make me popular!" cried Gene. "Everybody makes fun of me!"

"But you want to prove them wrong and you don't care which Ails you hurt to do it," said Fred.

"I'll keep that in mind next time I *don't* steal a name from your address book," said Gene.

Sighing, Fred clucked his tongue again. Every time they saw each other, the old man seemed even more disappointed in him. "So, are you going to come visit my booth at Comic Mania next week?"

Comic Mania was a crummy little comic convention held annually at the Santa Rosa Holiday Inn. Despite his lack of success with the *Arachnid Boy* comic, Fred continued to write and draw issues from his trailer in Crater Park. Every year, like clockwork, he set up a small card table inside the ballroom of the hotel and handed out free copies. Gene had promised to attend the convention several times but had never showed up.

"School is keeping me pretty busy," said Gene.

"If only I believed that," murmured Fred.

"Don't you believe anything I tell you?" asked Gene, irritated.

Fred clucked his tongue. "Nope," he said.

• • •

A few minutes after they'd said good night to Fred, the boys snuck back to the rear of the Airstream. They waited until Fred was safely engrossed in his nightly reruns of *Star Trek* before climbing in through the back window of the trailer. Behind them, the sun slowly sank down into the rolling desert hills.

Vince braced himself against the side of the trailer as Gene stood on his shoulders, pawing around inside Fred's nightstand for the address book. This was how they'd always done it. It wasn't graceful, but it was effective. Paging through the faded black address book, Gene searched for a name he didn't recognize, an alien they had yet to interview. The flashlight beam wobbled as he tried to read. "Hold still!" he hissed at Vince, who was holding his legs. "And stop touching my butt!"

"I'm trying not to drop you. Hurry up," Vince replied. He was acting as the lookout. Trying to stay balanced, he kept an eye on the back of Fred's head through the window at the other end of the Airstream.

On page forty-seven, Gene found a name he didn't recognize and wrote it on the palm of his hand in black marker: *Crumble Bun*. Then, shutting the address book with a puff of dust, he gave the sign—a whistle—and Vince brought him back down to earth.

In a hurry, the two of them walked away from the trailer to where their bikes were parked at the end of Fred's dusty driveway. Mounting up, they began to slowly pedal down the curving road leading out of Crater Park and back to Highway 10. As they coasted, they heard a call of, "Catch you dogs later," through an open window. Arachnid Boy lay sprawled on the dirty futon.

"What does Fred know, anyway?" grumbled Gene, riding over a white lawn gnome. "He spends half his day watching the Game Show Network."

Vince had a strong opinion on this subject, but he kept his mouth shut.

Sensing this, Gene shot his friend a look. "Do you think he's right or something?"

"I don't know," said Vince, dipping through a pothole. "You're kind of lying to him. He trusts you."

All of the anger and confusion that Gene had been carrying since earlier in the day exploded out of him. "What do you know about trust, dude!" he shouted. "You're a traitor! I saw you with Lucy. I saw the two of you flirting and laughing!"

Vince's eyebrows shot up with anger. "No way!" he protested, barely able to contain himself. "She compli- mented my novella. She was being nice. But I got up and left. Why? To honor the pact, that's why!"

"Yeah, right," Gene said, hitting his brakes. He ground to a stop in the gravel. A dust cloud rose up around him. "Since when did you call it a 'novella'? That's Lucy's word, not yours. You don't even know what that means."

"I swear, Gene, I—"

But Gene cut him off. "Next time you want to steal my headline and future girlfriend in the same day, let me know. Okay?" He pointed his finger right in Vince's face.

That's when Vince noticed a string of skin hanging from Gene's fingertip. "What's wrong?" he asked. "Is everything okay?"

Gene glanced down with shock as the last of his fingerprints unraveled from the index finger of his left hand. "Don't try to change the subject!" he snapped, self-consciously hiding his hand behind his back.

But Vince didn't respond, he just shook his head and rode away in a blur toward the highway, his gears clicking.

"Okay, fine!" shouted Gene as he watched him go. "You're forgiven for the Lucy thing! Hey, come back!"

Vince rode away on the shoulder of two-lane Highway 10.

"Did you hear me?" shouted Gene, feeling lonelier the farther away his friend got. "All is forgiven!"

Glancing around anxiously, Gene started to pedal again. It was almost completely dark out, and he didn't want to get caught in the dunes with all the wandering ghosts. Not that he believed in nonsense like that.

MOST MORNINGS, GENE WAS IN TOO MUCH OF A HURRY
to sit and eat. It was something his mother never stopped
worrying about. Instead, Gene might slurp a can of Coke
on his way out the door. Or he'd munch on a bag of
cheese curls as he waited for the bus, topping it off with
a mouthful of popping purple candy rocks. His dentist
called Gene "the greatest challenge of his career," and he'd
written several articles about him for a journal called *Your
Teeth and Gums*. Needless to say, Gene had a sweet tooth.

Out of all the sugary delights in the world, Gene's
secret weakness was doughnuts. He loved the colored icing,
how the powdered sugar stayed on his clothes long after he
was finished eating. When he found the time—and the
money—Gene would bike to Dippin Donuts for a special
breakfast of pastry.

That Friday morning, however, Gene was biking to

Dippin Donuts for a special breakfast *with* pastry. Her name was Crumble Bun, and she was an alien from the planet Waldorf in the Centrino System.

Sweatshirt hoods up, Gene and Vince steered their bikes down the old gulch road, avoiding potholes and shouting over the whir of their spinning tires. They headed for Dippin Donuts as fast as they could pedal. It was a beautiful morning, but they hardly even noticed the bright sunrise as it rose over the giant metal doughnut in the distance. That's because they were on the job. They never seemed to be anything else.

"So Crumble Bun turns stuff to pastry?" asked Vince.

"No, she crumbles things she touches, alters their molecular structure or something," said Gene. "I didn't have time to read Fred's notes. I barely understand them anyway."

Vince shook his head. "That's got to be the world's worst superpower."

"I don't know," said Gene. "Remember that kid who occasionally floats away?"

Both of them remembered back to the time they wrote a cover story on Hover Boy, a pudgy alien from the nearby town of Fulton. All during their interview, Hover Boy kept drifting into the nearby trees, until he caught a trouser leg on a rain gutter. Gene and Vince had to climb onto the roof to pull him down before he floated into the power lines. It had been one of their more irritating adventures and one of the more boring newsletter cover stories.

Swerving into the Dippin Donuts parking lot, they buzzed the front windows and coasted around the building. The back lot was just a small square of black asphalt, empty but for a pair of Dumpsters overflowing with trash bags. A box of day-old doughnuts sat out back for anyone who wanted to snatch one. By now the birds and raccoons had torn the dough to shreds, leaving nothing but red filling that was teeming with ants.

"Yum," said Vince as he passed the box, sticking out his tongue.

They buzzed the lot again. When Gene saw for sure that no one was waiting for them, he slammed on his brakes. "She's not here, man!"

"Too bad," said Vince, and he circled the Dumpsters. "Guess we'll have to make another appointment."

"We don't have time for that," said Gene, growing impatient. He slumped over on his handlebars. "We have to publish another issue by next week."

Vince came to a stop with a squelch of his tires. "We'll

just be a few days late. It's not a big deal." He eyed the posters of pink frosted snacks on the back wall of Dippin Donuts. "Besides, we deserve a vacation."

"We can't wait," said Gene sternly.

"Why not?" asked Vince.

"Because," said Gene, "all the kids who think the stories are fake will think we've given up. It'll be like they were right."

"Who cares?" asked Vince. "I thought the *Globe* was supposed to be fun."

This made Gene laugh. He turned and glared at his friend. "I forgot. You're a traitor now who's writing novellas for Lucy."

Vince returned the glare. "You still got that wrong, but traitor or not, I want a doughnut," he said, opening his bike's kickstand. "You want one?"

"Always," said Gene as he checked his watch.

Tugging his wallet from his jeans pocket, Vince hopped off his bike and hurried around to the front of the store. A minute later he returned carrying a blue-and-white-striped Dippin Donuts bag. Gene was right where he'd left him, perched on the handlebars of his bike, scowling at the Dumpsters, as if staring harder was going to make an alien appear.

Vince sat next to Gene on his own bike and began to eat. After a few bites and a few more minutes, he finally spoke. "Shouldn't we go?" he asked, licking icing off his hand. "You know, to school? It starts in about twenty minutes. I want to get there in time for the test."

"We're waiting until she gets here," said Gene.

"*You're* waiting until she gets here," said Vince. "I'm waiting until eight o'clock, and then I'm leaving for the math test."

"Traitor," murmured Gene. "I'll make you stay. Then you can try to get the front page again. You're welcome."

"Whatever," said Vince as he unzipped his backpack and took out his geometry textbook. He opened it to chapter fourteen. Then he flattened a study worksheet against Gene's back so he could write on it. Uncapping his pen, Vince tried to concentrate. "Okay, so if a is the area of the large square, and b is the area of the small square, then what is a divided by b?" As he talked, he sprayed powdered sugar from the doughnut he was eating across Gene's back.

"Hey, control the crumbs," said Gene, brushing his shoulder. He was busy watching the driveway. If Crumble Bun was still coming to meet them, she'd come from that direction. It was the only way into the back lot.

As Gene waited, focused, the flurry of crumbs continued falling. "I said watch it," he grumbled. "You're getting junk all over my best Hogwarts shirt. I got this at a book signing, man." Even as he protested, the white powdery pieces kept coming, like a sweet, sugary snowfall. He swiped at his shirt some more. "What are you, a buzz saw? Slow down, or you're going to choke on your wrist."

There was a tap on Gene's shoulder. "What?" he barked. When he spun around to face Vince, he saw that his friend's face had gone white, the color of the egg salad his mom always packed in his lunch bag.

"Dude, my doughnut's gone," said Vince.

The boys looked up into the rain of crumbs, craning their necks to see where it was coming from. A girl stood above them on the Dumpster. She looked to be about fifteen, was pleasantly plump, cute, even. And when she raised her hand to wave, crumbs sprayed from inside her sleeve and also tumbled out the bottom of her coat.

"Sorry I'm late," she said.

Crumble Bun wore a black trench coat the size of a small tent. It had been buttoned all the way up to her neck. The dark sleeves and collar were streaked with powdered and brown sugar. This was evidence of her alien powers to turn everything she touched into a substance that looked a lot like coffee cake.

Whether or not this substance was actually coffee cake remained a mystery. No one had ever eaten it, not even those who knew Crumble Bun well. This isn't surprising. Few people find the idea of snacking on their friends appetizing.

"Crumble Bun, it's an honor," said Gene, looking up in awe but also brushing falling crumbs from his face.

"Call me Cathy," said the girl, who smelled of cinnamon and cat food. She wore black gloves that stretched all the way to her elbows.

"*Cathy* Crumble Bun?" asked Gene, still swiping at his face. "Is that your full name? Is that how names work on Waldorf?"

"No. My name's just Cathy," she said. "And I'm not from Waldorf. I'm from Ascot. It's two moons over."

The boys wheeled back a few feet so they were safely out of the crumble trickle. Vince stuffed his geometry worksheet into his backpack and took out his notebook. Then he glanced at Gene, waiting for him to start the questions. Gene glanced back at Vince, making sure he had his pen ready. This was how they always did it. They were a team.

Gene waved. "I'm Gene," he said, "and this is Vince." Then he gazed around the deserted parking lot. "Do you want a ladder or something, so you can come down?"

"Or a doughnut?" asked Vince, holding up his crumpled bag.

Gene elbowed Vince hard, still flashing his friendly smile. "You think she needs a doughnut?" he hissed. "She practically *is* a doughnut."

"I don't need a ladder," said Crumble Bun. Slipping one of her bare feet from its special sandal, she tapped a toe against the second Dumpster and turned it into a ramp of sliding brown crumbs. This happened silently, and if the boys had looked away for more than a second, they would have missed it.

"Awesome," wheezed Gene, as she came down the ramp.

Once Crumble Bun's sandal touched concrete, she stared awkwardly at the bag of doughnuts in Vince's hand. "You can have one if you like," Vince offered again. Cautiously, like a deer taking food from a person's hand, she reached out a black gloved hand to take the doughnut he offered and nibbled at it shyly, crumbs falling to the ground. "Sometimes I get so lonely," she said between swallows. "I dream about eating myself." She took quick breaths between bites. "I wouldn't need anybody because I would just need me. Can you imagine that? All I'd have to do would be to start nibbling a finger, and then it'd be all over."

This made Vince feel a little sick to his stomach. He let her keep the rest of the doughnuts.

As she finished what was in the bag, Crumble Bun looked around nervously. "Is anyone with you?"

"No, why?" asked Gene.

"I don't want to get snatched up," she answered.

"Mold Man said something about that too," said Vince.

Crumble Bun nodded. "I haven't seen Alan in days. I'm worried he was taken."

Vince started to scrawl notes on the top sheet of paper.

"Who's taking all the Ails?" asked Gene.

"The one who was sent to find us, to bring us back," said Crumble Bun. "I knew it was going to happen some-day, but all my friends said the chances were slim. Look at us now—afraid, lonely." She dabbed at an eye. "I'm *so* lonely, so tired of hiding. You know? I don't even care any-more. I'd let myself get seen by other humans if it meant finding some friends."

"Is the one looking for you a bad alien?" asked Vince, writing.

"The worst," said Crumble Bun, nodding. "Mean as they come."

Gene and Vince looked at each other. After almost a whole year of interviewing aliens, the recent accounts of *other, meaner* aliens were the first the boys had heard. This news affected the boys in two very different ways. Gene saw it as an opportunity, and he immediately started daydreaming about uncovering a dangerous intergalactic conspiracy. Vince, on the other hand, saw another group of aliens as one more thing that would keep him up at night and get in the way of his schoolwork. They looked back at Crumble Bun.

Vince checked the deserted parking lot one more time. "There's no one here but us," he said.

"That means you can tell us everything," said Gene.

Crumble Bun nervously chewed the finger of one of her gloves. "No, I've already said too much," she said. "I don't want anyone else to get hurt." She balled up the paper bag in one hand and tossed it into the remaining Dumpster. "I probably shouldn't even be here." Shaking her head, she started to climb back up the ramp of crumbs.

"When did you come to Earth?" asked Gene.

"I don't know," she said. "A long time ago. There were hats, a lot of tricornered hats."

With a grunt, she reached the top of the Dumpster, and then stepped up onto the white brick wall behind it. "I never should have come to meet with you. I guess I just got lonely. That happens a lot." She gave a little salute. "See you later, boys."

"Hold on one minute!" said Gene, raising a finger. "How would you like to meet some other kids, make some friends? It would be totally safe. I promise."

Vince looked at his friend in shock. "Where are you talking about?" he asked.

"At school," said Gene. "She can meet some kids and then leave." A look of shy excitement rippled across Crumble Bun's face.

"Don't do that, Gene," said Vince. "She's obviously lonely."

"She deserves to meet some kids. There's no federal agents, no scary alien leaders, just kids. People like us."

Crumble Bun thought about this for a moment, and then said smiled. "Yes, please," she said, a tumble of crumbs bouncing over her lips and down the front of her trench coat.

"Terrific. Let's go," Gene said.

"Hold on," said Vince, who was finishing his last few lines of notes. "What's your power? Does it have something to do with the gloves you're wearing?"

"My gloves are special," said Crumble Bun. She tugged the left one off her hand and then clenched and unclenched her fingers. "If my bare skin touches something, it will turn it to crumbs."

"Everything, and always?" asked Gene.

Crumble Bun nodded.

"That's amazing," said Vince.

A second passed before Gene said, "Do it. Make something else crumble."

"Are you crazy?" said Vince.

"Stop doubting!" said Gene, punching his friend in the shoulder. "Analysis is paralysis! Stop thinking about everything, and just act from the gut. Be confident!"

"No," said Vince. "Sometimes you have to stop being a bonehead and think about stuff before you do it. Like, 'Look before you leap,' or, um, 'Considering the consequences is awesomeness . . . sss . . .'"

"Wait," said Gene, squinting. "Are you trying to make that rhyme? Are you trying to make that into a catchphrase or something? Because it's lame and so is what you're saying. You don't get anywhere by thinking. You get places by *doing*."

Then he nodded at Crumble Bun. "Go on, touch the building, Cathy."

At that very moment a hunched old woman stepped up to the door of Dippin Donuts and lifted a trembling hand to open the door. Hardly glancing up, Crumble Bun reached out to grab the handle and tug the door open for the old woman.

In less than a second, the entire building had fallen into crumbs. One second the walls were there and the next they were gone. Cash registers clanged to the ground. The drink refrigerator toppled to one side. A banner advertising the World's Fullest Jelly Donut blew down the street on a light breeze. Booths of stunned breakfasters gazed around in awe at the heaping piles of sugary dough. Many of them looked down at the doughnuts they held, made a face, and then tossed the pastry aside. Others, however, finished their doughnuts and then started to eat the building.

"Maybe we should go," said Gene, holding his box of doughnuts, which now seemed entirely pointless.

"Maybe we should," agreed Vince.

The trio hurried away from the scene before anyone

could see them. In fact, they were in such a hurry that neither of them noticed Vince's and Gene's geometry textbooks lying on the ground beside some trash cans, right where they'd left them.

The thirty students in Ms. Belkis's first-period geometry class heard Gene and Vince coming from five blocks away. This was because Crumble Bun hadn't serviced the brakes of her Dodge Plymouth Voyager in nearly ten years. Before anyone even saw her minivan, they heard its high-pitched *screeeeeeeeeee* sound as it turned into the parking lot. It was the kind of noise that caused people to cover their ears, which is exactly what Gene and Vince did as they rode inside with Crumble Bun.

"You look young, how did you get a license?" Gene asked.

She glanced at them as she drove. "I've been here a long time," she said.

"Oh, yeah," said Gene, "since the days of three-corner hats and powdered wigs."

"So . . . ," Vince started.

"She's been a teenager for a long time," Gene said, finishing the thought.

In the classroom, Ms. Belkis's students breathed a sigh

when the *screee* sound stopped and turned their attention back to their tests. The peace and quiet didn't last long. A few minutes later they were disrupted once more, this time by Gene and Vince arguing outside the classroom.

"Stop touching my hair!" hissed Gene. "I want it to look sweet!"

"I didn't touch your hair, I'm trying to stop you from making a big mistake," argued Vince.

"You touched my hair when you were trying to stop me," said Gene.

"Your hair looks like a bottle cap, forget your hair," said Vince. "We shouldn't be doing this, it's a bad idea."

"Well, your hair looks like rigatoni, man," grumbled Gene.

"Why is it a bad idea?" said a girl's voice none of the students in Ms. Belkis's class recognized.

"He's wrong," said Gene. "It's not a bad idea. It's a *great* idea."

"Why don't you try *not shouting* for a change," said Vince. "So we have a chance of slipping into class quietly."

"I think it's too late for that," said Ms. Belkis. She was leaning far back in her chair, peeking around the doorway into the hall. Her short gray flattop haircut shined with sweat as she pointed her ruler at the two boys. "Get in here *now*!"

Gene and Vince jolted in their shoes and hurried into the classroom while, outside the doorway, Crumble Bun stood out of sight watching the action heat up.

"Get to your desks and start your tests," said Ms. Belkis.

Vince sprang into action and began to walk down the classroom aisle. That is until Gene threw an arm out to stop him. "I'd like to offer an alternative to the test," he said, raising one hand. In the classroom seats, Lucy, Linus, and Quiet Matt sat staring, stunned. They'd seen Gene pull plenty of stunts, but this one was on its way to becoming particularly memorable.

"There is no alternative," said Ms. Belkis. "Everyone's taking the test, even people who are late."

"How about you allow a brief intermission?" asked Gene. "So people can meet a very, very, *very* special person?"

"Sit down, Gene," said Ms. Belkis. This was a direct order. The debate was over.

"But this is a *superspecial opportunity*." Gene couldn't help singing the last word, that's how excited he was to finally show all the nonbelievers that the Ails were real.

That would shut all the kids up and get him some respect at last.

"Sit or you're going to the principal," said Ms. Belkis coolly.

Gene knew that he was already in trouble. It was now or never. They were on the verge of changing the whole world's minds about aliens. How could he possibly pass that up?

"Ladies and gentlemen!" he began like a circus ringmaster. "Today our class has a special guest, a visitor from a faraway planet in the Centrino star system, which is, for those of you interested in astronomy, located way over on this side of our Milky Way. . . ." He picked up a piece of chalk and started to draw on the blackboard.

"Gene!" Ms. Belkis was starting to lose it.

"This is as important as equilateral triangles, trust me!" said Gene.

"The test is on circles," muttered Lucy.

"Yes!" Gene said, making it up as he went. "And what would a test on circles be without meeting a being, a creature, a person, who can crumble anything into countless crumblike spheres? A sphere is a circle right?"

"Yes," said Vince drily. "A sphere is a circle."

One boy in the front row whose name was Horace

Appleton turned to the student next to him and whispered, "Gene makes a good point." It should be mentioned that Horace was failing geometry.

"That's enough!" said Ms. Belkis, stepping in front of the class. She slapped a red detention slip into Gene's open hand. Then she handed one to Vince. "I want you to take this and go see Principal Mahoney—*both* of you."

"Wait, what did *I* do?" asked Vince, looking at his slip.

Gene, ignoring this, wound up his introduction with an echoing shout. "Now, she's a very shy girl, so let's give her a warm welcome. Please say hello to Crumble Bun, who likes to be called Cathy."

Everyone in the room held his or her breath, even Ms. Belkis.

Nothing happened.

"Crumble Bun?" said Gene meekly.

As everyone looked at the door, Cathy, a.k.a. Crumble Bun, slowly leaned her head into the room. She gazed at the bewildered students with awe and curiosity. At first it seemed as if she might run away.

"Come in, come in, please," said Gene, taking Crumble Bun by the arm. She shuffled in through the doorway. "Cathy lives alone and doesn't get out much to meet many kids. Most of them are like that, because they're different. But Cathy's nice. She's just from another place, a very *other* place."

Crumble Bun stood shyly in front of the classroom, shifting her weight from one foot to the other. Ms. Belkis rubbed her forehead and squeezed her eyes shut like she was having a migraine headache. She quickly opened her drawer, took out two aspirins, and swallowed them with a gulp from a water bottle.

"She's just some chubby girl!" barked Kevin Jurgenson, a basketball player. His comment started the whole class giggling.

"That's not very nice, Kevin," said Gene, holding up his hands. "Not that being nice has ever been your strong suit."

Crumble Bun stared down at her feet, blushing. But when she finally looked up, she found that not everyone in the class was laughing. In fact, one boy gazed up at her with a friendly, open face, his eyes as blue as Easter egg dye. It was Quiet Matt. The two of them seemed to connect from across the room, even as all the other students seemed lost in their tittering cruelty.

Now it was Gene's turn to look confused.

He quickly composed himself and gestured to the guest

at the front of the class. "Crumble Bun, would you please crumble something?" he finally managed to say.

She didn't answer but instead continued to stare deeply into Quiet Matt's eyes. Now Matt was the one who was blushing. Lucy and Linus turned to each other and silently mouthed "No way" almost in unison.

"Cathy's DNA is a tad different than ours," Gene explained, "but a tad goes a long way in this world. Cathy, what do you say, how about crumbling this test for us? I'm sure that will make you quite a few friends." Kids sat forward in their chairs, eager to see what would happen. This spectacle was growing more interesting by the second. It was even better than the time Lisa Perkins's bag of baby rats got loose in life science.

Obeying Gene, Crumble Bun tugged off the long black glove from her right hand. She was about to reach out and touch a desk when two large police officers came stomping through the classroom door.

The pair of gigantic policemen was followed by a smaller man with a short red beard, a pair of cowboy boots, and a pink dress shirt tucked into the waistband of his jeans. Around his neck he wore a tie painted to look like a fish. It was a hard outfit to take seriously. Unfortunately it belonged to Principal Mahoney.

"Officers, how can I help you?" said a flustered Ms. Belkis, now putting two more aspirin into her mouth and chewing them, this time without even drinking water.

The beefier of the two police officers held up a math notebook with GENE BRENNICK clearly written on it in large thick marker you could read from across the room. The book cover was a mess of doodles—flying saucers, planets, and galaxy swirls—all drawn by none other than Gene.

Vince covered his face with both hands and began to moan.

"These books belonging to a Gene Brennick and a Vince Haskell were found at a crime scene," said the beefy officer.

"What crime scene?" Gene asked, clueless.

"There was an incident at the Dippin Donuts down on Clark Street," said the beefy officer, "and we have some questions for you."

"I hate doughnuts," said Gene quickly, hoping this would prove his innocence.

"These are the boys," said Principal Mahoney.

"One more thing," continued the beefy officer, turning toward Crumble Bun. "This young lady here seems to fit a description we took down from the witnesses at Dippin

Donuts." He reached for the handcuffs on his belt. "We're going to have to take her too."

There wasn't much time to wonder, because, like some extraordinary, unlikely last-minute end-zone catch to win the Super Bowl, what went down next seemed to happen in the blink of an eye. Quiet Matt—Quiet, Unassuming, Never Says More Than One Line, Just Gets Everyone Sodas like the Shy Office Gopher He Is, Matt—leaped from his chair. In a single fluid motion, he grabbed Crumble Bun by her gloved hand and pulled her to the windows to escape. Fortunately the classroom was on the first floor.

When the window didn't budge in spite of Matt's straining, Crumble Bun reached out with her ungloved index finger and touched the wall. In an instant, the windows, the hanging diagrams of triangles, the California state flag, all of it disintegrated into a pile of marble-size crumbs on the floor. The sound of birds and the smell of grass lay before them, along with the sight of freedom. It was all just a step away, a step that Matt, pulling Crumble Bun, took with great speed as they bolted through the bushes.

And before anyone could say "Dippin Donuts," they were gone—just like that. Even the police looked stunned.

The beefy one, who wasn't very fast, made a lumbering effort to follow, and then he too disappeared through what once had been the fourth wall of Ms. Belkis's room.

"Wow," said Gene. "And I thought this place was drafty before."

A pair of hands came down on Gene's and Vince's shoulders. "That's enough out of you two," growled Principal Mahoney. "You're going downtown with Officer Martinez." The smaller of the two police officers grabbed Gene and Vince each by the arms and started to drag them out of the classroom.

As the boys passed in front of the class, Kevin Jurgenson flipped a pencil and hit Gene in the head. It made a wooden clicking sound as it bounced off his skull. "Nice alien powers, Brennick," said the power center. "I saw a magician do that to a wall when I went to Vegas with my parents last summer."

"Are you out of your mind?" Gene shouted. "That wasn't Vegas magic! It was real, totally real!"

"Nah," chimed in Missy Brannigan. "I saw some TV show where they did that. It's old news, all CGI graphics."

"What's the matter with you people?" shrieked Gene, beside himself with frustration. "I brought an alien to class, and you think it's a magic trick!"

"I guess it's not your day, kid," said Officer Martinez as he shoved Gene and Vince out the door.

Gene shouted during their whole long walk down the hallway to the parking lot. Vince, however, remained silent. He wasn't even that scared. He was just hoping Ms. Belkis would cancel the test after all the craziness. Maybe then he could squeeze in a little more study time in jail.

"HEY, I RECOGNIZE YOU," SAID THE POLICE OFFICER,
snapping his fingers as he tried to remember the stranger's
name.

The stranger, a man dressed in a loose-fitting white
shirt, olive suit, and striped necktie, closed his cell phone.
The plastic was hot. "Yes" was all he said. This sort of
thing happened all the time to Walter Sparrow. His name
was always on the tip of someone's tongue.

Another officer looked up from where he was working
on a computer and pointed. "You're the school counselor
guy, the one from Fulton Junior High."

Walter smiled and raised both his hands in air as if he
was being arrested. "Guilty," he said. "I believe we've met
before, gentlemen. I was here a few weeks ago to help out
some of my students."

He flashed his winning grin. "The name is Walter Sparrow."

At the name, the officers smiled back. Of course, how could they forget?

Walter ran his fingers through his hair as he scanned the room. When he didn't see the person he was looking for, he began to get nervous. Sitting down on a bench, he ran his fingers through his hair again.

The alien called Walter Sparrow had the power to topple mountains, to infect whole populations with disease, to hurl planets into the sun. But hanging around a police station gave him the willies. And when he had the willies, Walter Sparrow played with his hair.

Every few thousand years, he liked to try a new hairstyle. Just for fun. In 44 BC, after helping stab Julius Caesar to death, he went and got a haircut. He had it styled to look like Caesar's, which he did out of spite. Caesar had been so *annoying*. Many years later, in the 1700s, when he was living in the United States, Walter grew very fond of a powdered wig that he nicknamed Gertrude. Unfortunately, he was forced to throw her away when she became infested with lice. Then there was his time in France in the 1980s. He'd worn a Mohawk and played bass guitar for a punk rock band, the Plungers.

Walter eventually turned the band's lead singer into a badger and was kicked out of the band. After that, the Mohawk went bye-bye.

No matter what was going on in his life, Walter always seemed concerned with his hair. Perhaps it was simply because all human beings worry about their hair. And after thousands of years on Earth, Walter had become just like them. In many ways, Walter Sparrow was human.

Upon arriving in Santa Rosa, California, fifty or so years ago, Walter had taken a new form. This was something he did often. It was to blend in but also to stay hidden. There were plenty of folks he was trying to avoid. The galaxy was a big place. If you were smart enough about your appearance, you could stay hidden for centuries. He knew that from experience.

"Excuse me, Mr. Sparrow," said one of the officers. "Who are you here to see?"

Reaching into the pocket of his brown corduroy jacket, Walter took out a piece of paper. "I'm here for these two low-life criminals," he said, showing the names.

Two doors away, Gene and Vince sat in a white room with white lights and a white table. It was the police interrogation room, where the cops interviewed bad guys. But Gene and Vince weren't bad guys. They were just really hungry. That's because it was past lunchtime and all they'd had to eat that day were doughnuts.

Neither Gene nor Vince had said anything since they arrived at the police station. Everything they could have said they'd said before, the last time they were arrested. That time, the boys had been interviewing the Shock Brothers, a pair of aliens from Omega, the Mechanical Planet. Gene accidentally spilled his Coke on the Shock Brothers' megaconductor and ended up frying half of Santa Rosa's power grid.

The police had found them standing outside the electric plant, arms raised, hair sparking. Vince was so scared he couldn't talk. Not Gene. He just kept asking for a new Coke. The cops of the Santa Rosa PD didn't really know what to make of the two nerds and their alien newsletter. Most of them wondered why the boys couldn't just toilet-paper people's houses like other kids.

The door to the white room opened, and a cop named Officer Barnes stuck his head inside. He wore an ugly, unconvincing hairpiece, which sat on his bald head like a beanie. "I've got Fred on the phone for you," he said.

"Thanks," Gene said, and took the cell phone from the officer's beefy hand. He put it to his ear. "Fred?"

"Gene!" said the voice on the other end. "Gene, what in the world is going on?"

"Nothing," Gene said, squinting at the officer. "We're totally innocent."

Across the table, Vince buried his head in his hands and groaned.

"If you're so innocent, then why is the news saying that the Dippin Donuts turned into a pile of crumbs?"

"Don't ask me," said Gene. "You can't trust what you see on the news. You should know that, Fred."

Still groaning, Vince rested his cheek on the dirty table-top and decided to start whimpering instead. "Tell him to come get us," he said. "My mom can't find out."

Gene nodded. "You have to come get us," he said into the phone.

There was silence on the other end of the line, followed by a shuffling of paper. It sounded like someone thumbing through the pages in a book. "I did better than that," said Fred. "I sent someone."

"What do you mean 'someone'?" asked Gene skeptically.

"Don't you trust me?" asked Fred.

"I don't know how to answer that," said Gene.

The phone was filled with the clucking of Fred's tongue.

"Have a good night," he said, sounding chipper. "And I'll see you at Comic Mania."

Gene didn't like the sound of that and started to protest. "There's no way I'm going to—" But the line went dead. Furious, he handed the phone back to the police officer in the doorway. They were toast.

Gene and Vince were used to being in trouble, but never this bad. Once, a few months ago, they'd gone into the sewers under the town to flush out the Fish Man of Fulton. Not only did they scare him out into the open, where he crashed two slumber parties and a prom, but they also backed up toilets throughout Santa Rosa. Both boys were grounded for that whole month, meaning they couldn't even talk to each other on the phone. That part had been agony.

"Incoming," said Vince, lifting his head from the table.

A stranger entered the room, bringing with him a cloud of cologne. He didn't appear to be a police officer. In fact, he looked more like a professor at some cool college that let kids go to school barefoot. The man was tall, handsome, and hip with a rumpled brown suit and a pair of reflective sunglasses. "Hi, boys," he said, extending his hand. "My name is Walter Sparrow, and I'm here to help you."

Gene and Vince looked at each other.

"Are you a policeman?" asked Vince. "You don't look like one."

"No, I'm not a policeman." Walter laughed. "Not exactly."

"Then what are you doing here?" asked Gene. "It's called a police station for a reason."

"I'm here to help you," said Walter again, starting to fill out some forms on a clipboard. His fingernails were perfectly groomed, the ends long and slightly curved. A little longer and they could have been claws.

"Why would you help us?" asked Vince.

"Because you need it," said Walter. "You see, I'm the guidance counselor over at Fulton Junior High. I work with the local police departments, helping with at-risk kids." He read something on one of the clipboard sheets and began to shake his head.

"We're not exactly at-risk kids," said Vince, really hoping he was right. If his mom found out he was at risk, he'd be in so much trouble.

"Yeah," said Gene. "We're reporters."

Walter smiled. "Well, you're reporters who are about one step away from spending some time in juvenile hall." He raised one leathery finger. "Luckily, I just made a little deal with the police, and they're not going to charge you with any crimes. But this is your last warning." As he spoke, the silver lenses of his sunglasses glinted in the fluorescent lighting. "The cops are a little tired of chasing after you two troublemakers."

"But, mister," said Gene, "you can't help us. We don't go to your school. We think Fulton is for total wieners. We bleed Santa Rosa blue."

"Well, not me," added Vince. "I bleed type O negative."

Walter smiled, signing his name on three different forms. "That's okay," he said. "I agreed to cross school districts for you guys, since you're a special case. We don't get a lot of alien hunters in these parts. I thought it would be fun." Clicking the pen closed, he tossed the clipboard aside. "You can thank me later."

"This is all Gene's fault," said Vince.

Walter looked surprised. "It didn't take long to turn you against each other, did it?"

"He's the one who gets us into trouble," said Vince.

"So says the coward quitter who still wants front page credit," said Gene.

"I'd prefer to write novellas, if I had time," Vince explained.

"You hear that?" asked Gene, pushing at Vince with

his elbow. "Shakespeare here is too good for us. And he's a traitor!"

The two boys began to wrestle while still sitting in their chairs. This was as difficult as it sounds, as they kept scooting farther and farther away from each other across the room. They kept this up until Walter slammed his fists down on the table with a bang. *"Enough!"* he roared. The sound was loud enough to make the two-way mirror tremble, and the whole room suddenly got stuffier, as though Walter had breathed fire. *"Can't you guys go ten minutes without fighting?"*

"No," said Vince, his voice little more than a whimper. "We counted once. We can only go seven and a half."

"Bottoms in your seats, mouths shut!" roared Walter. The boys obeyed, frightened. They sat rigid. They said nothing. The laid-back, rumpled rock star of a guidance counselor was gone, replaced by someone else. This man, this Walter, was different.

"The police don't believe your stories about the teenager who can crumble things," said Walter. "Even Officer Martinez is skeptical, and he was at the school when the girl ran off. He's convinced some vapors from the chemistry class across the hall got to him, made him see things."

"It really happened," said Gene. "She's real."

Walter stared back, unmoving. "It doesn't matter if I believe you," he said. "What matters is that in order to avoid any more trouble, you have to meet with me for a counseling session. You only have to do it twice."

"Tomorrow's Saturday," whined Gene.

"I don't care!" shouted Walter. It was loud and grating enough to make the fillings in the boys' teeth ache. "Tomorrow, five o'clock!" he went on. "Be at my office at Fulton Junior High and don't be late!"

The boys cringed. "Okay," they said together. Their voices came out hoarse and weak, as if they'd spent the day shouting at the top of their lungs.

Then something odd happened. Blinking, Walter seemed to realize that he'd been yelling and that he'd scared the boys nearly to death. This did not seem to sit well with him. He ran his hand through his hair and cleared his throat. "Um, sorry, guys," he said softly. "Sometimes I get a little worked up. I don't mean to."

"It's okay," squeaked Vince. "We're used to it. Everyone's always mad at us."

Walter snatched up the clipboard. "Let's get you home," he said. He signaled to the officer behind the door to let them out.

And at that moment, Gene saw *it*.

Walter, who was in the act of waving, accidentally bumped his sunglasses with one hand. They fell away from his face and down the bridge of his nose. It took no more than a second, but that was all the time Gene needed.

The room's two-way mirror captured everything. In its reflection, Gene saw that Walter's eyes were different colors. One was a bright red and one was a bright purple. Both flashed with rage as Walter rushed to fix his sunglasses. They swirled with an otherworldly flame.

And at that moment, Gene *knew*. That Walter was different. That he was definitely not human.

When Gene walked into his house that evening, his head was a whirlpool of questions. *Who was Walter Sparrow? Why was he a guidance counselor? Was he an alien? What kind of alien was he? Was he a good alien, or one of the bad ones that Fred warned him about? Was he kidnapping other Ails? Was his hair real, or a wig? What product did he use in it to get that newly washed shine?* All of these and more spun around in his head and banged against his skull as he hurried down the hall toward his room.

Outside, the police cruiser honked once before backing out of the driveway and speeding off. Mrs. Brennick stood at the window and watched it leave. Shaking her head, she closed the curtains. One of her curlers slipped free and fell to the carpet. There were more gray hairs in it than she was used to seeing. Gene passed behind her in a hurry.

"Someone called," said Mrs. Brennick, following after him. "His name was Walter Sparrow. He was very nice. He explained everything, about the police station, about your appointment tomorrow." No matter how fast she shuffled, she couldn't seem to catch up to him. "It sounds like he's really looking out for you."

"I guess you could say that," said Gene, removing his backpack and hurling it onto his bed. "He probably wants to fatten me up before eating me."

"What?" his mother asked.

Gene glanced up, confused. "Oh, nothing," he said.

Mrs. Brennick sighed. "That man was so kind and polite. And he sounded very educated." Pausing, she waited to see if Gene would say anything else, and then asked, "Do you know if he's married?"

This caused Gene to glance up, suddenly listening. "What? No. I have no idea," he said. "I don't really care." Then, focused again, he began to close his door. "Mom, I'm really sorry about what happened. From now on I'm living life on the straight and narrow."

"But, Gene, we need to talk about this and—"

Before his mother had even finished talking, Gene had shut the door and clicked the lock button.

"This isn't over," said Mrs. Brennick, her voice muffled.

"I know," said Gene, "but later."

Flipping open his cell phone, he speed-dialed number 4. It rang for a few seconds before someone answered.

"Hello," said the voice on the other end.

"Lucy?" said Gene.

"Gene?"

"Yes, it's me," he said. "How did you know?"

"I have caller ID, Gene," she said. "Are you okay?" she added. "I heard you spent all afternoon at the police station."

He scratched his head. "How did you hear about that?"

"Vince called," said Lucy.

Gritting his teeth, Gene shook his fist at his traitor of a best friend. "Awesome," he said, trying to sound okay with the fact that his two friends were talking so regularly, and about him. "You know," he said, "that's not the half of it. We met this really weird guy when we were there."

"Most people in jail are weird."

"No," said Gene. "This guy wasn't in jail. He was some guidance counselor from Fulton Junior High." He pictured Walter's rumpled suit and shaggy haircut. And then he remembered the eyes, how they glowed a crackling red and purple. "And he had these crazy glowing eyes. I have to find out who he is."

"Glowing eyes," Lucy said, thinking.

"Didn't the Dime tell us something about that?" asked Gene, trying to remember.

"Wait," said Lucy. He heard the plastic creak as she opened her laptop, and then the hum of its power source coming to life. "Aren't you hanging out with the guidance counselor at our school too? You must need some serious guidance, brother."

"How did you know that?" asked Gene, feeling a little weird. That kind of information was private.

"Vince," she said.

Gene's phone beeped. "Hold on," he said, and he clicked over to his call-waiting.

It was Vince. "Dude, can you believe this?" he asked. "Who was that guy? He was a total Ail."

"I know, it's insane," said Gene. "I'm on the other line trying to find whatever I can from our old files."

"Who are you talking to?" asked Vince.

"Nobody," said Gene. "Hold on."

Switching back over, Gene apologized to Lucy.

"Who was that?" she asked.

"Nobody," said Gene. "Listen. If anyone can find some dude with glowing eyes in our database, it's you."

"You mean the database you said we didn't need?" asked Lucy.

Gene felt the blood run out of his face. He had to learn to keep his big mouth shut. "When you're right, you're right, Lucy," he said. "Now, can you find anything?"

He heard the click of her fingers on computer keys. "That detail came up in a bunch of the interviews this winter. A lot of the other aliens seem to know about this guy with one red eye and one purple."

"Really?" asked Gene. He was the one who conducted all of the newsletter's interviews. Yet he didn't have a single recollection of hearing about an alien with discolored eyes. Maybe Vince was right. Maybe he didn't pay enough attention.

"I'm accessing the entire database of Ails," said Lucy, talking him through what she was doing. "Then I'm going to cross-reference the keywords 'purple' and 'red.'" There was more clicking. "All I have to do now is remove all the stories about aliens outside Santa Rosa." She did. Her breathing grew faster, more excited. "It's a short list," she said. "There aren't many aliens with that feature."

"How many are there?" Gene asked.

"Just one," whispered Lucy.

"Who is it?" asked Gene, almost afraid to know.

Lucy read the name once. Then she read it again to make sure that they'd both heard correctly. "It's Vargon's nephew."

"*Vargon's* nephew," repeated Gene as a hum of excitement began to travel up his spine. "You mean Vargon the Atomizer? Vargon the Eater of Worlds? Vargon, Exploder of the Pure? Like, *the* Vargon, the most horrible alien in the entire galaxy? I thought he was just a legend."

"I don't know about Vargon," said Lucy, "but apparently his nephew's real."

Gene sat totally still. All of the questions about Walter Sparrow that had been racing through his brain disappeared. None of them mattered anymore, because he knew what he had to do. It wasn't strange for Gene's mind to be empty. However, it was rare for him to have a single thought driving him. This was the moment he'd been waiting for all along. This was the headline of headlines.

The kids at school didn't think a girl who could turn a doughnut shop to crumbs was anything special. Just wait until they met one of the galaxy's most ferocious villains, a creature that once set a whole planet on fire simply because he had the chills. Sure, he could have just put on a sweater, but the story goes that he thought the horizontal stripes made him look fat.

Taking a deep breath, he clicked his call-waiting back to the other line.

"I was just about to slip into a coma," Vince shouted.

"Be quiet and listen," said Gene. And then he told his best friend everything.

8

FROM THE OUTSIDE, FULTON JUNIOR HIGH SCHOOL LOOKED like a chain restaurant. There was no denying it. It was due to the stucco walls and the neon sign. Anyone who saw the building from a distance suddenly had a craving for cheese sticks. Once, in the 1990s, a woman actually walked her family into the front lobby expecting to be seated and given menus. This was unfortunate, because Fulton Junior High School was one of the better schools in that part of California. And it was one of the better schools because of Walter Sparrow.

If there had been such a thing as a weekly celebrity magazine about guidance counselors, Walter Sparrow would have been on the cover two out of four times a month. He was *that* good. Everyone in Fulton agreed. If it wasn't for the miracles that Walter Sparrow seemed to work with troubled kids, the town would have been a dump.

They knew this because before Walter Sparrow had started working at the school, Fulton had been just that—a total dump. He had changed everything for the better.

But that wasn't to say there weren't issues surrounding Walter. Not that anyone would ever bring those things up. They were the kind of things that everyone knew about but no one wanted to mention. Like the times when he left smoking footprints after leaving a room. Or the way small animals scampered away the second he came near. Or the way the school public-announcement system shrieked with feedback whenever Walter ate his lunch. Little things like that.

No one was more familiar with Walter's oddities than the principal of Fulton Junior High School, Principal Pinkus. The two men had been friends for more than a decade. They had been through good times and bad times. But as the principal would have pointed out: You can't really know someone you haven't played racquetball with. And he hadn't played racquetball with Walter. So despite his fondness for Walter, Principal Pinkus always knew the guidance counselor would be trouble.

Principal Pinkus's feelings about his friend came to mind that Saturday evening when he saw two strange boys walk onto the campus of Fulton Junior High. One of the boys was short with a terrible bowl haircut. It looked like he'd been sheared by an apple peeler. The other boy was tall and stooped with curly hair. At first glance, he resembled the portraits of cavemen one often found in science textbooks.

Principal Pinkus had no idea who these two kids were, but he had a pretty good idea who they were there to see. Who else did the weird kids go to see? The kids with tight pants, shaved heads, switchblades, clubfoot, no tongues, or wizard cloaks? No, not Mr. O'Leary, the Spanish teacher. Not Ms. Combs, the librarian.

They were there for Mr. Sparrow, of course. It was always Walter.

Vince had to jog to keep up with his friend, and when he did, he tripped on a crack in the sidewalk and nearly tackled a mailbox. "You really think we should do this?" he asked. He steadied himself, readjusted his backpack, and kept moving.

Gene didn't even slow down. "This could be the biggest story we've ever covered," he said, throwing his arms in the air. "Imagine it!" Fingers curled into air quotation marks, he spoke the headline. 'Boys Expose Local Alien Mastermind!' This might finally get us the attention we deserve."

"I think we already get the attention we deserve," said Vince. "People laugh at us. I'd probably laugh at us too."

That's when Gene stopped, whirling around, one finger (without fingerprints) stuck in his friend's surprised face. "Don't you wimp out on me, Vince," he said. "This is one scoop we can't screw up. This guy has been kidnapping Ails, man. Don't you remember what Crumble Bun said? Someone's been hunting down her friends, someone really bad. And Walter Sparrow is that someone."

"We don't know that," said Vince. "He's a school guidance counselor. How bad can he be?"

"He's Vargon's nephew, idiot," said Gene, turning back around and speeding off again. "And he's a guidance counselor at our *rival* school. If that doesn't say something about him, I don't know what does."

"And you're not at all afraid about him inflating your head or setting your intestines on fire?" asked Vince, still trying not to fall behind.

"This is important," said Gene. "That means we've got to be brave."

"Or stupid," said Vince.

Entering Fulton Junior High, something Gene and Vince had sworn never to do, they looked around the front hallway. Next to them, by the drinking fountain, stood the school mascot, Fulton the Aardvark, a huge furry monstrosity dressed in a Fulton wrestling team singlet. His googly eyes seemed to follow the boys as they walked by in silence, nervous. Gene was convinced that a gang of Fulton punks hid behind the trophy case and that they would leap out and clobber the two of them with heavy Fulton field hockey trophies. Luckily, the school was empty, as it usually was on Saturdays. The boys proceeded without incident to the front office.

Several minutes later, Gene pushed open the door to Walter Sparrow's small office with a creak and poked his head inside. The place was cramped, and it smelled like a twenty-four-hour convenience store, like sweat and heat. "Hi," he said, looking around nervously. "Is anybody home?"

Across the room at a small wooden desk, Walter Sparrow glanced up, surprised. His conservative purple striped necktie hung a little crooked, and there was a coffee stain on his shirt front pocket. Other than that, he didn't appear any different than your average junior high school teacher caught grading papers.

"How are you boys doing today?" asked Walter, setting down his pencil. "Is it that time already?"

"Looks like it," said Gene, slipping into the room.

"How's it going, Mr. Sparrow?" said Vince, smiling weakly as he entered and pulled the door shut behind him.

Walter Sparrow's office looked just as one would expect of a guidance counselor. In other words, it was nothing like the office of Dr. Jinks. Two cheap gray metal shelves lined one wall, overstuffed with leathery, yellowing books. On the floor lay a square of cheap red carpet that did a bad job of hiding the dirty tiles beneath. Above Walter's desk, an air-conditioning unit almost completely blocked the window. It dripped steadily into a saucepan that had been placed on a stack of encyclopedias.

However, there was one thing that seemed out of place in Walter's smelly little room. In fact, this object would have seemed much more at home in the office of Dr. Jinks. In the far corner, next to a chipped armoire, stood a fancy wooden screen with an ornate Chinese dragon carved into it.

Neither Gene nor Vince thought much of the screen. They were too preoccupied with the idea that Walter was one of the most feared and powerful creatures in the entire galaxy. That kind of detail often distracted from the furniture.

"Have a seat, boys," said Walter, gesturing to two

folding chairs that faced his desk. "What should we talk about today? Should we start by chatting about what happened the other day at school, or the incident at Dippin Donuts?" He shrugged. "Is there anything you want to know about me?"

This was just the intro Gene had been hoping he'd get. "About that," he said. "I was really wondering if you could tell us about—"

"That trick we pulled at school," interrupted Vince, who had suddenly, typically, and in this case, wisely, gotten cold feet about Gene's plan. "We wanted to talk about how wrong that was and how bad we feel about it."

Gene shot Vince an icy stare. "No," he said slowly. "We want to know if it's true you're—"

"The world's most awesome guidance counselor," interrupted Vince again, forcing a laugh. "Really, I've heard *great* things."

None of this seemed to faze Walter. If anything, he seemed mildly amused. "Is everything okay, boys?" he asked, getting up from his desk. "What are you trying to say?" He walked behind them and locked the office door. Then he began to pace, his wornout old brown shoes making scuffing sounds on the square of carpet. It was creepy, to say the least.

And it was enough to send Vince into a panic. "We should go!" he said, jumping to his feet.

"And why is that?" asked Walter, raising an eyebrow. "Hate to break it to you, but you can't go. You're required to spend an hour with me today."

Realizing that they were trapped in the office, Vince raised his finger and pointed at Gene. "He wants to write an article about you because—"

"Shut up, stupid!" shouted Gene, also leaping to his feet.

"You shut up!" shouted Vince.

Walter chuckled and crossed his arms. "Boys, why would you want to write an article about *me*?" he asked.

This was too much for Gene, and he turned to face the guidance counselor. His heart beat wildly, but he was not afraid. That's because he knew the truth. "You're Vargon's nephew!" he stated, saying it in his best TV-lawyer voice.

But when the words came out, they didn't sound quite as terrifying as they had the night before on the phone. That was because the word "Vargon" was actually pretty silly. In fact, for the briefest of moments, both Gene and Vince wondered if they had made a mistake, and Walter was just some cool teacher with nice hair and not related to a powerful alien warlord. Silence fell upon the room as the boys waited for a reaction, all the while terrified of what it would be.

When that reaction came, it wasn't at all what Gene and Vince were expecting. They were preparing for laser beams, lightning bolts, or even tentacles. Instead, Walter started laughing so hard that he almost cried.

Circling back to the desk, Walter sank into his chair and propped his feet on the windowsill. Sunlight streamed in through the glass. It made him appear faded, like a picture that goes through the wash in your pocket. He stared outside—right into the sun—without blinking. "Let's play along with your little fantasy, Gene," he said without feeling. "Let's say, hypothetically, I *was* this Vargon's nephew. Now, who is this guy Vargon again, as far as you know?"

Gene was about to speak but instead looked at Walter nervously.

"Please, go on," Walter encouraged him. "I want to hear this. It's all part of the counseling session."

"Okay, well," said Gene, fidgeting in his seat. "From what we know, he's like the worst alien in the whole galaxy."

Walter stared at Gene. "And *I'm* his nephew, a guidance counselor working with kids?"

Vince bit his lip. He agreed with Mr. Sparrow. The whole story was starting to sound pretty crazy.

"I'm a peaceful guy, a counselor," said Walter. "So tell me. How would Vargon's nephew turn out to be a peaceful school counselor?"

Gene shrugged. "Maybe he's not really a peaceful school counselor."

"So I'm pretending to be this guy, *hypothetically*," said Walter. "But I'm really what, evil?"

Gene tilted his head and nodded. "Hypothetically," he said.

"I'd like to leave now," Vince said, standing.

Walter pointed at Vince's empty chair. "Sit," he said. "You're required by law to be here, unless you'd prefer to go to juvenile court."

Vince sat and swallowed hard.

"Can you think of another possibility," Walter asked them, "other than the 'Walter is so evil' thing?"

"Like what?" Gene asked.

"Well, we're speaking hypothetically, right?" asked Walter. "As if this were true, which it's not, right?"

"Right, hypothetically," Gene said.

Walter sighed. "Well, what if I didn't like my cranky old uncle and my evil family, and I wanted out of that life?"

"Okay," said Gene.

"Well, do you think it would be easy breaking out of the Xenon star system?" asked Walter. "No. First I had to work for the outer Vargons, who randomly explode planets. Sure, it got me out of the house, but it was pretty depressing. From there I spent a few hundred years in hiding with the Particle Demons. When they found out who I was . . ." He shivered. "They have cannons that shoot space sharks, Gene. *Space sharks!*"

Leaning back in his chair, Walter's face twitched once, as if he was going to cry, and then spread into a smile. "I spent thousands of years running around wreaking havoc, trying to find my place in this world, until . . ." He paused, a warm look dawning across his face. Gene and Vince quickly noticed that it wasn't just a smile that made Walter appear to glow. His face actually radiated a soft reddish light, as if he'd stuck his head into a bonfire and pulled it out again. "Until I heard a rumor about a wonderful place, a watery blue sky place with beaches and snow and summer days. They called it Earth."

With a squeak, he sat up in his chair, alert. "So I came here, took this bodily form. That's that."

"Are we still pretending, or is this real?" asked Vince, confused.

"That's not what you really look like?" asked Gene, taking out his notepad and starting to write.

"Hypothetically, if I was an extraterrestrial, you couldn't comprehend what I really look like," said Walter. "It would be a mass of explosive gases combined with acids, solvents, poisons, and bloods."

"Gross," said Gene.

Getting up, Walter walked around the room until he stood right in front of them. "Do you have any idea how hard it is to start a normal life after everything I've been through?" His eyes met Gene's, and then Vince's. "Sometimes you only decide to change when you find something worth changing for." He grinned. "Isn't that right, guys?" The boys nodded enthusiastically. Of course, they would have agreed with him no matter what he said. After all, he was the nephew of an alien that once ate an asteroid as an after-dinner mint.

The boys stared unblinking at the guidance counselor, and he stared back. No one said a word for a minute.

At last Vince opened his mouth. "Are you going to kill us?" he squeaked.

Patting Vince on the shoulder, Walter shook his head. "No, I'm not going to kill you," he said. "I've devoted centuries of my life to going against my family's evil ways. It appears that you've discovered my secret, but that doesn't mean I'll hurt you. I no longer kill, maim, chop, burn, sear, *destroy, vaporize, or otherwise disfigure people!*" He took a deep breath, calmed down. "So, no, I don't plan on changing back now."

"Wait," said Vince. "So you're not the big bad alien Fred told us about?"

"Heavens no," said Walter.

"Yeah, right," said Gene.

"Honest, I'm not," said Walter.

Just then, the black phone on Walter's desk began to ring shrilly. Turning away from Gene and Vince, he snapped the receiver off the cradle and placed it between his ear and shoulder. A woman's voice could be heard chattering on the other end of the line. "Yes," Walter said as he opened a desk drawer and plucked up a chewed pencil. He scrawled a few words on the closest piece of scrap paper, which happened to be a copy of the *Globe* that neither boy had noticed sitting there before. "All right, then. Goodbye," he finished, and hung up.

"I have to leave," said Walter, kicking off his old shoes and crossing the office. "The astronomy club is holding a fund-raiser, and they need a teacher for the dunk tank. It seems Ms. Sanders chickened out." He walked right by them and stepped behind the wooden screen with the carved Chinese dragon. With a swish of corduroy, he removed his jacket and hung it over the top of the divider.

"Um, do you really want us here when you're changing clothes?" asked Gene.

"I'm not changing . . . my *clothes*," said Walter.

From behind the screen came a shriek and a groan. A pair of eyeballs plopped to the floor and rolled a few inches before a hand felt around for them and snatched them back up again. "Sorry," said Walter. This was followed by a fizzing sound, like a can of soda being cracked open. A rumpled suit of human skin fell to the floor in a heap. It lay there for a few seconds before being snapped up again. "Almost done," said Walter.

But the boys hadn't heard him. From their positions to the side of the changing screen, they had a view of everything going on behind it. And judging from the looks on their faces—pale, waxy, wide-eyed—they'd never seen anything like it. Before he could forget to do it, Gene fumbled around for his cell phone and snapped a few pictures.

Finally, a scaly red hand reached out and opened the door to the nearby armoire. Inside hung a series of clean brown suits on brass coat hangers. Walter tugged one free of its hook and pulled it behind the screen. "That'll do it," he said.

When Walter came out, he looked almost exactly the same as he had going in. Only his suit was different. "It's not hard to hide who you really are," he said, almost in a sad way. "But it's a shame you sometimes have to."

Restless, Gene picked up a picture frame sitting on the desk. "What's this?" he asked. "I don't see anything. It's just a big white blob."

"That's my mother," said Walter, taking the photo and putting it in a drawer. "Isn't she beautiful?"

Both boys had seen balls of snot that were better looking, but they chose to keep this to themselves. It wasn't wise to insult a man, or alien, who wore a suit of human skin like it was a Halloween costume.

On the inside of the armoire door hung a full-length mirror. Walter stood in front, rotating from side to side. He ran his fingers through his hair. "I need you to make me a promise, guys," he said. "Now that you've discovered me, you can't print anything about me. It's too dangerous, for you, for me, for everyone."

Gene closed his phone with a click and slipped it into a pocket. "And what if we did?" he asked.

The expression on Walter's face didn't change as he

continued to check himself out in the mirror. "I'll destroy you in some horrific way," he said. "You might get pulled apart by rabid dogs. Or maybe I'll bring back a golden oldie, like the bubonic plague. Perhaps I'll just have you repeatedly run over by a steamroller for all of eternity." Then he flashed a grin. "I'm kidding."

"Can you do all that?" asked Vince, trying not to faint. "That's horrible."

Walter shrugged, unimpressed. "I've done *so* much worse."

"Really?" asked Vince.

"Remember boy bands?" asked Walter, raising one eyebrow.

"Wow," said Vince. "That *is* worse."

"But you're not the one who's kidnapping all the other aliens?" asked Gene.

Walter shook his head. "Of course not," he said. "The aliens that are being kidnapped are my friends. This is the work of someone else, and I think I have a good idea who it might be."

Hands clasped behind his back, Walter stared out through the sliver of window that wasn't blocked by the air-conditioning unit. He gazed out at Fulton Junior High. The sun was starting to set in the distance. It cast a soft haze over the campus. In that light, Walter looked as human as someone could possibly look.

"I've been running my whole life, and it's not fun," he said in a thoughtful voice. "So have my friends. We come from a place where you can get in trouble for just being yourself." He took a deep breath. "There are those out there who want to find us, to bring us back. But we can't let that happen, right?" His voice grew grave, and he looked at the boys, a fire in his eyes. "Neither can you."

Walter turned back to the mirror. Pleased with what he saw in the reflection, he straightened his necktie. Then, starting to whistle happily, he grabbed a peppermint candy from a tin on his filing cabinet. Untwisting the piece from its wrapper, he popped it into his mouth. He held his hand in front of his mouth and smelled his breath. Then he flashed a grin. It was as if nothing had changed. Walter Sparrow, as the world knew him, was back.

As he left Fulton's campus and crossed the street to Opal Avenue, Vince walked with a spring in his step. It was more than that. He felt like dancing. He felt like singing at the top of his lungs. He felt like spinning around in a circle until he barfed. He felt like doing any number of things that someone who just survived a terrifying experience feels like doing—cartwheeling, playing air guitar, eating a tub of ice cream, or kissing puppies. This was because Vince was lucky to be alive. And he knew it.

"Wow, I'm glad that's over," he said, glancing over at Gene. "At first I believed you," he said. "I figured Vargon's nephew had to be behind all the kidnappings—had to be totally evil. But he's a really good guy." He laughed. It felt so good. It felt *alive* good. "That was a close one, though. Remember that time we took those pictures of Kid Crusty, and he chased us with his lawn tractor for, like, fifteen blocks? That was close." Then he raised a finger in the air. "But *this*, my friend, this was closer."

But Gene wasn't answering. He wasn't even looking at him.

"I have to write about him," said Gene.

"Are you crazy?" asked Vince.

"We wrote about the Shock Brothers, the Dime, the San Diego Dwarf, Hover Boy, and now Mold Man," said Gene, staring at the sidewalk, lost in thought. "Why does Walter get some sort of free pass? Listen. We can make it a special issue. It'll be great." Then he looked up, excited. "You'll help me, right?"

Vince did not like where this was going. Not one bit. "Are you crazy?" he said. "You can't write about that guy!

He's totally insane! He's not evil anymore, but he's still bonkers."

"I can't do this without you," said Gene. "You know I can't write. Don't be a traitor, not now."

Vince stopped in the middle of the sidewalk. "Didn't you hear anything he said? He's going to toss you to wild pigs or something!"

"It was wild dogs," corrected Gene. "Plus, I doubt he'd go to that much trouble."

Grabbing Gene by the shoulders, Vince shook him roughly. "He asked us not to. Didn't you listen? He's trying to stay hidden; he's being chased."

"But imagine what this story could do for us," said Gene, pulling away. Then, amazingly, he started to smile. "We have his real name, and photos. We even know where he works." He began to nod, convinced. "No one would ever laugh at us again."

"Believe me, I'm sick of that too," said Vince, "but writing about Walter isn't the way to stop it. He's off-limits."

"Why?" asked Gene.

Vince clenched his fists in anger. "What if you get it *wrong*, Gene?"

Both of them stood there by their bikes considering what this might mean.

"What if he really *is* helping kids?" asked Vince. "What if he really wants to be a better person? Do you really want popularity so much that you'd risk ruining that guy's life, and also risk him killing us?" Shaking his head, he started to push his bike again. "We should just leave him alone."

"You just want to scoop me!" Gene shouted after him.

"Nope," said Vince, not stopping. "I don't care about headlines."

"Liar!" shouted Gene. "Traitor!"

But Vince kept right on walking.

A short time passed before Vince realized that his friend wasn't behind him. He turned around. Gene stood alone at the end of the sidewalk, a puzzled expression on his face. It was a look that Vince had never seen before. It was confusion.

Finally, after a minute or so of this, Gene came out of it. He rushed to catch up. "You're right," he said as he pulled alongside. "I don't know what I was thinking."

Smiling, Vince patted him on the back. Then the two friends pedaled off together.

9

SMACK!

The sun hadn't risen yet, but Gene was wide awake and speckled head to toe in ink. He followed the bright, wobbly beam of a miner's lamp he'd attached to the front of his bike helmet. Despite the light showing him the way, Gene had trouble steering because he was so tired. It was a miracle he hadn't crashed his bike into a parked car—or worse.

Without his friends to help him complete the newsletter, Gene had stayed up later than ever before. Quiet Matt, who normally helped print and staple the pages, hadn't answered his phone when Gene called. (Gene could have sworn he heard Crumble Bun laughing in the background of Matt's new voice-mail message.) As for Lucy and Linus, Vince had scared them off. Neither of them agreed to help with the special issue. They thought it was a "bad idea." So Gene went all night without a wink of sleep. Now he rode his bike, shortly before dawn, cutting across driveways and through alleys.

Puffing madly, he hopped a curb, and then shot across a crosswalk to the other side of the street. He grabbed another copy of the *Globe* from his shoulder bag and sent it spinning through the air. His ink-stained hands left prints on the front of his gray sweatshirt. On one shoulder he wore a backpack stuffed with plastic-wrapped newsletters weighted down by stones he'd stolen from his mother's rock garden. Even with the smell of the ink making him dizzy, Gene felt better than he'd felt in a long time.

The eyes of the world were about to be opened. When it happened, Gene Brennick would be a hero, and he would be taken seriously. No more jokes. No more wedgies. No more insults. From that day forward, life would be different. He was sure of it. Well, mostly sure.

Gene sped around the corner of Sixth and Thorn Apple streets and pulled out another newsletter. Aiming, he sent the bag twirling through the morning air, where it landed with a satisfying plop on Mr. Reeves's doorstep. Gene smiled. Mr. Reeves had once laughed at him for saying he talked to aliens, calling him a "space cadet." Now it would be Gene's turn to laugh.

Of course, he would still mow Mr. Reeves's lawn come August. The guy paid him twenty bucks. And twenty bucks was twenty bucks.

In the center of downtown Santa Rosa, a pile of blue bags landed beneath Buddy Argyle's newsstand on the corner of Chase and Patterson streets.

Buddy was a short, hook-nosed man who insisted on wearing cowboy boots every day, even with shorts. When he saw the newsletters, Buddy got up from his folding chair. He ambled over to the bundle and stuck one of them under a scrawny arm. Stealing a look at the front page of the *Globe*, he grumbled. Normally the *Globe* came on Fridays; what was it doing here on a Sunday?

Still, Buddy stuck the pile of flimsy two-page school newsletters on his newsstand. He placed them on a shelf between a Japanese financial newspaper and a sports magazine. There was no good reason why he did this every week. Maybe it was because his childhood dream had been to write for a fancy newspaper. Or maybe it was because nearly every sentence on the front page ended in an exclamation point. He wasn't sure.

Regardless of why he did it, Buddy set the *Globe* out every week with the rest of his product. He charged a quarter for each copy that the kids gave him for free, not that any ever sold. However, on that particular Sunday morning, something very peculiar happened. Within fifteen minutes of the newsstand opening, five of the six issues of the *Globe* sold.

Buddy had to buy the last copy back from a customer, just so he could see what all the fuss was about. Retreating to his lawn chair, he sat with a loud stretch of the straps and pulled open the pages. He read the first few lines of the featured story and grunted.

The article was about a local man named Walter Sparrow, a guidance counselor, an upstanding member of the community. He had even been grand marshal of the Fulton Christmas parade—twice. He was also, according to the story, from another planet.

Walter was a lot of things, including one of Buddy Argyle's best customers.

In Lodestone State Park, off Highway 10, Alan, also known as Mold Man, emerged from the bushes. Several days before, he had escaped from his captors and once again gone into hiding. He'd spent the time since in disguise, wearing a pair of flannel pajamas he'd stolen off a sleeping camper. They seemed to fit snugly, as though they were several sizes too small. This might have been because he still wore his special transparent body suit underneath them, making the fit extra snug.

Mold Man had stolen a hat too. It was a hunter's cap with ear flaps. He wore the cap on top of his helmet, so altogether—head, helmet, and hat—he probably stood about seven feet tall. This was not the best way to stay unnoticed. It was also not the best way to walk around an area filled with low-hanging tree branches.

Tiptoeing along the dirt path, Mold Man made his way toward the small blue bag that lay on the gravel of the parking lot. In his haste, he stepped on a twig. It cracked loudly. He froze in his tracks. A group of tents stood a short distance away. Campfires burned with rippling red heat. Someone strummed a guitar. It was an inviting scene, but the last thing Mold Man wanted was to be kidnapped again. Not after he'd found such a great pair of pajamas.

When he reached the blue bag, Mold Man picked it up and shook out the thin newsletter inside. He made a point to always read the *Globe*, if for no other reason than the personal ads. There weren't that many cute alien girls to date. The last girl he went out with had kept one of her heads hidden under her dress the whole time they were at dinner. And boy had that head been ugly.

He unfolded the newsletter. Then, taking one look at the cover story about Walter Sparrow, he began to sweat. This was not good.

"Who are you?" said a voice. Mold Man spun around and found a young boy standing next to him. The boy was about eight years old and wore pajamas. The pattern was similar to that on the pair Mold Man had stolen.

"I'm just getting the newspaper," said Mold Man, not knowing what else to say.

The boy blinked. Then he began to scream. *"It's Bigfoot!"* he screamed. *"It's Bigfoot dressed as an astronaut and in my dad's pajamas!"*

"No!" shouted Mold Man. "I'm not Bigfoot. I'm an alien."

The boy stopped screaming and stared.

"It's an alien!" the boy screamed.

"Rats," said Mold Man as he took off at a sprint, the ears of his hunter's cap flapping.

For the most part, Gene's special edition of the *Globe* went as unread as any of its other issues. Most people who found the blue bags on their doorsteps emptied them over their recycling bins. Then they used the bag as a sack for dog poop. The revealing story about Walter Sparrow, the guidance counselor at Fulton Junior High, went largely ignored. At least, that's how it appeared at first.

What neither Gene nor Vince realized was that they had a fan. His name was Bernard Wax, and he lived in a basement apartment underneath the sub sandwich shop across from the coin-operated laundry.

That Sunday, when he heard the sound of the *Globe* landing on the steps outside his unit, Bernard went to his door to fetch it, shaving cream still puffy and white on his face. He was surprised. The newsletter only came on Fridays, yet here was a special issue sitting outside his door. Shrugging, he took the blue bag inside and set it on his kitchen table. He would read it over breakfast. The *Globe* made any morning just a little bit better. It was like the cream in his coffee, the syrup over his waffles.

Bernard Wax had first stumbled upon the *Globe* when he moved to Santa Rosa from Los Angeles. A stray copy had stuck to his shoe as he boarded the bus one morning on his way to work at the *Santa Rosa Examiner*, the town's premier newspaper. It hooked him almost instantly. The headlines were outrageous. The writing was delightful, messy but energetic. As for the aliens, they were some of the most ridiculous, and hilarious, characters he'd ever read about.

From that day forward, as far as Bernard Wax was concerned, Gene Brennick and Vince Haskell were geniuses in the making. That's why every Friday he looked forward to that little blue bag.

As he sat down to breakfast that Sunday morning, Bernard opened his special issue of the *Globe* newsletter. He began to read, chuckling at the "photographs" of the strange alien behind the changing screen, stepping into its skin like a normal person might step into a pair of pants. According to the article, the alien was a local guidance counselor. Bernard thought that was an especially clever touch. The piece was brilliant. Like every other issue.

Before he'd reached the bottom of the first page, Bernard had made up his mind. For months he'd considered writing an article for the *Santa Rosa Examiner* about the two high school students who published a fake alien newspaper. Now he was sold on the idea. Without even finishing his breakfast, he got up from the kitchen table and walked back to his office, the cereal in his bowl turning soggy.

The *Globe* was not getting the attention it deserved; neither were Gene Brennick and Vince Haskell. That was all about to change, whether they liked it or not. Far down at the bottom of the fourth and final page of the newsletter was a small square box that said: GOT ALIEN TIPS? CONTACT

GENE @ AIL-TIPS (555-8477). Below this, in small print, the ad continued with: NO MORE PRANK CALLS, PLEASE.

Taking his chipped gray cell phone out of his bathrobe pocket, Bernard dialed the number. It rang once, twice, three times before anyone picked up.

"Is this Gene Brennick?" asked Bernard. He listened to the voice on the other end. "No, I'm not on the football team. No. Really, I'm not lying." He listened some more. "No, that wasn't me who let the air out of your bike tires.

"Listen!" he interrupted, straightening up in his chair. "My name is Bernard Wax. I'm a reporter for the *Santa Rosa Examiner*."

There was a pause, and then the voice on the other end said something.

"No," said Bernard. "This isn't Linus playing a joke."

Bernard cleared his throat. "Hear me out, Gene. I'm a real journalist and I want to interview you for an article."

The voice on the other end began to cheer, and then it went back to chattering.

"No, I haven't called your friend Vince yet," said Bernard. "I wanted to start with you. Wait, you *don't* want me to call him?" The voice said something, and Bernard shrugged. "Okay then, sure."

Yawning, Bernard hunkered down over the table. It

was time to get comfortable. He took out his lucky scoop pencil, licked the tip, and then turned over his phone bill and prepared to jot some notes. His cat, Garcia, zipped across the table and nearly upset the sugar bowl. "So tell me more about this Walter Sparrow," he said. "This Vargon's nephew character."

One elbow in a puddle of milk, Bernard listened. He listened to a story about alien warlords and fiery planets and faraway galaxies and guidance counselors who could suck people's insides out through their mouths.

And very slowly, Bernard Wax began to realize that perhaps the *Globe* wasn't the story after all.

10

AT SIX THIRTY THE NEXT MONDAY MORNING, MRS. HASKELL, Vince's mom, threw open her front door. She balanced a mug of coffee in one hand and a baby in the other. Both needed a refill. As her youngest daughter shrieked into one ear, the other three shouted in the kitchen. They'd just ended what would become known as the "microwaveable oatmeal incident," and the walls were covered with streaks of brown sugar and cinnamon.

"These are my purple Capri pants!" Susan shouted from the kitchen. *"You know I need them for public speaking!"*

"No one wants to look at your ugly face!" screamed Sharon.

"I'm not worried about my face!" shouted Susan, bursting into tears. *"Those pants make my butt look smaller!"*

"That's what you think!" screamed Sharon.

Mrs. Haskell took a deep breath. She leaned across the doorway into the apartment hall and grabbed the end of the yellow newspaper bag, pulling it off the floor. Then she went back inside. With the *Santa Rosa Examiner* hanging from her fist, she headed down the hall. As she passed each bedroom, she banged on the door like a prison guard rattling the bars. "Wake up, lazybones! It's time for school! It's time for work!"

Vince's mattress springs squeaked as he rolled over in bed. "Five more minutes," he groaned.

In the kitchen, Mrs. Haskell pulled out a chair and sat at the table. The aftershocks of the morning battle still shuddered across the room. Three of her girls clustered around the counter like birds around a pile of crumbs, snapping up food and screeching.

"Don't you dare take that blueberry yogurt!" snapped Susan, slamming the fridge on Sally's fingers. "Blueberry is mine. Plain gives me weird breath and I can't have weird breath around Tate."

"I wouldn't worry about that," said Sally, flipping her hair. "Tate likes Sharon. He calls her every night after you go to bed."

"What!" Susan shouted, and then leaned her head against the wall. "Was it my yogurt breath?"

"No way," interrupted Sharon as she finished packing her backpack. "It was your giant butt."

Susan grabbed another nearby bowl of uneaten oatmeal, raising it back as though she was about to throw. *"I'm going to tear out that nasty nose ring!"*

"Don't bother," murmured Sally as she slipped on her earphones. "It's not even real. It's a sticker."

As it was every morning, the girls went about their business. And as it was every morning, Mrs. Haskell hoped to find some peace in her daily newspaper. She shook it out of the yellow plastic bag and gazed at the front page, sipping her lukewarm coffee. A feeling of calm settled over her even as the baby squirmed on her knee.

Then Mrs. Haskell saw the article written by Bernard Wax. It was situated far down on the page, below the weather graphic and next to a picture of a dog eating a little boy's ice cream cone right out of his hand. The article bore the title "The Secret Life of Walter Sparrow," and it featured a strange photo of a man stepping out of his skin as though it were a dingy bathrobe.

"Girls," said Mrs. Haskell quietly, as she kept reading.

The sisters did not stop. By now, Susan had maple

syrup in her hair, and Sharon was covered in flour. Sally wept in the corner.

"Girls!" yelled Mrs. Haskell.

Her daughters froze. They looked at their mother.

"Go wake your brother," she ordered.

11

WALTER SPARROW WAS A LOT OF THINGS, BUT HUMAN wasn't one of them. He was a cat lover. He was a big fan of the bluegrass band Rusty Watering Can. He was fond of wearing monogrammed hankies in his breast pocket. But none of that mattered. Since he was nothing more than a collection of loosely joined atomic energy particles, Walter Sparrow rarely, if ever, felt fear. A creature that can explode a person from the inside out doesn't scare easily.

That morning, however, Walter Sparrow was sweating. Yes, sweating. He'd already soaked through two undershirts, and his hair was beginning to droop. Lying in the chair by his door was a copy of the *Santa Rosa Examiner*. It was covered with his sweaty fingerprints.

Walter stood before his desk at Fulton Junior High School, emptying the contents of his drawers into a suitcase. First he grabbed the picture frames and the yearbooks. Then he took his degrees and teaching certificates. Last he emptied his entire candy jar into one of the suitcase pockets. Walter had always resisted the urge to eat any of the sweets, since they were for the students. But since he probably wouldn't live to see the sunset, he thought he could break one of his office rules—just this once.

A knock at the door made Walter jump in his loafers. If he'd had a heart, it would have skipped a beat. When he didn't answer, a quiet voice called from outside in the waiting area. "Walter, it's me." The voice belonged to Principal Pinkus, one of Walter's oldest and dearest human friends. "Let me in, please!"

Now, Walter knew better than to open the door. He'd been in Salem, Massachusetts, during the famous witch trials of the 1690s. That had been a pretty bad scene, and he'd gained important lessons from it. He'd learned what frightened humans did to those who were different: They burned them, hanged them, crushed them, or drowned them. None of these outcomes sounded very appealing to Walter. He liked to spend his evenings watching cop shows on TV and eating ice cream out of the carton. Getting burned alive would certainly put a kink in those plans.

A few minutes passed. Then, as Walter was in the middle of gathering his extra shirts and ties, he heard the voices—a crowd. He could just make them out through the wall. Closing his eyes, he tried to focus. "Relax," he told himself. He knew that if he let his worry, his anger, loose, then Fulton Junior High School would have a lot more to worry about than finding a new guidance counselor.

"Freak!" shouted someone outside his door. At least that's what it had sounded like, but Walter couldn't be sure.

He hated that word, "freak." His purple eye flashed with rage. A large brass clock on his shelf sprang up, hovered in the air, and then rocketed across the room. It slammed into the far wall with a fiery crash. After the clock burst, its inner gears and springs floated in the air for a few seconds on puffs of hot air. Then they shot out in all directions, sticking in the wall plaster like tiny metal darts. The whole room trembled as Walter took long, deep breaths, trying to get a grip.

Again, Principal Pinkus knocked on the door. "Walter! Let me in *now*!" With a flip of the lock, Walter opened the door and allowed his friend to slip inside.

Principal Pinkus was a large, red-faced man with a balding crew cut of silvery hair and eyebrows that always seemed to be raised. He had the boring look of a 1970s football player who's become a football commentator.

Resting against the door, the sleeves of his dress shirt rolled up around his large arms, Principal Pinkus stared at Walter. "You really got your back to the wall this time," he said.

"I know it," said Walter.

"Was that really you," asked Principal Pinkus, "in that *Examiner* article?" When Walter nodded, his friend whistled loudly. "This is bad," he said.

"Do you think it's really *that* bad?" asked Walter.

"Walter, you sank Ms. Cranston's station wagon in the pool!" said Principal Pinkus. "All she did was ask if you'd seen the newspaper today."

Walter threw his hands in the air. "It wasn't on purpose," he said. "Sometimes bad things happen when I get upset."

"Well, *this* is bad," said Principal Pinkus, mopping his brow. "This is the worst."

Walter went back to his desk. He zipped up his suitcase and dropped it to the floor. "Well, it can't be as bad as that time I accidentally sent that e-mail about the cafeteria food to the whole faculty."

Hanging his head, Principal Pinkus sighed. "Walter," he said, "Ms. Cranston was still *in* her station wagon when you sank it. It took the entire water polo team to get her out. They emptied the bench, and you know that they never make Bobby Tipper swim because of his asthma."

Sinking into his office chair, Walter buried his face in his hands. He couldn't believe his rotten luck. Everything he'd built for the last fifty years. Every good deed he'd done. Every young person he'd helped. All of it was about to be flushed down the toilet, all because of Gene and Vince.

"Listen, Carl," said Walter, "you know me. I'm not all bad. True, I am the nephew of the cruelest and most powerful being in all of existence. True, I have done some things I'm not proud of. Like that planet in Alpha Sector Seven that I threw into the sun—not the best idea. I know that now." When he next spoke, he tried extra hard to keep his eyes from flashing, which they did when he felt stress. "I'm not a threat to anyone." Even as he said this, the crowd in the hall began to chant.

Principal Pinkus scratched his chin. "But, wasn't it you who made the pages in all the library books disappear?"

"Yes, yes," said Walter, waving his hand. "And they didn't disappear. I burned them up when someone stole my cream cheese out of the teacher's refrigerator. But that's not the point."

"Then what is the point?" asked Principal Pinkus.

He looked nervously over his shoulder. The sound of a mob, shouts and stomping, had reached the office door. The words "Fire him!" were being repeated again and again.

"I get it," said Walter. "I can't work here anymore. Not with my secret out. Not with people fearing me."

"I'm sorry, pal." Principal Pinkus looked away.

It was clear that his friend still didn't understand what Walter was getting at.

No one was safe. Not if people knew who and what Walter really was. Despite being a creature of extraordinary powers, Walter was lonely and moody, and he had a terrible temper. When he got mad, awful things happened. Everyone gets mad sometimes. But when Walter Sparrow got mad, he got *evil*.

If he ever harmed the kids that he'd grown to love, he'd never forgive himself. That meant he had to go.

As is the case with most angry mobs, this one wouldn't be stopped. Their chanting of "Fire him!" grew so loud that Walter and Principal Pinkus had to start shouting to hear each other. As the two men were preparing to say their last good-byes, the office door flew open with a bang.

The mob of about twenty angry teachers and parents shoved their way into Walter's office. They found him standing by the window, suitcase in hand, as Principal Pinkus stood in front to protect him.

"I would never want anything to happen to your kids; I care for them deeply," Walter said to the crowd. "I'm sorry this is what happened."

"Where are his suction pads?" shouted one irate mother.

"And his horns?" shouted another.

"Put him in jail!" called a man in back.

"Let him go peacefully," said Principal Pinkus. "He's served this community well and he's still my friend."

The mob took a good look at Walter Sparrow. They saw that he looked about the same as he always did—maybe a little sick, as if he'd missed too many nights of sleep. *It would do him some good to go to the gym and work out,* one woman thought. *Mr. Sparrow might want to start dying his hair,* thought another. *Oh,* that's *Mr. Sparrow,* thought one man. *I thought we were here for a different guy, the ceramics teacher.*

Regardless of how many knew why they were there, the people were upset. Most of the teachers were shocked to learn that one of their own might be from another planet. Not that it was too surprising. Some of the teachers were pretty weird. The history teacher, Mr. Rickles, carried an empty lunchbox with him wherever he went. Nobody knew what that was all about. Nobody really wanted to.

Most of the parents were shocked to learn that the school guidance counselor was not who he said he was. And what if he was an alien, as the newspaper article suggested? These parents wanted only the best for their kids, and there was no way that Walter could have gotten the right training anywhere but on Earth. Wasn't Jupiter almost all gases? Mercury was just a bunch of burning craters. How could any of those experiences help Walter work with kids who ate paper or who talked to people using only puppets? They couldn't. He seemed to love his work, but he was weird. And weird was always bad. That was the one killer about Earth.

"Who are you?" demanded one woman near the front.

"Yeah, how about a little truth for a change!" shouted someone else.

Being a creature that is made up of pure energy, Walter could have burned a hole in the ceiling of the school and rocketed away. He could have drawn a circle of fire on the floor and traveled back or forward in time. He could have summoned a flaming phoenix from the swirling gases of the lobster nebula. At the very least, he could have taken out his cell phone and dialed Ernesto's Taxi Service at 301-CAR-ERNE (Monday–Saturday, twenty-four hours a day; Sunday, 8 a.m.–8 p.m.).

But Walter knew he'd already made enough of a scene and that the only way he might ever earn back the trust of these people would be to do things the hard way. He also didn't want to do any more damage. Apparently he owed Ms. Cranston some money for her station wagon, and guidance counselors don't make a lot of money.

Ignoring the angry mob, Walter climbed up on his desk and slipped out through the open window. He dropped to the ground and, with a mournful sigh, took off running toward the large clump of trees at the far end of campus. He moved fast, as powerful aliens often do, and was safely in the shadows within a matter of seconds.

Before departing forever, Walter gazed back a final time at his beloved Fulton Junior High School. It was a special place to him, a place he thought of as a home. Then he turned away.

As he hiked into the shady forest, Walter's eyes began to burn with a red and purple glow, like the ashes of a dying fire. He considered his next move. As he did, he went from sad to angry to evil, all in the span of five minutes. Only one thing in his life made sense anymore, and that was getting even.

"Gene," he said in a growl.

Walter Sparrow may not have been human, but he most certainly could feel hatred.

12

OCTAGON
You'd better put down that pair of pants,
Technocrat.

TECHNOCRAT
And why would I want to do that? Everyone
needs pants.

OCTAGON
Not a cyborg. Not anymore.
*Technocrat lunges for the key to the airlock,
but the parrot, Ms. Beasly, beats him to it,
pecking his hand.*

MS. BEASLY
And you wonder where he got that hook.
Caw.

It was lunchtime, and Vince had wicked writer's block.
It was something new for him. Every time he sat down,

powered up his laptop, and started to type, the words fizzled out after a paragraph. For two days straight he'd been stuck on page twenty-five of his graphic novel *Days of the Octagon*. After a whole year of trying to find more time to write stories, he suddenly couldn't even think of any to write. His mind was too jumbled with real-life problems to focus on fiction.

"Darn it," said Vince, pulling at his hair until it stood up in wavy stalks. "What are the natural enemies of pirates? Cyborgs hate pirates, right?"

"What are cyborgs?" asked Linus. She hunched over in her chair, stapling copies of the *Globe* together—two sheets, five stories. After every ten, she bundled them with rubber bands and inserted them into her backpack. Then she would start the next batch. She included all of the best issues: "Stilt Walkers Need Work!" and "My Uncle Dates a Warfblatt!" and even "Blob Runs for City Council!"

"What are *cyborgs*?" said Vince. "They're half-human, half-machine. Come on, get with it."

"I don't know," said Linus, frowning. "I'm not really into that stuff. I have a life."

Vince sat at his desk in room 113, surrounded by stacks of flyers and note cards with the *Globe* tabloid logo stamped on them. Comic Mania, Santa Rosa's annual comic convention, started that afternoon. Linus had come up with the bright idea to set up a small table in one of the hotel exhibit halls and pass out free copies of the newsletter. She figured that if dorks in costumes could appreciate imaginary aliens, they should probably appreciate real ones, as well.

As Vince typed, Linus stopped stapling and swiveled in her chair. She started combing through a box of pens to give away to convention visitors. On the side of each pen were printed the words: THE FINEST IN ALIEN REPORTING. She had skimped on the pens, so most of them didn't work, but they did look pretty snazzy behind a person's ear. In an attempt to add some flair, she spent an extra ten bucks for some women's lip balm with the *Globe* logo on the lid. She doubted this was going to be a hot item at a comic convention, though, since most geeks were mama's boys.

"So what did you think about the *Examiner* article on Walter Sparrow?" asked Linus, trying to act busy, even though she was clearly curious about Vince's reaction. "Did you even see it? Wow, did that reporter ever scoop you guys. He mentioned you, though. Sounded like he thinks you're cool. I guess that makes sense. Dorks probably find other dorks cool."

Vince groaned.

Oh, he'd seen it all right. His mother made a point of waving her copy of the *Santa Rosa Examiner* in front of his face the second he walked into the kitchen that morning. Never in his life had he seen her more agitated. Ordering him to sit down at the breakfast table, she had proceeded to read the entire Bernard Wax article out loud, as the rest of the family just sat there, eyes empty, mouths hanging open. Vince didn't say a word. Not even when his mother ordered him to quit the newsletter and spend less time with Gene.

He didn't say anything because he agreed. It was time for him to take a break.

Of course, Vince's sisters had a delightful time making fun of his newfound fame. At last, after years of telling him that he was the world's biggest loser, it had been confirmed by the local media. However, Vince had a suspicion that the girls were also secretly jealous. Each one of them had the same goal in life of becoming a reality-show contestant and then cutting a pop album. As far as they were probably concerned, a short piece in the crummy local newspaper was one step further down the road to stardom.

"That good, huh?" said Linus.

"I didn't like being written about; it made me feel weird," said Vince. "Like I was walking around in my underwear."

Reclining in his office chair, Matt grunted. "You're

going to hate being popular," he said, reaching over to take a fresh stack of flyers from the printer. "I was popular once, back when I was captain of the chess team. It was such a drag." He shook his head slowly. "Way too many parties, man." Then he smiled. "That's why I hang out with Cathy now. She likes quiet evenings at home."

Linus took the printouts from Matt and began to go through them, stapling. She'd finished only two of them when there was a noise at the door to room 113—a thud against the wood and whispering.

Everyone glanced up and saw the same thing; a group of strange students peering through the small square window. Elf ears were visible bobbing up and down behind the glass. A boy dressed like Darth Vader reached up and waved with his gloved fists. "You've got fans," said Linus.

"Why are they dressed like that?" asked Vince.

"I'm guessing that most of them are heading to Comic Mania after school," said Linus. "The nerds."

"Wow, this would make Gene's day," said Matt as he watched more kids gather outside the door to room 113.

"Where is Gene, anyway?" asked Vince. "He's got some explaining to do."

None of them had seen their friend that day. And while it wasn't odd for Gene to show up at school late or not at all, they figured he'd want to be on time that Monday, to suck up all the attention the *Examiner* article was generating.

Almost as if on cue, Gene swaggered into the news-room followed by a group of about ten other Santa Rosa Junior High students, a mixture of ages, and both boys and girls. Almost all of them carried a copy of the *Globe* or the *Santa Rosa Examiner*. Gene wore oversize sunglasses and a thin leather jacket that had once belonged to Vince (he'd grown out of it). He also appeared taller. Looking more closely, Vince realized that this was because Gene was wearing special shoes his mother had bought him when they thought one of his legs was shorter than the other.

Sliding onto his desk, all casual, Gene accidentally knocked most of his own junk, and Vince's too, onto the floor. He pretended not to notice and pulled open a drawer to grab around for a black permanent marker. When he found one, he waded back into the small crowd of students and began autographing whatever he could find—socks, backpacks, homework, bagels, faces. He did this whether or not the kids were asking him for his signature.

The funny thing was that many of them really *were* there to see Gene, to ask about the article in the newspaper, and even to get him to write his name on something as a souvenir. And they weren't all Comic Mania nerds either. Some of them were stylish punks with leather bracelets and nose rings; a couple were actually jocks. There was even a cheerleader—an honest-to-God cheerleader.

"Wow," said Matt, stunned. "He's a star."

"One of those dying stars that's about to explode, maybe," said Linus, capping a pen.

"Are those your mother's sunglasses?" asked Vince.

"No!" Gene took them off, embarrassed.

"They are too," said Vince. "I've seen her wear them plenty of times."

"I think they look good," said Linus.

"Thanks, pretty lady," Gene said, nodding in her direction.

"*Pretty lady?*" said Vince. "What is this, a bad movie?"

Then, as the rest of the staff watched, Gene jumped up on a chair and began to make a speech. "I'm throwing a huge party tonight at my house!" he said. "Tell your friends. Tell people who aren't your friends! It's going to be sweet! There's going to be guacamole and everything! Seven o'clock at my house! If you want to know more information, visit the party's website at W-W-W-DOT-GENE-IS-AWESOME-PARTY-DOT-COM." He waved and flashed two peace signs. "Thank you!"

Just as he was about to start offering to have his picture taken with people, Vince stepped in. He walked up behind his friend and grabbed him by his hood, dragging him off the chair and into a corner of the studio.

"What did you do, dude?" asked Vince, spinning Gene to face him.

"What do you mean?" asked Gene as he reached over to sign a copy of the *Santa Rosa Examiner* that was being thrust into his face. "This is awesome."

Vince glared at him. "How did this journalist, Bernard What's-His-Face, even find out about Walter, about us?"

"He called me, but only after he read my special issue," said Gene.

"I thought we decided *not* to do the Walter Sparrow story," said Vince.

Gene huffed. "*We* never decided that. Neither of us said anything like that."

"It's called an unspoken agreement," yelled Vince. "You're not *supposed* to say anything. You're just supposed to know, because we're such good friends."

"Well, I'm sorry if I can't read your thoughts," said Gene. "I'm not Mind-Master Melvin."

"Who in the heck is Mind-Master Melvin?" asked Vince.

"That kid who worked at the video store," said Gene, shaking his head. "We interviewed him in August, remember? He moved to Pittsburgh last month."

Vince could barely contain his anger. He tightened his hands into fists, and then tried to tighten those into something but without much success. "Listen," he said, giving up and hanging his head, exhausted. "I can't work here anymore. You do whatever you want, and you never listen to me."

"Sure, I listen to you," said Gene. "It wears me out, but I do it."

"That's my point!" growled Vince. "You hear me out, but then do whatever you want. You're selfish. You care only about yourself. You don't care about me, and you don't care about the Ails we write about."

"What are you complaining about?" asked Gene, completely missing his friend's point. "The *Globe* is selling like hotcakes!"

"The newsletter is *free*! It's not selling like anything!" shouted Vince.

Unfortunately, none of these arguments seemed to be making an impression on Gene, who gestured wildly at the crowd of kids. "Look at this, man," he said. "People know who we are! And they came here to hang out with *us*! They don't want to be jerks. They don't want to make fun of us. They want to be friends." He grinned excitedly. "This is what we wanted."

Instead of returning the smile, Vince glared at his friend. "Well, it's sure not what Walter Sparrow wanted," he said flatly. Then, grabbing his backpack, he headed for the door. "I quit!" he called over a shoulder.

The rest of the *Globe* staff watched, stunned, as Vince pushed through the door and vanished down the hallway. Even Gene seemed a little surprised by this development. Eyebrows scrunched in a puzzled expression, he watched his best friend go. It didn't stop him for long, however. Raising his black marker, he walked back into his group of fans. "Who's next?" he shouted.

Dr. Jinks glanced up from where she shuffled through a stack of papers on her desk. "And where were you this morning?" she asked. It was three in the afternoon, time for her appointment with Gene, the same Gene who had been absent from school since the homeroom bell rang.

Entering the spacious office, Gene dropped his backpack on the floor by the chair. "I was sick," he said, shrugging. Of course, this wasn't the case at all. In fact, Gene had spent the better part of the day updating his page on the social networking site Mugshot. He'd added a link to the *Santa Rosa Examiner* article about him and Vince and changed his status to "Gene Brennick is . . . looking for superstardom."

Not stopping what she was doing, Dr. Jinks smiled knowingly. She slid open her desk drawer and took out a small pink slip, then slid it across the desk to him. "Nice try," she said. "I'm pretty good at spotting forged signatures, and yours was one of the worst I've ever seen. Next time you write a fake note from your mother, remember that the name Judith is not spelled J-U-D-E-E-T-H."

Punching his palm, Gene cursed the name of Vince Haskell, who had told him how to spell his mom's name.

Chuckling, Dr. Jinks relaxed back into her cushy leather chair. "Now, where were you really?"

"Fine," said Gene, also sitting. "I was at the comic shop downtown for some of the morning, and then at the offices of the *Santa Rosa Examiner* for the rest." He kicked his legs up on the puffy armrest of the overstuffed chair, sinking deeper into the cushion. "Funny how life changes, isn't it?" he said. "One day you think the world is against you and you want to drop your best friend off a bridge. And the next, you're a celebrity."

"I don't know what you mean," said Dr. Jinks, not

seeming very interested in what he was saying. As she spoke she examined a pair of open file folders on her desk, each of which overflowed with photographs and handwritten notes. "I've been out of the office, following some other leads."

"What do you mean 'leads'?" Gene asked, confused.

This snapped Dr. Jinks out of her distracted haze. She straightened up and slid the two files away. Then, adjusting her black jacket, she made eye contact with Gene for the first time. "I'm sorry," she said. "What I meant to say is that I've been busy with other students. There are a lot of people who need my attention, Gene. You're not the only one I'm interested in."

"Should I be jealous?" said Gene jokingly.

"I wouldn't," said Dr. Jinks, drifting off into her paperwork again. "If you only knew how many leads I've had to follow through the centuries, each of them leading me step by step to where I am now. Poor souls, I vaporized most of them once I gained the information I required."

"You what?" asked Gene.

"Oh, nothing," said Dr. Jinks, waving one hand. "There were others. That's all."

"Okay," said Gene, feeling a little hurt. After their few sessions together, he'd started to grow quite fond of Dr.

Jinks. It didn't matter that she had weird habits, such as picking her teeth with scissors or occasionally barking in a high-pitched voice, like a seal. She was pretty, and she treated him like he was special—and not in the bad way either.

"So what were you saying?" she asked.

"The article in the *Santa Rosa Examiner*," said Gene. "It's pretty cool. It's about me and sort of about Vince and about the newsletter." The issue had been out for hours, and he'd just figured everyone had seen it.

"I don't read the newspaper," said Dr. Jinks, waving her hand again. "Earthly news sources are far inferior to others in the galaxy."

"What?" Gene asked.

Dr. Jinks's eyes grew wide, and then she began to laugh. It was clearly forced, and Gene half expected her to start barking like a seal again. "Nothing," she said. "I'm just being silly. I didn't have my usual cup of hot water and coffee grounds this morning."

"Right," said Gene, looking at her suspiciously.

"So what's this about an article?" she asked.

Gene pulled his backpack closer to him and yanked out a yellow plastic bag—he had four copies stuffed into the big pocket—and dropped it on her desk. It landed with a loud thump, and some of her paperwork fluttered. Dr. Jinks glared at him for a second, irritated, but then went about shaking the newspaper free and opening its droopy pages.

He waited as she read the first few lines.

"This is about you and the *Globe*," she said matter-of-factly.

"Yeah," said Gene, grinning. He couldn't help himself.

She glanced at him from around the front page, her face a sickly green color. "It says here that you met someone claiming to be Vargon's nephew. Is this true?"

"Yeah," said Gene. "He's this guidance counselor over at Fulton. He's kind of a nutcase. Not surprising, though. I mean, it's *Fulton*." He started laughing but stopped when he saw how Dr. Jinks's tightening fists were starting to shred the newspaper.

"Why didn't I read this in *your* newsletter?" she demanded. Her voice jumped in volume and became squeaky, like car brakes in need of a checkup. "Did I miss an issue of the *Globe*? You're not supposed to publish another issue until Friday. It's a Friday publication!"

Growing anxious, Gene reached into his backpack again. This time he took out a blue plastic bag containing the special issue of the *Globe*. Leaning out of his chair, he slid it across the desk into her waiting hands. "It was a special issue," he whispered. Before Gene could even release the bag, Dr. Jinks had clawed it up and torn through the blue plastic. She unfolded the two-page printout and began to read.

When the guidance counselor said nothing for a full minute, Gene assumed this meant that she was waiting for him to start talking. So he did. "You're probably wondering what my friend Vince thinks about all of this fame," he said. "Well, since you asked, let me just say that I'm disappointed he doesn't share my excitement. Can you believe he tried to talk me out of writing that article about Walter Sparrow? That's the article that's putting us on the map." Gene shook his head. "It's sad. Vince and I started the newsletter together. He helped me tackle the San Diego Dwarf when she pickpocketed my iPod. I thought he was my best friend."

Dr. Jinks said nothing, her face growing greener. She turned the page and continued reading.

Gazing out the window at the kids passing to and from class, Gene thought about Lucy. "It's funny," he said. "There's this girl, a friend of mine, and she's really nice. I thought she was pretty before, but now . . . She has freckles on her nose. I'd never noticed them before. Freckles! They're kind of cute, not like the ones on Linus's face. Lucy's freckles are, like, wow."

But Dr. Jinks was still not listening. Not in the slightest.

When she finally finished the article, Dr. Jinks carefully folded the newsletter and placed it back on the desk. Then she cleared her throat in order to get Gene's attention. "So, this man, this Walter Sparrow, he's at Fulton Junior High School right now?"

Now it was Gene's turn to be distracted. He was still talking about Lucy. "And when she eats potato chips, she munches them bit by bit with her two front teeth, like a hamster, and it's pretty cute. Is it weird that I think so?"

"Gene," said Dr. Jinks, raising her voice. "Where is Walter Sparrow now?"

"Don't get me started on her smell," said Gene. "I could go on forever. It's like someone lighting a can of room deodorizer on fire. It's nice."

"Gene!"

The voice that came out of her mouth sounded nothing like the woman he'd come to know. It was low, deep, and fuzzy, like someone shouting through an intercom.

"What?" Gene asked, looking up.

Then Dr. Jinks stared at him so hard her eyes looked electric. "Is this article true? Is all of it *true*?"

Gene didn't know how to respond. "Yes," he said, shrugging. "My articles are always true. How many times do I have to tell people that?"

This answer seemed to satisfy Dr. Jinks. Briskly, she began to hurriedly pack papers into the open briefcase on her desk. She slipped a cell phone out of her jacket pocket. "We need to end our time a little early today," she told Gene, standing up.

"Really?" asked Gene. He couldn't keep up. One second Dr. Jinks was packing her paperwork, and the next she was standing by the door, wireless headset in her ear.

"Yes, come on," she said. "Let's go. Go."

"Okay," said Gene, unsure of what was happening. Zipping his backpack, he got up from the overstuffed chair and headed for the hall.

"Yes, yes, I need two teams," Dr. Jinks said into her phone. "Six agents."

Gene paused outside the door. He opened his mouth to thank her for listening to him. More than that, he wanted to ask her whether or not it had been a good idea for him to ignore Vince's warnings about Walter Sparrow. Frankly, he was still a little nervous about the whole thing. Despite the cool article about him in the *Examiner* and the popularity it brought, he had a sour feeling deep in his gut that wouldn't go away.

Unfortunately, as soon as Gene's shoes hit the hallway tile, the door to Dr. Jinks's office slammed shut behind him. He heard the loud bang before he felt the rush of wind that followed. That was that. "Guess she's in a hurry," he mumbled to himself as he walked off toward his locker.

Gene had been right. Dr. Jinks was in a hurry. That's because for the last five thousand years she'd been searching the galaxy for the alien known as Vargon's nephew. Now, at long last, she knew right where to find him.

At the Holiday Inn in downtown Santa Rosa, Gene's cousin Fred slipped out the back door of the ballroom to catch a breath of fresh air. If he'd learned nothing else from twenty years of attending Comic Mania, it was that fans of the superheroes Platypus Lass and Brain Scan rarely bathed. After a whole morning closed in a room with hundreds of sweaty nerds, you started to smell like nerd too. It was his least favorite thing about comic shows. It was second only to seeing all those middle-aged men wearing tights.

Hands in his pockets, Fred sat on a metal railing and watched the endless line of people dressed as robots and pixies march toward the hotel. It never ended.

As he often did, Fred imagined what his life could have been if he'd published *Arachnid Boy* first. First of all, he'd be rich. Second of all, legions of comic fans would worship him. Third of all, he wouldn't be living in a trailer along Highway 10. Last, and most important, he wouldn't have to deal with aliens anymore. No longer would they drop by and ask for help. No longer would they keep him from doing what he wanted in order to protect them from society and from the government.

True, Arachnid Boy and the other aliens were his friends. But after so many years of protecting other people, Fred was getting worn out. What had they ever brought him but trouble and heartache?

As he daydreamed in the afternoon sun, Fred spotted a figure leave the crowd of comic fans and walk toward him. It was a man. He was tall and slender and wore a dark suit and dark sunglasses. Almost immediately, Fred recognized the man as Agent Park from the BSSM. His heart sank.

Agent Park stopped in front of Fred. "Good afternoon, Mr. Brennick," he said.

"Agent Park," said Fred. "What can I do for you?"

The man reached into his suit pocket and removed a small silver device that looked remarkably similar to an electric nose-hair trimmer. "Since you asked," he said, "there is something you can do."

With the flip of a switch, a bolt of lightning exploded from the device and struck Fred in the chest. It made a hissing sound, like bacon on a grill. Moaning quietly, Fred lost feeling in his legs and fell to the sidewalk as his hair began to smoke.

"You can join me in my truck, if you don't mind," said Agent Park with a smile. His eyes narrowed into two yellowish slits as he tossed Fred over his shoulder.

On the way back to the parking lot, Agent Park passed a whole crowd of nerds in costume. No one gave a second look to the man in the black suit carrying the old dude. After all, it was a comic book convention. Just five minutes before, a pair of wizards had fought a duel on the sidewalk over a limited-edition Platypus Lass action figure.

"Humans," mumbled Agent Park as he dumped Fred's body into the back of his black SUV.

13

"GOOD AFTERNOON, THIS IS CINDY CORNFIELD OF ACTION
Six News, Santa Rosa, coming to you live from the house
of Walter Sparrow. Or, as he is known today: Vargon's
nephew!" The pretty news lady bent sideways and adjusted
her hair in a van mirror. She straightened the collar of her
attractive blue suit jacket. Then, burping, she tightened
the waistband on her holey gray sweatpants, which no one
watching TV could see. "Can you see this zit?" she asked
Mike the cameraman.

Mike the cameraman closed his eyes and shivered.
When he'd gone to college to direct blockbuster movies,
he never thought it would end like this. "You look . . . ," he
started, and then paused. "Um, *good*?"

Cindy glared at him and took a drink of water. She was
not known for being "good." She was known for being the
face of Santa Rosa news.

Scattered in camps out in front of Walter Sparrow's house on Carmelina Terrace were members of the media. They had been sitting there on his lawn and sidewalk for nearly twenty-four hours. So it was a given that no one looked good, not even Cindy Cornfield, who had won the Anchorperson of the Year award for the last five years straight. A group of soundmen from different stations had started a poker game on a foldaway card table. A burrito truck had pulled up onto a neighbor's lawn and was selling food. It was quite a scene, topped off by the Fulton police, who had surrounded the whole area with yellow tape. No one could get in or out.

Not that the yellow tape could ever stop Walter Sparrow.

Inside his garage, Walter sat behind the wheel of his car, keys in the ignition. He couldn't bring himself to leave. Everywhere he looked there was something that brought back memories. On his visor hung a photograph of him and some of the students at Fulton. The flowers in his dashboard vase were ones that Pam Masters, the algebra teacher, had picked for him. (He'd always kind of had a crush on Ms. Masters.) Even the socks he was wearing were a pair he'd borrowed from Principal Pinkus.

For Walter, leaving Fulton and Santa Rosa County

would mean leaving who he was. He liked living there. He liked that there was a free community picnic in Fleet Park every Saturday. He liked that people smiled at you when you walked by, even when you looked terrible and were wearing gray, holey sweatpants. Most of all, he liked how people here didn't make him do bad things like create black holes or crash star cruisers into satellites. Stuff like that.

He liked that Earth made him good. Not Cindy Cornfield "good" but the kind of good where you find joy in doing kind things for other people.

Now he had to leave, all because of Gene.

Wiping his eyes, Walter pressed the button on the garage door opener. With a chugging rumble, the door lifted. A sea of people waited for him in the driveway. The crowd was so thick he couldn't even see the asphalt beneath their feet.

Walter opened his window and leaned out. "Move!" he shouted, waving his arm. The car backed up only a few feet before it bumped against the swarm of onlookers. Still, people did not move. He tried honking. That only seemed to make them more excited. After a lot of braking and bumping, Walter finally reached the street.

"Set something on fire!" a person shouted.

"I saw him throw a teacher's car into a pool!" yelled a kid.

"Yeah, throw a car!" the first person screamed. "Throw a car!"

"Into a pool!" someone added.

Suddenly the crowd came apart, and before Walter knew what was happening, two black SUVs screeched up next to his car. One swerved in front and the other pulled in behind. Unable to move, Walter now found himself trapped.

The driver-side doors of both SUVs squealed open at the same time. Out jumped two men wearing black suits and sunglasses. Something about them bothered Walter. They moved strangely, jerkily, as if they weren't quite sure how to get around in their own skin. At first he thought they might be robots, because he had met plenty of robots during his travels in outer space. But robots usually clanked when they walked, and they never, ever wore human clothes. That was considered gross.

One of the men grabbed the door of Walter's car and yanked it open.

"Hey, back off!" shouted Walter.

"Walter Sparrow, you will come with us!" said one of the men.

"That's not going to happen," said Walter, trying to close the door again.

"Wrong!" said the man. "It has been ordered by the Secretary of Homeland . . . er, the Department of . . ." The man turned to his closest companion and asked, "Which group are we with? There are so many government agencies, I've lost track."

The second man shoved the first out of the way. "The BSSM," he said.

Walter raised an eyebrow. "The BSSM?" he asked. "I've never heard of that one. What does it stand for?"

"It's classified," snapped the second agent, who had a shaved bald head.

"What do you want?" asked Walter.

The two men looked at each other for a few seconds, and then the first shrugged. Instead of answering the question, he reached in and grabbed Walter by the striped necktie. "You're coming with us," he said coldly.

That's when things got ugly.

A burst of flame erupted from Walter's palm and sent the man flying head over heels into a nearby flower bed. Screaming, the man leaped up and tore off his burning coat. Then he rolled around in the mulch like a dog that had found a dead bird. The second man dove for cover behind a pair of trash cans, but he wasn't fast enough. Stepping from his car, Walter raised his hand. The trash cans lifted off the ground and floated on a warm current of air. He brought them crashing back down again, right on the man's head.

Walter's eyes flashed red and purple, and he smiled that evil smile. It was so easy to go back to being bad—*too* easy.

With a chorus of screams, the crowd of onlookers ran in all directions. News reporters tripped over themselves to flee the scene, leaving cameras and microphones behind. The party was over.

But Walter was not done. Raising the metal trash can lids off the ground, he spun them like saw blades, and then fired them through the windows of the black SUVs. The men inside ducked down low in their seats to keep from having their heads sliced off. Then, with one last twist of his hand, Walter rolled the trucks as though they were toys. Rattling loudly, the SUVs landed upside down, and a rain of empty coffee cups and loose change fell on the passengers inside.

Walter dusted off his hands and turned back to his car. It was on fire. Not that there was anyplace to drive. At that very moment a parade of white police cars was pulling onto Carmelina Terrace, sirens wailing.

Just when he thought his day couldn't get any worse, Walter now had to make his escape on foot. Walter started to run and was out of breath by the time he reached his backyard. It was a pity he'd let his gym membership expire.

Several blocks from Carmelina Terrace, a third black SUV slowed down but did not stop. It continued rolling forward until it crushed a picket fence, flattened an empty lemonade stand, and uprooted a mailbox. When the truck finally came to a stop, its driver-side door opened.

Out stepped the man known as Agent Park. His gelled hair reflected the sunlight, and his navy blue suit was missing a button. He would have looked perfectly normal if not for the red forked tongue that occasionally flicked from between his lips.

Agent Park stared at where he'd parked the truck on top of the mailbox, but he did nothing about it. Walking around to the other side of the SUV, he opened the passenger-side door.

A high heel stepped down to the pavement, and out slid Dr. Pamela Jinks.

She watched the action in front of Walter's house, one hand on her hip. She did not seem pleased. While she waited, the men in dark suits and sunglasses—her agents—hurried over. They were still a little dizzy from Walter's swooping trash cans. One of the men had a trash can lid sticking out of the side of his head. It didn't seem to bother him.

When the agents reached Dr. Jinks, they bowed. "Did you do it without drawing attention to yourselves?" she asked.

"Well, it hasn't *actually* been done yet," said one agent, who went by the name of Wurtel.

"And there may have been some teensy-weensy explosions," said one who went by the name of Vonker. He removed the trash can lid from his head and turned around, revealing that the back of his wig was on fire. "Yes, there were a few fires."

Dr. Jinks shook her head. She never should have hired Bozons.

Bozons were lizard men from the Salamander System. They were the cheapest hired thugs in the galaxy but also as dumb as moon rocks. You couldn't rely on them to get anything done, unless you wanted someone to accidentally blow up your home planet. You get what you pay for, even with moronic alien henchmen.

Dr. Jinks turned away from her agents and scanned the street, searching for movement. Then she saw him—

Walter. He was barely a speck in the distance but she knew it was him. She watched as he sprinted toward a backyard fence, hoping to climb it and reach the alley beyond.

Her eyes narrowed. Then her face crackled, as if she'd just been zapped by static electricity. In a flash, another face became visible. It existed behind her pretty smile, bright and bony and red, with blazing eyes. The real Dr. Jinks could be seen for a split second before vanishing again behind the makeup.

"I don't think so," she whispered. And raising her hand, she began to lift one of the crashed SUVs into the air as if it were on invisible strings.

Walter heard the SUV before he saw it. The sound started out as a faint whistling and grew louder. Then it became a whoosh.

As he climbed the back fence, a truck fell to earth. It fell from out of nowhere, landing on its grille and making a loud honking sound, like a goose getting stepped on. The SUV teetered upright, and then dropped to one side in a flurry of twisted metal. The smell of hot oil filled the air.

Walter gawked. The truck had just missed him. His gaze shifted to where the truck had come from, across the street. Then he saw the woman—*her*.

She glared at him with hate in her red, burning eyes. It was a glare he knew all too well.

"Great," said Walter. "Fine time for a family reunion." He turned and hopped up onto the SUV, over the fence, and down into the alley. Then he was gone.

Of all the people they could have sent after him, they had to send his sister.

Far across the street, Mike the cameraman for Action Six News watched as the black SUV burst into a ball of fire. "Wow," he said, looking over his shoulder. "Did you see that, Cindy?"

But Cindy Cornfield had fainted dead away on the lawn, right next to a lawn gnome. It looked like she might not win Anchorperson of the Year a sixth time after all.

14

FAR ACROSS TOWN, AWAY FROM THE CHAOS ON CARMELINA
Terrace, Gene sat on a bean bag that was the color of a
tongue. He wore a shiny purple silk shirt—his party shirt.
The room was lit by soft red lights. A stereo on the shelf
played slow, soothing new age music. During the day, this
room was his mother's yoga studio. That night, however, it
was his party room.

Gene was nervous. Every few minutes he glanced at the
clock on the wall. From time to time he sniffed his armpits to make sure his deodorant was still working. He'd
bought the antiperspirant stick on sale, mostly because it
was Adventure scented. He wasn't sure if something that
cost ninety-nine cents could really keep him dry. Not
when he seemed to be sweating more than he'd ever sweat
in his entire life. And Gene was a big sweater. He sniffed
his pits again. It was not a good smell. Buying that cheap

deodorant was one "adventure" he regretted taking.

Gene counted down the minutes until the clock struck 7:00. As he did, he tried to calm his nerves. It was weird sitting there alone. Vince was usually with him. They were almost always together, even when they weren't doing anything in particular. Life had been that way for as long as he could remember.

Sighing, he wondered if Vince would even show up to his party, considering he was afraid of girls. Not that he was even invited, the traitor.

Gene had always wanted a have a party in his basement. He wanted to be one of *those* kids, the kind who threw big shindigs, wore stylish clothes, had nicknames, and found dates to school dances three months ahead of time. Gene just had the nickname, and it wasn't the kind of nickname you bragged about. It was Pumpkin Butt, and whenever he heard it, he felt like crying.

He got up off the bean bag and walked in a circle, feeling a little dizzy. The strains of the music from the other room didn't sound right. Everything sloshed and echoed as if Gene were underwater. Sticking a pinkie in one ear, Gene drilled around inside. When he pulled the finger back out, the tip dripped bluish ooze. "That's not good," he said to himself.

Upstairs the doorbell rang. Gene forgot about his ear and, practicing his hellos and how's-it-goings, walked into the finished portion of the basement. The room had been decorated with streamers and balloons for the party. A disco ball spun from the drywall ceiling, whirring quietly with the beat from the stereo system. Gene had even gone so far as to borrow a smoke machine from his neighbor Ted, who was in a rock band called Robot Butler.

He heard the front door open and the sound of voices. Leaning against his dad's old pool table, Gene crossed his arms and tried to look cool. His back began to itch like crazy, and he felt the steady drip, drip, drip of sweat falling against the silk of his purple party shirt.

Vince and Lucy arrived at the house at just the same time. It had rained earlier, and small silvery puddles spotted the driveway. The moon hung huge and white in the sky. Every so often a warm breeze blew through the trees, moving the branches and shaking drops from the leaves.

"Hey," he said to Lucy as she walked over.

"Hi," she said. She wore a lime green sundress with thin straps. She looked fantastic, like a model in a Back to School ad.

"How are you doing?" asked Lucy.

"Fine," said Vince. Why was she asking? Had she been thinking about him? What did she want him to say? Had he said the wrong thing? Questions bubbled up in his brain like fizz in a soda.

"Good," she said. "I was worried about you."

"Why?" asked Vince.

"You seemed a little freaked out today," she said, "after everything that happened with Gene and that article in the paper."

Vince thought back to lunch, when the group of students had showed up outside the office of the *Globe*. He didn't know if it had freaked him out or not, but it certainly hadn't made him happy. Instead of being punished for his selfishness, Gene was being rewarded for it. It didn't seem fair, especially after Vince had always tried to do the right thing. What was the point in being a good person if bad things always happened to you?

"Nope," said Vince. "I'm okay, just had a little writer's block, that's all."

"Good," said Lucy, and she stepped closer to him. "You're a nice guy," she went on. "You really care about people, about your friends. And I like that. You think about other people's feelings."

"I do," said Vince. "Other people's feelings are the best."

He really had no idea what he was saying. He wanted to hear more about how much she liked him.

She stepped even closer, so close that he saw the whites of her eyes. So far that night, everything had gone normally for Vince. That was before Lucy reached out and took his hand. For the next twenty steps they walked up the driveway hand in hand, which was much, much different from just walking down the driveway next to each other. It meant you're *together*.

Vince had a hard time relaxing. He had never held hands with a girl before. With every step he wondered if he was squeezing too tightly or too loosely. He wondered if his fingers were too chilly, because they certainly felt cold to him, like a clump of frozen fish sticks. He thought about letting go to dry his sweaty palms on his pants, but he didn't want to seem like he wasn't enjoying holding hands.

Most of all, Vince didn't want to leave a sweaty streak on his pants, which he'd picked out especially for the party. They were black velvet. In his opinion they said both "Let's party" and "But quietly and without bothering the neighbors." Vince had never had much of a social life. The only party he'd ever been to was the restaurant kind, as in "Haskell, party of seven, your table is ready."

As they neared the house, Vince began to worry. He

wasn't cool enough to go to a big party with a girl as pretty as Lucy. It didn't matter that she was his friend. People would wonder. But that wasn't even the issue. Vince wasn't nervous about being seen with Lucy. He was nervous about being seen *by* Gene.

A few steps before they reached the patio, Vince pulled Lucy aside.

"What's wrong?" she asked.

"Nothing," said Vince. "I feel weird."

"It'll be fun," she said, smiling that wonderful gap-toothed smile.

The grin was infectious, and Vince couldn't help feeling lifted by her good spirits. "Thanks for being my date," he said, squeezing her hand.

Lucy was silent. Again, Vince couldn't see her but could imagine what she looked like. She was frowning. Her forehead was scrunched up. The dimple in her chin had gotten deeper. This was the annoyed expression she got whenever she was waiting for an article Vince was trying to finish. After three years of friendship, he knew what her silence meant. It meant she was mad.

Just like that, her smile vanished. "We're not a couple," she said. "We're just friends, Vince." She eyed him suspiciously. "You know that, right?"

Vince's heart pounded against his rib cage as he searched for the right words to say, knowing he was going to choose the wrong ones. "Yeah, sure," he said at last, nodding stupidly.

"You're my best friend," said Lucy.

"You mean, like I'm a girl?" asked Vince.

Lucy frowned. "Well, no, not exactly. It sounds bad when you put it that way."

"You mean you *do* think of me that way?" squawked Vince.

"No," said Lucy, not looking at all convinced by her words. "I don't think about you like a boy or a girl, just as a friend."

"That's worse!" said Vince. "You don't even think of me as a boy!"

"Come on," said Lucy, starting to pull him toward the house again. "Don't be weird."

When she tugged, Vince didn't move. "Go on ahead," he muttered. "I'll be there in a second."

"Okay," said Lucy in a concerned voice. Then, with a whirl of that lime green sundress, she headed up the steps toward the door. In the blink of an eye, she'd been swallowed up by the stream of partygoers heading into the Brennick house.

Vince watched her go. He'd known about girls for his entire life, but aliens for only a year or so.

Aliens made a lot more sense.

Once again, Gene sat in his mother's yoga studio on a bean bag, staring at the floor. On that floor lay a copy of the *Globe*. It was the issue with Walter Sparrow on the front page. The guidance counselor stared out from the picture like an alien deer caught in a UFO's headlights. Dance music from the other room shook the walls. Gene could just make out the lyrics to one of his favorite techno songs, "Starlight Mirror is the Electric Dance Floor."

Listening to all the fun being had at his party, Gene wondered how he could still feel so confused. Everything was going his way. He had fame. He had thrown a party and people actually showed up. He wore a sweet, silky purple party shirt. What had he done wrong? And why did he still care that Vince was mad at him?

There was a thumping sound across the room, followed by a click. Gene looked up. The doorknob shook. It began to turn very slowly, and then unlatched. A ray of light crept across the carpet as the door inched open.

It was Lucy. She stood in the doorway, sparkles from the rotating disco ball rolling across her pale white shoulders.

"Hi, Gene," she whispered. Smiling, she stepped inside the room and closed the door behind her.

In his career at the *Globe*, Gene had seen many terrifying things. He'd faced a fat man whose mouth could spew lava like a volcano. He'd wrestled a trio of praying mantis sisters with claws for hands. Yet, despite all of that, nothing had prepared him for the terror he felt as Lucy walked across that room.

"Why aren't you out at the party?" she asked, sitting on the giant rubber yoga ball next to his bean bag.

"I was," said Gene, shrugging, trying to stay calm. "I was dancing up a storm." Then he added, "Check out all this sweat." He stood up and sat down on a second wobbly yoga ball next to hers.

Lucy raised her eyebrows and then nodded approvingly, a little surprised. "Wow," she said. "That's impressive."

"Yeah," said Gene. "You don't get this sweaty sitting in a little room all by yourself, that's for sure." When Lucy didn't respond right away, he saw that she sat with her hands in her lap, twiddling her thumbs. She looked almost as nervous as he was. "Are you having fun?" he asked.

"Sure," she said. "It's a great party. There are lots of people."

"And I know about six of them," said Gene, cracking a smile. They both started laughing.

"You know something, Gene," said Lucy. "I like you."

He shrugged. "I like you too."

She smiled sheepishly. "No, I mean I *like* you."

It took Gene far too long to understand what she was trying to say. And when he did, he felt appropriately stupid. "Oh, yeah," he said, sitting up on the bean bag. "What? Wait, really?"

"Yeah," said Lucy. "I've kind of always liked you."

This confused Gene. "What about Vince?" he asked.

"He's my friend," Lucy said. "Probably my best friend. But I like *you*."

Gene didn't know what to say. Never in a million years would he have foreseen this moment. Sure, he had day-dreamed about it and even acted it out a few times with his pillow, but that was because he didn't think it would actually happen. Now it was.

Instead of speaking, Gene chose to show his feelings. He leaned over to kiss Lucy. Eyes closed, he tightened his lips into a pucker—ready, aim, fire.

As soon as he'd leaned far enough, the big rubber yoga ball shot out from under him and dropped him lips-first to the basement carpet. The ball smacked off the closet door and bounced back to strike Lucy right in the face. She made a sound like "Unh" and fell to the floor.

After a few seconds, Gene rolled over. "You okay?" he asked.

Lucy nodded. Then she started giggling. "What about you?"

"I see double," he answered.

She crawled in close to him. "Then both of us are going to kiss you now."

And they kissed.

It was better than Gene had imagined. An electric shock crackled through his body, a sensation like freezing to death and burning alive all at the same time. His fingers and toes went numb, and he stopped sweating, even if just for a few seconds. All was right with the world.

Then the tickle started.

It started as a pesky itch at the back of his neck. He would have scratched, but he was too busy kissing.

In fact, he was so busy that he didn't notice the long blue tentacle rise up from between his shoulder blades and hang coiled in the air.

Unfortunately, when someone did notice, it wasn't Gene. It was Lucy.

• • •

Vince sat on the back patio watching Gene's neighbor Ted operate the big stereo system. He was winking at girls and playing only the music of his dorky alternative band, Robot Butler, which consisted of a drummer, a flutist, a guitarist, and a saw player.

Vince was having trouble enjoying the party. This was because he wanted to be at home working on his graphic novel. Writing was predictable. That was why he liked it. Plus he didn't need to wear fancy velvet party pants to do it. Worst of all he was disappointed about Lucy. He thought she had *liked him* liked him.

Being at home, writing his Mexican cyborg stories, never made him do crazy things he didn't want to do. They didn't fight him to get the headline. They didn't snap at him whenever he had an idea they didn't like. Of course, they weren't much fun either. And a graphic novel couldn't have helped him trick Hip-Hop Sasquatch into getting out of that car trunk. Not like Gene had.

Walking into the house, Vince thought back to that interview. He and Gene had hunted down Hip-Hop Sasquatch after he was spotted by hunters last autumn. Once they caught up to him, the boys convinced him to move in with the rest of the Santa Rosa alien population, so he wouldn't be lonely. After the interview was published in the *Globe*, Hip-Hop called less and less often.

As he remembered their hairy friend, Vince wondered what happened to him, if he'd gone to law school like he'd always wanted to. When he thought back to that adventure, Vince smiled. Those had been good times.

"Hey, Vince, why aren't you out on the floor?" asked Quiet Matt, walking over. He was out of breath from dancing. Linus trailed along behind wearing a T-shirt that said KISS THE KOOK on the front.

"I don't dance," said Vince.

"Neither does Cathy," said Matt, smiling. "It's a good thing she can't come to the party because she's in hiding. I doubt she would have had much fun. We usually spend our afternoons playing Scrabble or reading poetry to each—"

"Okay!" interrupted Linus. "I've heard enough about your honey bun. I liked it better when you were quiet."

"You should dance," Matt said to Vince. "It'll make you feel better."

"Do *something*?" asked Linus, always smiling.

"Whatever you do, don't sit here alone all night," said Matt, patting Vince on the back. Then the two of them hurried back out onto the dance floor with everyone else, where they seemed to be having a blast flailing around.

Only a couple of people laughed as they moved. People were pretty serious when they danced, Vince noticed. Maybe they weren't into it, or maybe they were nervous and afraid to look stupid. Either way, Vince was slightly jealous that someone was having fun.

That's when he decided to find Gene. If anyone could make the party more fun, it would be him. Besides, Vince was ready to patch things up, to let bygones be bygones. They could still be friends even if they didn't agree on everything all the time. Thinking otherwise was just silly. Yes. He would apologize and they would be best friends again. It was simple as that.

Feeling very proud, very grown-up, Vince left his spot near the wall and went on the hunt for Gene. He checked the dance floor. No Gene. He stuck his head in the bathroom. No Gene, although there was a funky smell coming from the shower. He visited the unfinished furnace room. No Gene, only a mouse with its neck caught in a trap. Finally he reached Mrs. Brennick's yoga studio at the far end of the basement hallway.

Vince knew that Gene's mom kept the room locked, so he was surprised when the knob turned with hardly a twist. The door fell inward.

On the floor lay Lucy. Next to her lay Gene. Their

heads were turned toward each other, lips barely touching in an innocent kiss.

At first glance, Vince didn't even notice the four blue tentacles sprouting from Gene's back. He didn't care about those. Only one thing mattered to him, and that was the sight of his ex–best friend making out with the girl he liked. Gene could have been forty feet tall and Lucy could have been made out of cookie dough, and still all Vince would have noticed was the kiss—the kiss, the kiss, the kiss. He could think of nothing else.

Of course, when Lucy saw the tentacles, she noticed all right.

"What in the heck!" she screamed at the top of her lungs, pushing Gene away.

Actually, she slapped him, hard. Gene grabbed his face and cried out. This made the tentacles flap around madly, as if they were reacting to his pain. One of them whipped back and knocked a potted plant against the wall with a crash. Another thrust forward and hit the carpet, throwing Gene backward and onto his feet.

That's when Gene too noticed what was going on. Looking up, he caught sight of two tentacles hanging over his head like a pair of floating fettuccine noodles. He kept turning around to get a better look at them, but they turned when he did. So he ended up spinning in circles until he lost his balance and fell into the bookshelf. As he did, a long, thin tentacle sprang out to steady him. Gene saw it and began to shout. "Get them off me!" he cried. "Get off!"

This whole time, Lucy never stopped screaming.

Face white with terror, Gene noticed Vince standing in the doorway. He reached out to his friend. "Vince! Help me, man! I don't know what's going on! Help me!"

But Vince only stared blankly. Not at the flapping tentacles, as one would expect, but at Lucy, who was huddled in the corner beneath a pile of dirty yoga tights. He stared, his thoughts jumbled up in knots. Nothing came easy. Not being friends. Not being ex-friends. Nothing came easy, except writing stories.

So that's what he decided to do. He decided to write one more story.

Slipping his cell phone out of the pocket of his velvet pants, Vince pointed it into the room. The tangle of blue tentacles appeared on the small LCD screen, flapping crazily. With a flash, he captured them, and he captured Gene.

15

EVEN FROM FOUR BLOCKS AWAY, GENE COULD STILL HEAR
Lucy screaming. Or maybe he thought he heard it, because
that sound would haunt him for the rest of his life.

Ahead of him, Vince scrambled over a low wooden
fence, tearing his black velvet pants in the process. A huge
patch of cloth in the shape of Nevada was left dangling
on a bent nail. Vince paused at the top long enough to
look down and mouth the words, "My party pants." Then
he was gone again, pushing off and disappearing over the
other side. Leaping with all of his strength, Gene followed
him over, taking great care not to rip his shiny silk shirt as
he went.

This mattered little, however, as the next lawn was
under fire from a series of sprinklers. They hit every inch
of grass with their arcing spray. Yelping like a puppy, Gene
wrapped his arms across his chest and bolted through the

sprays of water. He came out on the other end of the lawn with a splatter of black dots across his purple shirt.

Gene shook his fist at Vince. "My party shirt!" he screeched. "I kissed my first girl in this shirt, you jerk! I'll kill you!"

The next yard was an obstacle course of baby toys and dog poop. Both Vince and Gene hopped across the empty patches of grass. Neither wanted to get anything gross on their fancy shoes. It's not like they had a lot of nice clothes just sitting in their closets waiting to be worn. Both boys wore the same jeans and sweatshirts pretty much every day. Gene couldn't even remember the last time he'd put his underwear in a laundry basket. In fact, he couldn't remember the last time he'd worn underwear.

"Go away!" Vince called over a shoulder.

"Never!" Gene called back.

What kept him going, through yard after yard, was the picture. He had to get it off Vince's cell phone if it was the last thing he did. No one else could see him with those disgusting tentacles sticking out of his back. He didn't want to think about what would happen if someone did. It would be a disaster. If anyone knew what people could do to those who were different, it was Gene.

His focus on getting the picture back also helped

distract Gene from the tentacles themselves. Where had they come from? What in the world were they? The shock was too huge for him to wrap his head around the situation. All he knew was that one second he was bumping chins with Lucy, and the next he was Gene Brennick, teen squid boy.

After another three lawns, Gene was at last within diving distance of Vince. So he dove. It was something that looked easy on TV, in baseball games or in action movies. But in real life it hurt, a lot.

Gene's shoulder whacked against Vince's hip, and there was a loud thud as the two boys fell to the ground. Tumbling together, they rolled onto a slab of concrete beside a bean-shaped swimming pool. Even as they lay in a heap, they kept on swiping at each other, trying to get in kicks and punches. But since neither boy had ever been in a real fight, none of their blows landed, and instead of looking tough, they just ended up looking silly.

They jumped to their feet, tense, ready.

"Stop!" shouted Gene at last. "Just stop, okay!"

Resting against the wall of the pool shed, Vince stared back, furious. "You kissed Lucy!" he shouted.

"She started it!" shouted Gene. "She doesn't like you, she likes *me*!"

Growling, Vince plucked a plastic life preserver off the wall of the pool shack and bashed Gene over the head with it.

Not in three years of friendship had one of the boys actually hit the other. They stared at each other, amazed at what had just taken place. The rules had changed, and there was no going back. Dropping the life preserver, Vince bolted. He ran across the bouncy green pool cover and clawed his way over the next fence, Gene in hot pursuit.

The last lawn on the block was the messiest of all. Leftovers from a child's big birthday extravaganza were scattered across the ground. Dirty paper plates sat on a wooden picnic table, skittering across the concrete patio whenever a breeze picked up. A half-busted walrus piñata creaked from a tree branch. On the grass lay a bright yellow Super Slide water toy that stretched from one end of the yard to the other, shining with wetness. When Vince hit the yard running, he was looking behind him instead of ahead. This proved to be his undoing.

As soon as he set one foot on the Super Slide, his right leg flew out from under him and he went sliding sideways down the length of the plastic sheet. He ended with his nose in the dirt, giving Gene the chance to catch up again.

Gene jumped on top of the taller boy, and then moved into a sitting position on his chest. He jabbed Vince several times in the gut, just to punish him for running so far so fast and for forcing him get his purple silk shirt all nasty.

"Get off me, you dork!" shouted Vince.

"Give me the phone!" shouted Gene, grabbing at Vince's hands.

"Over my dead body," said Vince.

"Do it. Or I'll spray slime all over you!" shouted Gene.

"You can't spray slime," said Vince. He rolled out of the way so that Gene fell beside him on the grass. "You just have tentacles. And tentacles suck."

"No, they don't," said Gene. "They're awesome." He really hadn't given the coolness of tentacles much thought and was disagreeing with Vince just to make a point.

Vince leaped to his feet and glared down angrily at Gene, fists raised. "You think you're so smart, that everything you do is so smart! You act like you don't need anybody. But if it weren't for the rest of us, you'd be a joke. You couldn't do *anything*."

"Listen," said Gene, begging now. "Give me the picture before something bad happens. Remember, you've got to think. What's your catchphrase? 'Considering the consequences is awesomeness . . . sss . . .' or whatever . . ."

And he trailed off. "It's *your* catchphrase, man. You have to listen to your own catchphrase."

"No!" shouted Vince. "Shut up!"

Gene had never seen Vince so upset. His friend's hair stood straight up in brown corkscrews and his eyes were red with tears. As he yelled, his fists shook. "You don't care about anybody but yourself!" The more he talked, the louder he yelled. "Just you, that's all! Not even your friends! All you care about is getting the story!"

Taking the cell phone out of his pants pocket, Vince held it up so Gene could see the screen. His jaw was locked in a scowl. "Well, guess what? This time *you're* going to be the story."

That was it. Gene had to get the picture. And he had to get it *now*.

With a growl, he leaped forward to grab the phone, but Vince's fist met him halfway. It caught him squarely in the nose. There was a loud squishing sound from Gene's face as he flopped flat on his back, arms at his sides. "Ouch," he gurgled as blood began to seep from a nostril.

Once he saw what he'd done, Vince turned and ran.

Gene listened to his friend's footsteps pound away as he ran down the street with the phone, with the picture. With the truth about Gene and what he really was.

As he lay there, stunned, Gene began to slip slowly down the Super Slide. Once he reached the end, he came to a stop against the fence.

His fancy purple party shirt, among other things, was completely ruined.

16

ONCE VINCE HAD RUN FOR TEN MINUTES STRAIGHT WITHOUT
stopping, he'd gotten rid of enough anger to throw up, but
not enough to forgive his friend. Slowing down, he sank
to the curb, legs wobbly, hands shaking. He covered his
face with his hands and groaned. This normally made him
feel better, but not tonight. The groans became moans,
and then the moans became sobs, and for the first time
since he'd started working on the *Globe* newsletter, Vince
Haskell cried.

Every so often he looked up at the windows of Condor
Towers. He could make out the glow of his apartment,
301, three levels up and two squares from the corner. At
about this time of night, his sisters would be descending on
the kitchen like buzzards on a dead body. The last thing he
felt like doing was facing their ridicule. Still, he considered
going home. He wanted nothing more than to go talk to

his mom, to explain to her what had happened. She'd been right all along. Gene was about as good a friend as he was a writer, and now Vince was paying for it.

If only there was something I could do, thought Vince.

Of course, *doing* things had always been Gene's bag not Vince's. It had been that way with the Ails, with the *Globe*, with Lucy, and even with that stupid newspaper article about Walter Sparrow. Gene always had to make it happen, to get the headline. Vince, on the other hand, was just expected to write about it.

He took out his phone. The screen lit up when he touched it, showing the last picture he took. Gene stared out, eyes wide with shock, tentacles everywhere.

"I tell stories," said Vince aloud to himself. Then he dialed the number for Santa Rosa information.

"This is four-one-one," the operator said.

"I'd like the number for Bernard Wax, please?" said Vince, sniffling. "He works for the *Santa Rosa Examiner*."

Linus pounded on the door again. "Gene, get your butt out here!"

There was no answer.

Outside the bathroom, Gene's friends gathered around the door. This meant Matt and Linus, since they were the only two he considered "friends." Several other kids stuck around for a few minutes to see what would happen, if Gene would come out. But this grew boring fast. They'd come for a party, and when the only people left are camped out around the bathroom door, it's a clear sign that the party is over. Luckily Gene had managed to slink back into the house and the safety of the bathroom without anyone catching him, maybe because so many people had already left at that point anyway.

Katarina Lopez was gone first, not wanting to miss her favorite sitcom, *Sid's Friends Are Crazy*. After about fifteen minutes of waiting, Janet Kelly had wandered off to find a better cell phone signal. As for Bernie Klosterman, he hadn't even known whose party it had been. This left the staff of the *Globe*—two in the basement, one in the bathroom.

"Come out, Gene!" shouted Matt. "I'm tired and I want to go home. Cathy has been calling all night."

"No!" shouted Gene.

"I'm sure it's no big deal," said Linus. She pressed her ear to the door. "Remember when you got that zit on your eyelid? You didn't leave the locker room for two days."

"I don't remember that," said Gene.

"You probably blocked it from your memory," said Linus. "We sent firefighters in to get you. They used tear gas."

"That's not true," whimpered Gene. "You're lying."

Linus banged on the door. "Gene, stop being a drama queen!"

"Tell us what happened," said Matt. "Why was Lucy upset?"

"Everything is fine!" said Gene, his voice cracking.

Inside the bathroom, Gene dragged himself to a seated position against the toilet. The tentacles had disappeared for now. He knew they would be back. He didn't know when or why, but he knew they would be back. Hugging his knees to his chest, he tried to ignore his friends' voices. If they discovered his secret, he'd be completely alone.

"It's not a big deal," said Linus. "A lot of guys get nervous when they kiss a girl. I heard that the first time Tom Steiner kissed someone, he threw up on her face."

"It's true," added Matt. "I was there."

"Why were you there when Tom Steiner was kissing Becky Webb?" asked Gene.

There was silence, and then Matt said, "Never mind."

"I didn't throw up," said Gene. He was starting to get a little anxious, his face growing hot.

"Did you start crying?" asked Matt. "I hear that happens to a lot of people."

"I didn't start crying!" shouted Gene. He was sweating again.

"Did you throw up, and then start crying?" asked Matt.

He'd had enough. Rising to his feet, Gene fumbled with the lock and pushed open the door. "I did not start crying! I did not throw up! *And I was not kissing anybody!*"

No one in the basement spoke. There were no words to describe what they saw. What does someone say when their friend's back is sprouting blue tentacles? Since words were out of the question, all they could do was scream. So that's what they did.

Gene's tentacles had appeared only seconds before, when he'd gotten flustered. He hadn't seen them yet. So he had no clue what Linus and Matt were screaming about. Confused, he started to scream too. It seemed like the right thing to do in the situation. When he still hadn't figured out why everyone was freaking out, Gene started asking, "What is it?" and "Is there something on my face?" and "Is it the smell from the bathroom?" And finally, he tried the much clearer "Hey, what are you screaming at?"

He spotted the first blue tentacle when it grabbed an

empty two-liter bottle of Coke and started whacking Matt over the head with it. The plastic bottle made a bonging sound as it messed Matt's hair and sent the boy scurrying for safety.

"Tentacles!" screamed Gene, as if he'd been the first to spot them. Stupidly, he started to run, as if he could get away. He tried to mount the steps leading up to the ground floor. As he did, two of the tentacles reached out and seized the railings.

About three steps up, Gene felt a sharp tug and stopped abruptly. It felt as if he'd struck a brick wall. Suddenly he was flying backward through the air, the wind whistling past his ears. The tentacles had fired him down the steps like a stone from a slingshot. Landing hard on his butt, Gene lay on the carpet, his head spinning, wondering what to do next. Not that he could escape his own body.

Luckily for Gene, it was Linus who first found her calm. She backed away from him slowly, arms up in front of her face. "Stay calm," she whispered, putting distance between her and the tentacles.

Matt had his own way of dealing with the situation. It was called screeching like a bat and hyperventilating. "I knew it!" he shouted, eyes wild. "Vince was right! We never should have published that story about Vargon's nephew!"

Before Matt could say another word, Linus smacked him across the cheek. "Relax," she hissed. That was all it took. Matt shook his head groggily, and then seemed to calm down, at least enough to stop shouting.

Linus stepped toward where Gene lay sprawled on the carpet. She inhaled deeply. "Listen," she said. "Try to settle down. Slow your heartbeat, relax."

"That's a little hard right now," whined Gene. And as if the angry blue tentacles weren't enough, he was starting to feel hungry. Not for doughnuts or sandwiches or pizza but for metal. He felt like tossing nuts and bolts into his mouth like popcorn.

"Just try," said Linus.

Gene nodded and sat up. He didn't want to feel this way anymore, not tingly and itchy, not all alone even though he was surrounded by his friends. So he did as Linus suggested and closed his eyes.

"What do I think about?" he asked.

"Something that makes you happy," she said.

So Gene thought about chasing stories with Vince. It was what he enjoyed most. Like when they'd almost gotten flattened by Mold Man, or when Crumble Bun had turned the Dippin Donuts into strudel. Those were the memories that made him smile, even if he wasn't sure if he'd ever make any more of them. He and Vince were through. All Gene had to show for their friendship was a bunch of tentacles and a bloody nose.

Suddenly, he felt better.

Whenever Gene thought about Vince, the tentacles hung in the air, unmoving. But as soon as he got upset again—about anything—they began to whip around like crazy. They'd lash out and pull Linus's hair or try to force-feed Matt guacamole from the refreshment table. Still, he was making progress.

This control, as small as it was, gave Gene a tremendous feeling of accomplishment. It was something he'd never felt before, not even when he published the *Globe*. He'd done this all by himself. He hadn't told someone else's interesting story. He hadn't asked his friend to write an article for him. Best of all, he hadn't revealed someone's secret for the sake of his own popularity. He did this, no one else.

"Hey, check this out," he called, grinning broadly. He stood up. "I think everything's going to be okay!"

That's when a grubby face pressed against the window-pane behind him.

Its lips curled back in an evil sneer. Two scaly red

horns stuck up from the top of its head. The tips of its hair crackled with flame.

It was Walter Sparrow, Vargon's nephew, Santa Rosa's public enemy number one, and Fulton Junior High School's 2005 Teacher of the Year.

It had been a hard day for Walter, the hardest since the time eleven thousand years ago when he'd accidentally sank Atlantis. After escaping Dr. Jinks's agents outside his house, he'd gone on the run. It had taken him all night to slog across town to Gene's neighborhood. On the way he'd been hit by a taxi, struck by lightning twice, attacked by dogs, and spray painted by a couple of teenagers. All he wanted now was a nap and maybe a couple of Doritos from the refreshment table.

But there would be no rest for Walter Sparrow. As he lurched into the basement through the sliding glass door, there was only one thought on his mind: revenge. Unfortunately, he wasn't the only one with this thought.

"You did this to me!" shouted Gene, pointing at Walter. When he did, a giant blue tentacle reared up from his back and pointed too. *"You ruined my life!"*

"Me?" said Walter, shocked. It was Gene who had

written the article about *him*. It was Gene who had gotten *him* fired. It was Gene who had revealed *his* location to the aliens who had been tracking him for centuries.

All of Walter's energy—a power that could juggle asteroids for fun—returned in a rush. Eyes flashing, Walter crossed the room. "You *ruined* my *life*!" he roared at Gene, his voice shaking the foundations of the house.

The kids stood and watched in horror as the air around Walter began to crackle with sparks. The intense heat made their hair start to frizz and their spit taste like ashes. Within seconds, everything in Gene's basement—the mood candles, the disco ball, the black lights, and even a plate of baklava (which had seemed like a good idea at the time)—began to float on hot currents of air. The cloud of junk whirled around Walter. Then, with a pop, fountains of flame burst from his eye sockets like water spraying from a hose. They streamed down his cheeks, some even catching his ragged collar on fire.

People always tell you not to panic. But most people don't know what they're talking about, so you shouldn't listen to them. When a nephew of one of the most gigantic and powerful many-headed villains in the galaxy gets upset, it's probably okay to panic. That's exactly what Gene and his friends did. They totally, and without apology, freaked the heck out.

"I should boil your organs!" shouted Walter, venting his rage. "I should shrink your heads and make them into key chains. I should cast you down into the Pits of Flarg, where tiny flarglings will drown you in the tears of crying orphans!"

It was Gene who finally fell to his knees. "Please, Mr. Sparrow," he begged. "Please don't let the flarglings or whatever hurt me! I don't want to drown in anyone's tears. That would be gross." He hung his head. "Haven't you gotten your revenge? Aren't the tentacles enough?"

In an instant, the fountains of fire went out, and Walter was back to being a guy in a cheap suit that had been chewed by Dobermans. "Tentacles?" he asked in a normal voice. "What are you talking about?"

Gene looked back at him suspiciously. "*These* tentacles," he said.

Walter had been so tired, and then so angry, that he hadn't even noticed. Now that he saw what Gene was talking about, his jaw dropped. "Good grief!" he yelped, as a tentacle snapped at him. "What in the world happened to you?"

Closing his eyes, Gene seemed to concentrate. The tentacles grew limp and dropped down at his sides. Then he opened his eyes again. "Are you saying you didn't do this to me?" he asked.

Walter shook his head. "Why would I do this to you?" he asked. "Exactly how would this help me get my job back?"

"So you don't want to kill me for writing that article about you?" asked Gene.

This made Walter throw his head back and chuckle. "Of course I want to kill you," he said. "I'd love to kill you, eat you, and use your windpipe as a straw. But I'm not going to. Do you know why?"

Gene shook his head, frozen in terror.

"Simple," said Walter. "Because that was the *old* me. The old Walter made volcanoes erupt just for fun. The old Walter sent plagues of scorpions. The old Walter shrank Pluto from a planet to a *dwarf* planet, which is, like, *so* much worse. I don't do that kind of thing anymore." Then he began to wobble on his feet. A wave of exhaustion swept over him, and he found a seat on the edge of the pool table.

"So you're really not the evil alien Fred warned us about?" asked Gene.

"No," said Walter. "How many times do I have to tell you? I'm one of the good guys. Mold Man, Crumble Bun, Arachnid Boy—they're all my friends."

One of the tentacles scratched Gene's head for him as he thought. "I guess you're right," he said. "That does make you one of the good guys."

"My life was that school," Walter said sadly, thinking of better times. "I poured everything I had into those kids. And now it's all gone."

Gene sat down next to him and had to shift around in his seat to allow for the tentacles. They squirmed underneath him like a boxful of live fish bait. "So you don't know anything about this weirdness?" he asked, pointing to one of the tentacles.

"Not a thing," said Walter. He poked one of the tentacles, and it jerked back, almost as if it was angry with him. "But they sure are cool."

As Walter and Gene considered what this meant, the rest of the kids came and stood around them, listening, ready to start screaming and run for the door at a moment's notice. A layer of thick gray smoke hung at waist level in the room. It was the usual product of Walter's anxiety attacks and smelled like car exhaust.

Gene snapped his fingers. "Maybe it's from the mold,"

he said. "I got some of Alan's mold spores on me when we were interviewing him."

Grunting, Walter smiled and began to nod his head. "I heard about that," he said. "Alan is a good buddy of mine. But those have nothing to do with him. If he'd infected you, you'd be covered with spores, with mold. Not tentacles."

"Then what are they?" asked Gene.

Walter ran his fingers through his hair. The blackened tatters of his shirtsleeve brushed against his face. "Well, if I didn't do this to you, and Alan didn't do it, then who did?"

"Who's Alan again?" asked Matt, raising his hand.

"It's Mold Man," snapped Gene.

Matt bit his lower lip and looked away. "Remind me who Mold Man is. Is he the same as Bacteria Lad?"

"No, you idiot," said Gene, huffing loudly. "Mold Man is *Alan*. Bacteria Lad is *Bernie*. It's not that hard to remember which Ails are which."

"Yeah," added Linus, "says the guy who suddenly grew tentacles."

Distracted by the babbling of the kids, Walter tried to think through the problem. He turned it over and over in his head but didn't arrive at a solution. Aliens were born with their powers. Sure, occasionally an alien got hit by a falling meteorite and absorbed cosmic rays from another solar system or had powers injected into him by a mad scientist. But those were both pretty rare occurrences.

Gene had been born to human parents, which meant he was human. And as far as Walter knew, Gene hadn't been hit by a meteorite. The mad scientist option didn't work either. The closest thing Santa Rosa had to a mad scientist was a grumpy pharmacist that worked the graveyard shift at the local CVS.

"It doesn't make sense," said Walter. "What in the world turned you into this?"

No one had the answer. Not until a loud cough broke the silence. It came from the top of the basement stairs. "It's not *what* did this to him," said a familiar voice, "but *who* did it."

The group turned around to find a small figure perched on the top step in a fuzzy pink bathrobe and lacy slippers. "I think it was me," said Mrs. Brennick.

The next few minutes were tense. Gene watched his mom come down the steps slowly, looking as though she were just about to collapse into bed. On her forehead she wore a bright purple eye mask, and on her teeth was the special mouth guard she used to keep from grinding her teeth.

Gene stared at her as if *she* were the alien, and not Walter. When she reached the bottom step, his mom sat on the empty couch.

"Go home, kids," she said to the others.

At Mrs. Brennick's order, Linus and Matt rushed up the steps and down the hall toward the door. No one tried to stop them. As for Walter, he stayed put, leaning against the pool table and sipping Coke from a red plastic cup. It was as if he wasn't even there.

Once Gene's friends had gone, his mom began to take out her curlers, one by one. She talked as she unrolled. "I was in Paris studying art, painting, something I used to really enjoy doing," she said.

"Paris is nice," said Walter, sighing.

Gene's mom went on. "I met a man, his name was Henry. He was handsome and sweet and sensitive. He understood me in a way no one else seemed to, almost as if—"

"As if he was from another world?" interrupted Walter. He pulled out the tucked front of his shirt and used it to wipe his dirty face, leaving a grimy mask on the fabric. "That happens a lot. Aliens come down here for vacation or to sightsee, and they end up falling in love. Some get part-time jobs, just so they can get employee discounts."

"Things just happened," Gene's mom said, ignoring

Walter. "We fell in love. We got married. I always had a feeling he was different, I just didn't know *how* different."

The only person who hadn't spoken yet was Gene. He sat on the end of the pool table cradling the eight ball in his hands. If he could have, he would have just walked away. Only there was nowhere to go. This was something he couldn't walk away from.

Everything Gene had been through on that crazy day had made him feel things. Lucy's kiss had been warm. Vince's punch had hurt like crazy. Even the tentacles made him light-headed, and they kind of itched too.

His mother's news was different, though. It didn't make him feel anything. It left him cold. Like no feelings remained. After all the times he'd told his friends that thinking too hard about things made you weak, that analysis was paralysis, he was learning it firsthand.

"I am so sorry, honey," said Gene's mom, standing up and walking over to give Gene a hug. But his tentacles had other ideas. When his mother moved in for the squeeze, one of the tentacles blocked her from getting any closer. She stared at it nervously.

"Please, Gene," she said, but he was in no mood to talk. The tentacles did the communicating for him.

While Gene sat on the pool table ignoring his mother,

Walter paced. He didn't seem especially interested in the Brennick family drama. He kept peeking through the Venetian blinds. After a while, he settled down on the couch next to Gene and began picking M&M's out of the trail mix in a paper bowl.

After a while, Walter turned to Gene. "You heard from Fred in a while?" he asked, cracking a hard candy shell with his teeth.

"Fred?" said Gene, confused. "You know Fred?"

Walter gave him a sideways glance. "Um, yeah," he said. "We're poker buddies."

"I really don't *care* where Fred is right now," said Gene.

"You should," said Walter, standing up and checking his watch, which had a crack right down the center of its face.

"Wait, why?" asked Gene.

"Yes, why?" asked Mrs. Brennick, suddenly interested.

Chuckling, Walter shook his head in disbelief. "No offense," he said, "but the situation we're in here is bigger than your dad." When he said this, he pointed to Gene. Then he turned his finger on Mrs. Brennick. "And it's bigger than your husband."

"What do you mean?" asked Gene, forgetting his own issues long enough to wonder. Walter had been acting crazy all night, maybe even a little afraid. How scary must something be to have Vargon's nephew worried?

"That article you wrote ruined everything," said Walter.

"I know," said Gene, hanging his head. He felt really bad about it.

"It's why I'm here," said Walter.

Gene's face went white. "You said you weren't going to hurt me."

"I'm not," said Walter. "I came here to *help* you, not to hurt you."

"Really?" asked Gene.

"Really," said Walter. "Remember how I told you I was in hiding?"

"Sure," said Gene.

"Well, thanks to your article, I'm not in hiding anymore," said Walter hotly. "I'd been keeping my identity secret for nearly five thousand years. And if you think that trick's easy, then you should try it sometime. Now, thanks to you, everyone knows who I am." He paused. *"That's* why we need Fred. He knows where to hide me again."

"But where is he?" asked Mrs. Brennick, her voice weakening with worry.

The three of them sat and thought about the last time they'd seen Fred. For Walter it was the week before, when he'd let the old goofball use his telephone to make a few long-distance calls. For Gene it was a few days ago, when he and Vince had stolen Crumble Bun's information from his address book. For Mrs. Brennick it was last Thanksgiving, when Fred had fallen asleep in a dish of yams. None of them, however, had seen or heard from their friend lately.

Mrs. Brennick pulled her bathrobe around her for comfort. "I hope he's okay," she said.

"I'm sure he's fine," said Walter, lying through his teeth.

17

AGENTS FASOOM AND KARKLEY WERE NOT USED TO EARTH'S
potato chips. For one thing, there was the grease. It got all
over everything. And no matter how much you wiped your
hands on your navy blue suit pants, they always seemed to
be slick, salty, and covered with crumbs. Agents Fasoom
and Karkley were used to eating orbs of pure energy. These
didn't make your fingers greasy, but they sure could cause
a heck of a bellyache.

The two agents sat on folding lawn chairs out in front
of room 219 of the Crystal Ball Motel off of Highway 10.
They had been stationed there to guard the door. However,
in the last four hours they had done nothing but watch a
couple of college guys drop a couch into a Dumpster. At
one point, a woman came out of room 155 and stood on
the balcony to yell at a cat.

No one had paid much attention to agents Fasoom

and Karkley. This was because they were doing something uniquely human. They were hanging out.

The lizard men of Bozon were not used to being couch potatoes. They spent most of their lives toiling in the aluminum mines of Vector IV or clearing the rats out of space transport crates. They rarely snacked or just sat around on their duffs chatting. Usually they didn't have anything exciting to say. How could they? They spent the first twenty years of their lives eating the eggs containing their brothers and sisters. It was not a glamorous existence.

This is probably why they found Santa Rosa so interesting. First of all, there were cars. And while the lizard men had yet to understand exactly how to drive without crashing into something, they certainly enjoyed doing it. Then there was the food. Never had they seen so many free lightbulbs. Anytime they felt hungry, they could just unscrew a light and eat it. Santa Rosa was like an amusement park. For a town that had been voted Least Interesting Town in California by an airline magazine, it was a pretty fun place.

The motel manager walked out of his office. He bent down on one knee and began to repair a vending machine with his screwdriver.

"Greetings!" shouted Agent Karkley, waving. "We love your planet!"

The manager rolled his eyes. "Don't we all!" he shouted back.

Inside room 219, Fred Brennick sat tied to a chair. He was tired and grumpy and wearing a sweater vest that was far too itchy for something you'd want to be tied up in. A semicircle of three men in dark suits stood around him. At first Fred had assumed these men were government agents. However, as time passed, he was beginning to think otherwise. He knew cheap alien henchmen when he saw them.

The strange men had grabbed him in the parking lot outside Comic Mania, and they'd taken him here, to a motel that didn't offer cable and smelled like cat pee. Tying him to the chair, they threatened him. They made angry faces. They drank the hair conditioner in the tiny little hotel bottles.

Fred was confused. It was obvious that the men wanted to get information out of him. Only they were going about it the wrong way. Fred expected to have his fingernails torn out or to have his knees whacked with a hammer. Or at the very least, he expected to spend some time sweating in the heat of some interrogation lamps. And while the strange men had set up lamps and plugged them in, they didn't understand what to do next. Instead of turning on the lights, they spent the first ten minutes debating whether or not to eat the bulbs.

Even worse were their attempts to scare him. First, they'd tried tickling him, which, while uncomfortable, was hardly torturous. Second, several of them donned disguises and pretended to be his lawyer. They tried to gain his trust, even though he knew that they were the same men he'd seen moments before. Last, they'd tried to offer him potato chips to talk, as if chips were something special. Fred accepted the chips, and the men offered him as many as he wanted until the one-pound bag was empty. Soon they were out of snacks and didn't have any information to show for it.

The weirdest part of all was that Fred answered all of the men's questions, and willingly.

The leader of the men was Agent Park, who Fred had met on several occasions. The other men called him Prak now that they were in private. He glared down at Fred. "Does Walter Sparrow work at Fulton Junior High School?" he asked, circling the chair.

"How many times do I have to tell you?" said Fred. "Yes, he *does* work there. You know he does."

"But do *you* know he does?" asked Prak with a sly grin.

At first Fred thought this was a trick question. Then he realized that the man had no idea what he was talking about. "*Yes*, I do."

"Where is Walter Sparrow now?" asked Prak, sitting at the foot of one of the hotel beds. The springs made a squeaking sound as he did, and a mouse ran out from under the box spring. With a flick of a long red tongue, he snatched up the rodent and devoured it.

"Here is the arrangement," he said. "You tell us information about Walter Sparrow, or"—he got up and stood looking down at Fred—"we stare into these very bright lamps." He gestured to the tall interrogation lamps, which were now burning brightly but pointed out the windows. The other men nodded enthusiastically, thinking that this was a terrifying threat.

Fred sighed. It had been a long night.

"Shall I try the lawyer trick again?" asked the one who called himself Vonker. "I would certainly like to try that a second time. This time I shall wear a fake beard."

"And eyeglasses," suggested the one calling himself Wurtel. He was a small man who had spent most of the night standing in the corner licking the TV remote. "Eyeglasses are very convincing. Aren't they, Mr. Brennick?"

As he'd done all night, Fred agreed. Yes. Eyeglasses would be very convincing.

"No!" said Prak. He scratched his chin, and as he did, a piece of white makeup flaked off. Underneath, his skin was a scaly green. "I have another idea."

"Do tell us, Prak," said Wurtel, leaving the slobbery remote on the bedside table.

"I will use reverse psychology," said Prak, grinning at his cleverness.

"Reverse psychology?" asked Fred.

"Yes," said Prak, "meaning that I will try to convince you to tell me things by pretending I do not want to know about them."

"Sounds like a very good plan," said Fred.

"Yes, it does," agreed the others.

Before he began, Prak cracked his fifty-six knuckles. Then he rolled his neck and stretched his long lizard tongue. Everything was ready. Placing his hands on his hips, he began with his reverse psychology. "You do *not* want to tell us the whereabouts of Walter Sparrow," he said.

"That's right," said Fred.

"And you certainly don't want to tell us the whereabouts of his extraterrestrial friends," said Prak.

"That is correct," said Fred.

"And I don't want to know any of this information."

"Fine with me," said Fred, shrugging.

Prak rubbed his forehead, wincing. He turned to Vonker. "When will he begin to reveal the information we seek?"

"Perhaps we should try *reverse* reverse psychology," said Vonker.

"That is a good idea," agreed Wurtel, who had moved to the bathroom and was now standing in the toilet. He pressed some buttons on a glowing electronic pad and then stepped onto the bathroom floor again. Water sloshed across the tile.

"Yes," said Prak. "We shall try it." Taking a deep breath, he squinted down at Fred, trying to look scary. It didn't work. He looked more like someone who really had to use the bathroom. "You really want to tell us the location of Walter Sparrow," he said.

Fred shrugged. "No, I don't."

The agents looked at one another. Prak shook his head. "That method does not seem correct."

"It most certainly is," said Vonker, trying on his fake

beard. In his mouth he wore a set of oversize novelty teeth. "The idea is to ask the opposite of the opposite of what you wish to ask."

"It means you ask what you really want to know," added Fred.

No one said anything for a few seconds, and then Prak shook his head. "Well, that does not make much sense," he said. "And it's giving me a brainache."

"Then take a break, and let me pretend to be his lawyer," said Vonker as he pulled a large green cowboy hat onto his head. "Call me Sheriff Lawyer."

"Enough with the costumes," snapped Prak. To show that he meant business, he took a silver ray gun out of his pants and aimed. With a flash of blinding light the green cowboy erupted into flame and fell off Vonker's head in charred strips. "This is serious business," he growled. "We must learn where Vargon's nephew is hiding."

Things grew very tense very quickly. Fred could feel it. The other men stopped what they were doing and watched, on edge. Even Wurtel stopped flushing the bottles of complimentary mouthwash down the toilet long enough to wait and see what would happen next. In the silence, the large lamps fizzled and popped. They filled the small room with a thick, pulsing heat.

"Tell us, Mr. Brennick," said Prak, pointing the ray gun at Fred. "Where is Walter Sparrow?"

Fred didn't know what to say, except the truth. "I don't know," he mumbled.

Everyone waited. Fred's heartbeat quickened. A single drop of sweat fell from his chin onto his shirt.

"But we already knew that," whined Prak, throwing his hands in the air in defeat. "All of this talking is difficult. Besides, my human skull is beginning to throb. It reminds me of when a narf-hound whacks a pozner with a large mallet."

The other men nodded in agreement, understanding exactly what he was talking about. They too looked a bit under the weather.

Wurtel walked out of the bathroom wearing a see-through shower cap. "May I have permission to suggest a strategy, sir?" he said.

"Yes," said Prak, sitting down at the foot of the motel bed.

"I suggest that we rest," said Wurtel. "It is what these humans do when they wish to feel better. They take naps."

"Agreed," said Prak, and again, the other men nodded their approval.

Fred watched in disbelief as the three men stretched,

pulled back the musty motel sheets, and climbed onto the queen-size mattress. They snuggled up close to one another with their heads sticking out from under the covers. Almost immediately, two of the men fell fast asleep. They began to snore with a sound that reminded Fred of the loud hum that came from the power plant near his trailer park.

Prak, however, seemed restless. "Could you turn off those lamps, please?" he asked, covering his head with the comforter. "It is so very bright."

Fred wriggled around in the chair, thumping the legs on the floor. "I can't turn off anything," he said. "I'm all tied up."

The room was still for a moment. Then Vonker rolled out of the bed and trudged across the room, a hand covering his eyes. He moaned all the way, loosening his necktie but keeping his fake beard tightly fastened. Standing behind the chair, he untied each of the ropes binding Fred. As soon as he finished, he turned around and shuffled back to bed, slipping under the covers with a swish.

Amazed, Fred stood up. His limbs ached, but there wasn't time to dwell on it. He had to help Walter. He had to get the others.

As he gathered his belongings from the top of the TV,

Fred heard the sound of someone move under the covers. Then someone cleared his throat. It was Prak. "Could you be sure to close the door on the way out?" he asked, yawning.

"Sure thing," said Fred, and he left.

He closed the door all right. He *slammed* it.

18

GENE COULDN'T SLEEP. HE LAY ON HIS BEDROOM FLOOR,
knowing it was only a matter of time before the mob
appeared. That's how it always happened in old movies.
Rumors got around town. Torches were lit. Pitchforks
were taken down off the barn walls and sharpened. Then
everyone would assemble in the town square and march
to the monster's house, chanting something like, "Kill
the monster!" Or in this case, "Kill that bowl-haired kid
Gene!"

Of course, when he really thought about it, Gene
remembered that Santa Rosa didn't have any farms. And
he doubted anyone within a ten-mile radius owned a pitch-
fork. He didn't know if the same could be said of Fulton,
which he was pretty sure had a lot of hicks, but it was
the grisly end of the scene that mattered, not the specifics.
Soon enough everyone at school would know his secret,

and he would be history. His life as a normal junior high school student was over.

The only reason Gene could think of for why people hadn't shown up at his house already was the article in the *Santa Rosa Examiner*. If everyone, including some big bad alien, was after Walter, then they'd probably look for him in all the logical places. Gene had revealed the guidance counselor's true identity to the whole town. That didn't exactly make them friends. If anything, Walter should have wanted to stay as far away from Gene as possible. This meant that Gene's house was relatively safe—for the time being.

Closing his eyes, he tried to forget about the pounding in his temples. It was hard to think about anything else. Unfortunately, the only thing that made him forget his head pain was his nose pain. He still had bloody tissue paper stuck up one nostril, and the skin around the bridge of his nose had turned purple.

Gene still found it hard to believe that Vince had punched him, especially with enough force to cause a nosebleed. He knew the nosebleed would stop, but he wasn't sure if he'd be able to shake the memory of the punch, the look on Vince's face.

Lying flat on his back, Gene thought about his ex–best friend. He remembered their first assignment for the *Globe*.

They'd stolen from Fred the name and address of an alien called Towering Tatum. It had taken them three hours to find the right condo building, and when they did, the two boys scaled the large oak tree outside to try and snap a picture. Gene remembered how the spring air smelled of warm chlorine from the condo swimming pool. How, dangling from a branch, he tried to aim his camera into the large open window.

Eyes still closed, Gene smiled. He could still hear the creak of that oak trunk and feel the sway of its branches. Then, strangely, he actually *could* feel it—a movement as though he was swinging in a hammock in a cool evening breeze. It felt as if he was being rocked to sleep, as if he was moving. Wait. He *was* moving.

Opening his eyes a crack, Gene glanced around, and then let out a scream. The tentacles were back!

Working as a team, the four long, curling tentacles had sprouted from Gene's back and lifted him up off the ground. Now they were slowly carrying him out of his bedroom and into the hallway, his face toward the ceiling. They headed for the stairs to the basement, bringing Gene with them. Shrieking, he began to pedal his legs furiously even though he couldn't touch the ground. It was no use. It was one against four.

Gene threw out his arms and grabbed the stair railing. One pair of tentacles kept him up off the ground as the other encircled the banister at the foot of the steps. Working together, the tentacles strained against him, tugging with a sound like a rubber glove being stretched as far as it can before snapping. No matter how hard he tried, Gene couldn't keep his grip. With a squeak, his fingers slipped free, and he fell, tumbling down the steps and somersaulting across the basement carpet. Along the way he kicked over a basket of folded laundry and came to a stop against the wall, his legs in the air, and his head in a pair of underwear.

One of the tentacles—Gene was starting to call him Tricky—let out a whispery giggle. It curled down and plucked the underwear from Gene's face. Then it hurled them into the nearby laundry basket.

"Cute," said Gene.

He got to his feet and stood there wobbling. "Listen up!" he shouted angrily. "You might have ruined my love life, but you'll never ruin—"

Another tentacle—which was earning the name Hungry—snapped out sharply and snatched a bowl of pretzels from the hours-old party refreshment table. It began to shake the snacks over Gene's face. "No!" screamed

Gene as he swatted them away. "I don't want any!"

There were footsteps in the hallway, and Walter Sparrow appeared near the kitchen. He had showered and changed his clothes. Hawaiian shirts weren't exactly Walter's style. Neither were white linen golf pants. Leaping to action, he rushed down the steps to Gene's rescue.

"Calm down!" Walter shouted to Gene. "Just take it easy, and everything will be fine. Take a deep breath!"

"What are you still doing here?" asked Gene.

"I needed a place to crash for the night," said Walter.

As if sensing that Walter was trying to take control of the situation, one of the calmer tentacles suddenly lashed out. It socked him right in the face with a strong left hook that sent the guidance counselor soaring backward. He crashed into a bookshelf, showering the two of them with heavy hardback collections of Shakespeare.

"Wow," said Gene under his breath. "Nice shot."

In an instant, Walter had sprung back to his feet and was dodging and weaving as the tentacle tried to flatten him again. But he wasn't one of the most feared aliens in the galaxy for nothing. As soon as the tentacle coiled up to strike, Walter tackled it. Within seconds the others were on him, a nest of wriggling blue muscle.

"Stop," shouted Gene, wishing he could do something.

Then he remembered that he *could* do something, and he began taking huge, deep breaths. Anger surged through him. It tingled in his arms and legs and toes. So much had happened in a single day that it felt as though he'd lost all control of his life. *Almost* all control, that is. Feeling the anger fill him, he let it go.

The tentacles lifted off Walter. They coiled back behind Gene and waited there, as if expecting orders.

"Nice trick," said Walter, getting to his feet. He winced and touched a black eye. "Got any ice?"

An hour later, around five in the morning, Gene and Walter sat side by side on the ratty upstairs couch, uncooked steaks over their black eyes. Gene's injury was from Vince. Walter's from a tentacle. The steak trick was supposed to reduce the swelling. It really just made them look like a couple of guys waiting for a barbecue.

Gene watched as Walter tinkered with a jumble of electronics. On the beat-up coffee table in front of them sat a box of tools, circuit boards, tangles of multicolored wires, a cell phone, and a small satellite dish. With a series of snaps and twists, Walter began connecting pieces together. After a few minutes he'd created a strange contraption that appeared to be part science project, part garage sale item.

"This is the best you can do?" said Gene. "You build a giant cell phone?"

"It's complicated," said Walter. "You don't avoid your enemies for centuries by being predictable. All other forms of communication will be monitored, I'd imagine. This little doodad will help me send a message to the rest of my people without being heard. I'm telling them to meet at our safe house, so we can figure out what to do."

"Can't you just send them a message with your mind or something?" asked Gene's mom from the doorway. She entered the room in a pink sweatsuit and white sneakers, carrying two mugs of coffee. From the looks of it, she appeared to be doing a little better. She was showered and fully dressed, which was a start. As she passed Walter, she handed him one of the coffees, and then sat down on her old piano bench to watch him do his thing. Sunlight was just starting to shine in through the large front windows.

"Thanks," said Walter, looking up with surprise.

"Let's see," said Mrs. Brennick, placing a finger on her chin. "My son ruins your life, and I make you a cup of coffee. We're almost even." She smiled sarcastically, but the smile Walter returned was totally genuine.

Gene still didn't understand what Walter was doing.

He was doubtful the piece of junk would even work or that it would work without electrocuting someone first. "So no mind control, then?" he asked.

"No. I don't have that power here on Earth," said Walter. "And there is no alien Internet. Not yet, anyway." He set down the screwdriver and reached up to undo some of the buttons on his Hawaiian shirt.

That's when Gene recognized the shirt Walter wore as one that had belonged to his father. It came from the collection of clothes his mom stored in the hall closet, a door to which she always kept locked.

Yawning, Walter stretched. The clunky alien communicator was done, if that's really what it was.

"So who's after you, anyway?" asked Gene, getting up. He walked into the kitchen and started looking for something to drink. He had a weird craving for something metallic or greasy, like motor oil. He ended up mixing a Coke with some WD-40 machine lubricant. "You've been sneaking for all this time, but who are you hiding from?"

Walter turned around on the couch. "My twin sister," he said.

This caused Gene to stick his head out of the refrigerator. "What?"

"That's right," said Walter. "My sister. And trust me, she's trouble." He took a sip from his mug. "Now if only I knew who she was."

"You don't even know who your own sister is?" asked Mrs. Brennick.

Walter shrugged. "It's hard to stay hidden on Earth. If you change too often, people ask questions. If you never change, people ask questions. If you look strange, people ask questions. This is a tough planet. You've got to keep changing who you are." He shrugged again. "That's the price of fitting in, I guess."

"That's awful," said Mrs. Brennick in a sad voice.

"Well, it's worth it to be able to stay here," said Walter, smiling.

Gene came back and sat down. He carried a bowl of tinfoil that he'd torn into strips. So hungry he could hardly stand it, he plucked up a shiny wedge and gobbled it. Then he offered one to Walter. "Want one?" he asked.

"No, thanks." Walter laughed as he started to punch the buttons on his makeshift cell phone.

As Gene watched Walter work, he found that he liked the guidance counselor. Or he had come to like him, anyway. Walter was honest and funny, and he really cared about the kids over at Fulton Junior High. In fact, he was probably one of the best people Gene had ever known, even if he wasn't a real person.

That was when Gene really understood how selfish it had been of him to publish the story about Walter. It had ruined the guy's life, and he'd had a pretty good one.

Walter dialed several lists of numbers and then waited. The contraption began to beep continuously. A small indicator light blinked. That was all there was to it.

Gene and his mom waited, unimpressed. Nothing else happened.

"What is all this about, Walter?" asked Mrs. Brennick, leaning forward on the piano bench. "You're on the run. So was my husband, Gene's dad. And you keep talking about this enemy. But who are they? Who are *you*?"

This question seemed to strike a chord in Walter, and he thought about the answer for a long time before sharing it. "It's a birthday party."

Mrs. Brennick raised an eyebrow. "A birthday party?" she said.

"Not just any birthday party," said Walter. "It's my uncle's, the most evil, most horrible being in the entire galaxy. Oh, it's a big deal. He's turning fifty. One of our years is something like a million light-years for you humans. I don't know the exact numbers."

"So some big bad alien is having a birthday party, and you don't want to go?" asked Gene, gulping a mouthful of foil. "I don't get it. What's the big deal? I mean, I'd love to get invited to some birthday parties, man."

"It's not that," said Walter, resting his legs on the coffee table. The contraption continued its nonstop blinking and beeping. "The party is unlike anything that's happened before. My uncle started preparing for it long ago, the glory hog. He sent me and my brothers and sisters to capture three whole solar systems. Then he put all the planets to work getting ready. We had to destroy a couple of moons just to power the fireworks display." He sighed. "My uncle loves the fireworks that spell out things. So they had to do that, of course, to make old Pig Breath happy. From what I've heard, there's a giant firework that spells out: 'Nifty, nifty, look who's fifty!'

"Now there are billions of people working on it, people of all races. They toil night and day, building waterslides, practicing celebratory songs, and blowing up balloons. I mean, they wanted nine hundred trillion balloons per table! *Per table*, Gene!" Growing slightly depressed, Walter slouched forward and pushed his mug along the tabletop with one long finger. "Everyone became cogs in his big machine. There was no freedom. No individuality. And even worse, I was in charge."

Mrs. Brennick clutched her chest. "You were in charge?"

Walter smiled playfully, and then winked. "Until I escaped, of course," he said. "I took some of my friends with me, others who wanted to get out, to be free. Anyone else who gets out knows where to come to be on their own, to have a life. They come *here*."

"And now Pig Breath is after you," said Gene. It wasn't a question.

"No, not Pig Breath," said Walter, growing serious again. "Worse. He sent my sister." He grunted and flopped back on the couch. "She's a real piece of work, probably more evil than my uncle. That girl's been on my tail for thousands of years, and now she's right about to snap it off."

"She's the one who's been kidnapping Ails, isn't she?" asked Gene.

"Yup," said Walter, running his hands through his hair. "It's been hard for her to find me. I have a cloaking device I picked up at a flea market in Sector Q, and it's kept her off my trail for a long time. Apparently she's using good old detective work to hunt me down now. And it seems to be working. She's snatching us up one by one." He shook his head sadly. "I hate that screechy old bat."

The words "her," "find," "hunt," and "screechy" stuck in Gene's mind as he listened. And then suddenly he knew exactly who Walter was talking about. He didn't know how he knew, he just did. It was a weird rush of understanding, but it soon passed and left him feeling as clueless as ever.

"It's Dr. Jinks," said Gene.

"I don't know who that is," said Walter.

"You would if you saw her," said Gene. "Pretty, tall, says weird stuff."

Gene had known his own school guidance counselor was different, but not "has a UFO driver's license" different. However, the more he thought about it, the more the truth stared him in the face: the strange office, the barking sounds, the odd comments about black holes, and the strong interest in the *Globe*. All signs pointed to extraterrestrial—that or a foreign exchange student. "So, Dr. Jinks is a flunky for an alien overlord?" he said, nodding. "It makes total sense."

"I bet she hates Earth," said Walter. "I wouldn't be surprised if she planned on turning this planet of yours into something for herself. Like a vacation home or an intergalactic slave colony. She *hates* humans, thinks you're intolerant of other races."

"Well, we kind of are," said Mrs. Brennick. "Don't your people stay out of sight most of the time?"

"True," said Walter. "But humans like you and your son give me hope that people can change." He stood up and walked to the window, gazing out over the front lawn as the dawn began to break. "My sister believes that humans should pay for treating aliens like monsters." He smiled weakly. "Even if she really is one."

None of this sat well with Gene's mom. As the conversation had gone on, she turned more and more ghostly pale. Getting up, she tried to busy herself by picking up the empty mugs from the coffee table. This was difficult, as her hands were shaking. "So what do we do now?" she asked.

"We go someplace safe, and soon," said Walter. "And we go together."

As Gene sat and mulled over everything he'd learned, he heard a thump outside on the stoop. He walked across the room, head filled with images of the galaxy's largest and wackiest birthday party, with a circus big top the size of a star and more balloons than there were grains of sand on a beach. He pitied the Ails who had to inflate all of them. He'd once tried to blow up a camping bed all by himself and ended up passing out in a poison ivy bush.

Opening the door, he found a yellow plastic bag on the topmost step. Inside was the *Santa Rosa Examiner* daily newspaper. Sleepily, he shook out the thick stack of papers and unfolded them, yawning.

He looked at the headline, which he always did first, and then blinked. He looked again. Gazing at the front page was like looking in the mirror. This was because the photo on the front page was of Gene. He stared at the camera, mouth open, tongue sticking out like a snail that had ditched its shell. Tentacles sprang up in the background, filling the whole picture. Above the image was the headline: LOCAL BOY REVEALED AS ALIEN!

The byline read: BY BERNARD WAX, WITH ASSISTANCE FROM VINCENT HASKELL.

19

"ARE THOSE REAL TENTACLES?" ASKED THE GIRL WITH THE
shiny hair and the beauty mark. Vince thought her name
was Kimberly, but he'd been wrong before. Last time he
talked to her he called her Rebecca, at which she made a
scrunched hamster face and walked away. He didn't want
her to make that face again, because she was cute.

Girls had a habit of walking away from Vince. This
was something that had been happening to him for as
long as he could remember. He was so used to it that if
a girl actually came up to him, he felt the urge to correct
her by saying, "You don't want to talk to me," and then
sending her in the opposite direction. Not that this had
ever happened.

For this reason Vince was having a lot of trouble that
Tuesday morning. For the first time in his life, other
kids—girls *and* boys—wanted to talk to him. In fact, they

came to school seeking him out. Before that day, the only person who had ever looked forward to seeing Vince was the boy who kept asking his sister Susan out on a date. The kid wanted advice on what Susan liked and didn't like. So Vince told him that she liked "shoes" and didn't like "you." After that the boy stopped following him.

Now students followed Vince everywhere. When they finally stopped him to talk, it was in his homeroom, high on the third floor of Santa Rosa Junior High School. Before the first bell had even rung, he had talked to more of his classmates than he had during the entire year up to that point.

"So are they?" asked the girl whose name was probably Kimberly. Vince had already forgotten the question, having gotten lost in the shine of her black hair.

"Are they what?" asked Vince.

"Are the tentacles real?" she asked again.

"Yeah, they are," said Vince. "He's got four of them. They come out of his back."

"That's disgusting," a boy behind him said. His name was Riley Tucker. He and his friends were texting their friends in other homerooms, cocking their heads every so often to listen in on the conversation between Vince and the girl whose name was probably Kimberly.

"I think it's exciting," said a girl named Karen Bosworth who sat two desks away. "I wonder if he can climb up walls and stuff, like Arachnid Boy."

The other kids erupted in laughter. "Who in the heck is Arachnid Boy?" asked the girl whose name was probably Kimberly. No one answered. They were too busy sticking their noses into the most current issue of the *Santa Rosa Examiner*, which was causing quite a stir around school.

No one told the students to sit down or be quiet. Ms. Ambrose's homeroom was always a pretty wild place, because Ms. Ambrose rarely showed up for it. She preferred to stay down in the teachers' lounge until the last minute before coming up to take attendance. She was the kind of teacher that never should have been around children. Her favorite companions were cats, which is why she owned seven of them and why her students called her Catnip. She thought children were creepy, and if she could have had them declawed, she would have.

"Tell us again, dude!" shouted Bill Pittman, a kid who wore a bandage on his arm because of a staph infection.

Vince half smiled, which gave him a lopsided appearance. This was appropriate because he felt mixed up inside. Half of him was excited about the attention. The other half felt awful about why he was getting it. "I don't know," he said quietly.

"Do it!" urged Latoya Brown.

"Really?" he asked, looking around at all the interested faces.

"Get on your desk!" barked Grover Williams, the kid who dressed up as the school mascot and danced around during basketball games. Grover was known for being hyperactive. Last homecoming he'd tackled the homecoming queen, just because no one had stopped him in time.

Giving in, Vince climbed up onto his chair, and then onto his desk. Then he began to speak. He lowered his voice, and the class fell to a hush so they could hear him. For Vince, standing up there in front of all those kids was far scarier than any encounter with an Ail, even the most terrifying ones, like the Shock Brothers . . . or Walter Sparrow.

"So we were over at his place for a party," he began, going from a whisper to a mumble. "No one knew what was going on." The faces of his classmates shone up at him, wide-eyed, willing to go wherever he wanted to take them. So he went with it and spun a tale that was more about making his audience happy than it was about the truth.

"I'd gone to find the bathroom, and I saw him. He stood in the darkness, breathing heavily. I could make out the four tentacles slithering around him like a nest of snakes." One girl squealed at this detail and almost fainted. "His eyes burned red in the shadows. He'd been waiting for me. And before I could turn around or even speak, he attacked."

Vince clutched at his throat, wrestling an imaginary tentacle. The more he talked, the more confident he became. "The first one got me around the neck," he said, his voice becoming a raspy wheeze. "It tightened. It choked. It would have taken my whole head off if I hadn't gotten away. But sometimes you just have to act. You can't think. Analysis is paralysis. So, grabbing the giant tentacle, I threw him over my head, his whole body. But he was quick and landed on both feet, tentacles ready."

"Were you scared?" asked the girl whose name was probably Kimberly.

"Not really," said Vince.

"But he was a monster," she said.

"Well, not *really*," said Vince.

"Well, was he or wasn't he?" asked Grover Williams, raising one eyebrow.

Opening his mouth, Vince waited for the right words to come to him. When they didn't, he gazed down at his classmates, hoping to find some inspiration there. That's when he saw Lucy standing in the back with her arms crossed. She didn't look angry, exactly, just disappointed. It was the kind of face a mother made when she knew you were lying and had hoped for better from you. Maybe Lucy was practicing for one day when she would have a couple of kids. They'd probably have the same huge gap in their front teeth as she did.

"Well?" said Grover Williams, throwing his arms in the air.

Not bothering to answer, Vince climbed down off the desk and left the room. He'd tried fame, and it didn't fit. He preferred to stay in the shadows, where no one ever wanted to hear your story.

At eleven o'clock, Vince found himself standing in front of the office with DR. JINKS painted on the door. Unlike any other office in the building, this one had a doorbell. If Vince hadn't been as stressed as he was, he would have thought this was cool. Unfortunately, he was so worried about the article in the *Santa Rosa Examiner* that he thought nothing of the doorbell. Instead, he concentrated on his stomach and on keeping it from emptying his breakfast all over the hallway floor. He felt *that* guilty.

Several minutes after Vince rang the doorbell, the door fell open with a loud buzz. A warm breeze blew into the hallway from inside the office, smelling of fireplace smoke and a perfume called Austere. He only knew the name because he had two older sisters, and that's the kind of stuff a guy picks up when he lives with teenage girls.

"Uh, hello," called Vince, poking his head around the doorframe. "I'm here for an eleven o'clock appointment." When there was no answer, he stepped into the huge darkened room and felt around for a light switch.

The office was bigger than Vince remembered from the time he'd been caught outside spying. Actually, the more he thought about it, the more he could tell that the room was completely different. It may have just been his memory playing tricks on him, but there were suits of armor in this new office, and there hadn't been any in the old one. The new room had a library, complete with mounted globes and a ladder that slid along the wall. No such area had been part of the old office.

Vince even started to wonder how such a huge room could fit in the school. It was probably half the size of the gymnasium. And was that a domed ceiling up above him? Were those stained-glass windows? He scratched his head and slowly crossed the room.

Still marveling at the office—this time at a large display screen blinking with green digital numbers—Vince sat in one of the big overstuffed chairs near the hearth. The warmth of the roaring fire felt good. He unzipped his hooded sweatshirt and dropped it next to him on the Oriental rug. *Wouldn't that be funny if this were something unnatural,* he thought. *Like, if it was really just a room on a spaceship made up to look like an office.* Smiling, he realized how stupid that sounded. Even for someone who interviewed Ails on a weekly basis, it was pretty out there.

The doors to the office opened with a click, and in walked Dr. Jinks. She wore a ruffled white blouse and black slacks that made a hissing sound as she crossed the carpet. In her hands she carried a pair of manila file folders and a small silver device. The device looked similar to an electric razor, except that one end glowed with soft pink light like a hot coal. With a flash of her gorgeous smile, Dr. Jinks sat in her high-backed leather chair.

"You must be Vince," she said, winking.

This caught Vince by surprise, and he wasn't sure how to react. He was torn between winking back and reporting her to the principal.

"That's me," he said nervously. He'd never been too at

ease around adult authority figures. It didn't help that this one looked like a model and had an office bigger than his entire apartment.

"How can I help you today, Vince?" asked Dr. Jinks.

"I don't know," said Vince, leaning forward in his chair. "I was just thinking that I'd like to talk to someone. You seemed like a logical choice, being the guidance counselor and all."

"What do you want to talk about?" she asked.

Vince paused. "A friend of mine," he said shyly.

This made Dr. Jinks smile as she rotated slowly in her office chair. "Do you want to talk about Gene Brennick?" she asked.

"I guess," said Vince, curious how she knew this. Then something occurred to him. "*Can* I talk about Gene? Is there some kind of rule that I can't talk about another student who talks to you or something?"

"We don't have rules like that," said Dr. Jinks. "You can talk about whatever you want, such as the location of Walter Sparrow."

"I'm sorry, what?" asked Vince.

"Nothing," said Dr. Jinks. "Please continue."

"Well, I guess I do want to talk about Gene," he said, feeling kind of silly for having asked. "How can I not talk about him? The last year has been all about Gene. Gene. Gene. Gene."

"Does that bother you?" asked Dr. Jinks.

Vince thought about the question. "You know. I thought it did, but I'm not so sure now. He drives me crazy. He's loud. He's clumsy. He's totally clueless when it comes to other people's feelings. But he's also my best friend."

Dr. Jinks reached down behind her desk. With a hollow wooden sound she opened one of the deep drawers and took out a bundle of newspaper. It was still rolled up tight, a rubber band snapped neatly around the middle. Rolling off the rubber band, Dr. Jinks unfolded the front page and held it up. "Then why did you do this?" she asked.

Staring at Vince from across the room was Gene, or at least the picture of him from the front page of the *Santa Rosa Examiner*.

No matter how hard Vince tried to come up with a good answer to her question, he couldn't. That's because there was none. "I guess I just wanted him to know what it felt like," said Vince. It was the best he could do.

"Felt like to what?" asked Dr. Jinks.

"To have his whole life put on the front page," said Vince. "That it doesn't feel so good. That there is such a thing as a bad headline, especially if it's about you."

"Well, you succeeded," said Dr. Jinks, putting away the newsletter.

"I guess I did," whispered Vince.

Clapping her hands together, Dr. Jinks stood up. She walked around behind him, so close he could smell her perfume. Austere had a fancy, fresh scent, like a mall Christmas tree. "I'm afraid I'll be leaving soon," she said. "My work here is nearly done, and in time I will move on."

"You're leaving?" asked Vince. "You've only been here for a week."

"It was a very important week," said Dr. Jinks. He could hear the smile in her voice. "And I wanted you to know that your little newsletter had a great impact on me and my work."

Gene looked up. "The *Globe*, really?" he asked.

"Of course," she continued, examining the huge display screen and its digital readout. "I never would have found all of them if it hadn't been for your wonderful reporting. Now only a few of them remain at large, and I will bring them back as well. You have my word on that. They will return with me, dead or alive." She walked behind him, her heels clicking softly on the floor.

Then, suddenly, Vince felt her fingers on his neck.

She had a light touch but her fingertips were hot. Not warm but near scalding. He squirmed as she tightened her grip.

"I'm glad you liked it," said Vince, growing very anxious. "We aim to please."

"You can help me once more, if you wish," she said in a strange voice that seemed to come from everywhere at once. "I would be eternally grateful."

"Okay," said Vince. He'd do anything if it meant he could leave.

"Where is Gene?" asked Dr. Jinks. Her voice began to make him dizzy. It was like he was lodged in a space between sleep and wakefulness. "If he is truly one of us, then Walter Sparrow will seek him out."

"He's probably at home," said Vince sleepily.

"No," she said. "They have abandoned the house. It was a wise move."

"Then I have no idea," said Vince.

"Think harder," said Dr. Jinks, lowering her voice until it sounded so strange he wasn't even sure it was her talking anymore. "Where would he go? We've searched the home of Fred Brennick and that of Walter Sparrow. Where else could they dare hide?"

"I don't know," said Vince, yawning. "He might go see

Lucy. I think they like each other now or something." He huffed. "And *I'm* the traitor."

"Lucy who?" asked Dr. Jinks, now interested.

"Lucy Herman," said Vince. "She designs the page layout for the newsletter."

"I see," said Dr. Jinks.

"I feel weird," said Vince, his eyelids drooping. "This one time on vacation, my dad took us to this restaurant where a guy . . ." He yawned again, rubbing one eye with a knuckle. "It was this restaurant where there was this hypnotist, and he put one of my sisters to sleep and made her walk around like a crab. It was awesome." Falling forward, he bumped his head gently on the arm of the chair. "I bet she probably felt like this when that happened."

There was a loud barking sound, and the hot hands on his neck disappeared. Vince blinked. A feeling of crisp clearness snapped through him like a bucket of icy water getting dumped over his head. His eyes flew open. According to the clock on the wall, ten minutes had passed, yet he couldn't really remember what had happened in all that time. All he could recall was his sister Susan scurrying around on all fours like a crab, which he was pretty sure had happened a long time ago.

Vince pushed himself up out of the overstuffed chair and, still a bit woozy, started to walk toward the office door. Dr. Jinks had returned to her desk and was hard at work scribbling notes on a yellow legal pad. As Vince passed, his eye was drawn to a photograph lying on the messy desktop. It was the hairdo that grabbed him. Such a great head of hair could only belong to one person.

"Hey, that's Walter Sparrow," he said drowsily, as he placed his hand on the doorknob.

"Yes, it is," said Dr. Jinks. The corners of her mouth curled up in a smile.

"Hey, did you know that you're both guidance counselors?" asked Vince. "It's like you're twins or something. Ha." He stopped laughing, and then yawned for about ten seconds. "Funny, huh?" he said.

"Very," said Dr. Jinks with a knowing smile.

A goofy grin still plastered from ear to ear, Vince pulled open the door to the office. On the other side there stood a man in a dark suit and sunglasses. Without so much as a hello, the man poked Vince in the chest with a vibrating silver device.

"Hey," Vince said before a bolt of electricity made his tongue go numb.

He dropped to the hallway floor, and then began to slip into unconsciousness.

As he teetered on the brink of sleep, Vince was in some small way glad he didn't have to go back to class. He had a science test coming up, and he hadn't really studied for it. In his opinion, it was better to be kidnapped than to be a C student.

The last thing he saw was Dr. Jinks standing over him. The last thing he heard was her saying, "Humans are idiots. I should destroy them all." Then the lights went out.

20

IN 1957 A SPECIAL MILITARY BASE WAS BUILT IN THE DESERT
outside Santa Rosa, California. It was named Fort Dreyfus
after the important general who had come up with the idea
for it while flossing his teeth. The base was meant to be a
secret research station for unidentified flying objects, or
UFOs. But since none of the scientists working at Fort
Dreyfus had ever seen a UFO, they found themselves
bored rather quickly. Having a good idea and then making
it work don't always go hand in hand.

One night, however, a brilliant, flaming object fell from
the night sky above Santa Rosa. It plummeted to Earth, strik-
ing a sand dune and destroying a soda stand called Curly
Sue's. Within minutes, a team of army scientists rushed out
to the impact crater. They wore top-secret protective suits
that had numerous hoses and nozzles, none of which actually

did anything. They certainly looked impressive, though.

As the smoke cleared, a man stepped from the wreckage. He was handsome and tall with a shock of brown hair. He was also naked, but everyone fails to mention that when they tell the story.

A few years after that fateful night, the U.S. government flattened Fort Dreyfus and made it into a drive-in movie theater. A few decades after that, the Santa Rosa zoning committee decided to turn the crusty old eyesore into a trailer park. They named it Crater Park as a joke.

More than fifty years after the night he first arrived in Santa Rosa, Walter Sparrow pulled into the dusty drive of Crater Park and parked beside Fred's dented old Airstream trailer. He turned off the engine of the pickup and sat silently gazing out the window at the desert. There were so many memories out there, lost in the sweeping dunes, buried. The vast, yawning crater seemed to swallow them up.

Mrs. Brennick's rusty pickup wheezed and banged as it settled into the ruts of the sandy driveway.

"And why are we at the trailer park?" asked Gene, who sat in the backseat with his iPod jammed into his ears. He hadn't said a word during the whole ride, his hood pulled up so it hid his face.

"We'll be safe here," said Walter, shoving open the car door with his foot. He uttered a loud groan and stretched.

"You're right," said Gene, "because no normal person would ever come out here." Hopping out onto the sand, he wandered off in the direction of the Airstream.

Walter chose to ignore Gene's sarcasm and sat down on the hood of the car to watch the sunset.

Carpooling a family around was not something he was used to doing. He'd done a lot of strange things in his different lifetimes on Earth. He'd helped fake the Apollo 11 moon landing. He'd built the Egyptian pyramids to impress a girl. He'd even ordered and eaten the Gut-Buster Bacon Cheeseburger Super Special at the Burger Shack, just because he'd felt like it. In five thousand years, he'd done just about everything there was to do, except run away. But he was running now. Walter knew life could get bad, but nothing could have prepared him for sitting at a stop sign and watching Gene pick at an elbow scab with his teeth.

Above them the sun descended, casting an orange light over the trailer park. Closing his eyes, Walter took a deep breath and smelled the faraway scent of someone's campfire. It had been a good life. Too bad it was all coming to an end.

"What are you doing?" asked Mrs. Brennick. She was

walking past, her arms piled high with luggage. Walter immediately moved to take the bags from her.

He forced a smile. "Call me crazy," he said, "but I'm not in any hurry to go from one tight space to another. I like being out in the open. I don't get to do it all that often. Not when you're on the run."

Then Mrs. Brennick surprised him. She sat down next to him on the hood of the truck, placing the bags on the ground. "What do you want out of all this?" she asked. "If you get away from these bad aliens, where will you go? What will you do?"

There was only one real answer to this, and it had taken him a lifetime to find it. He smiled. Mrs. Brennick was a very pretty woman, but she had forgotten that. From the way she acted, it was clear that she felt about as lonely as Walter did. "To be honest," he said, sighing, "I just want my old job back."

"What did you do?" asked Mrs. Brennick.

"I was a guidance counselor," said Walter, laughing at how weird it sounded after all that had happened.

Again, Mrs. Brennick surprised him. She began to nod and to smile a little bit herself. "I bet you were good at it," she said. "You're good with Gene."

If Walter had been able to blush, he would have. But

his species of alien do not blush. "Thanks," he said, his smile growing wider.

There was a commotion from the big silver Airstream, and the front door flew open with a squawk of its hinges. The whole trailer shook as Fred came stomping down the front steps, his ponytail bouncing along behind him like a pet ferret. Once he reached the bottom step, he crossed his arms and squinted hard at everyone. There were red rope marks on his wrists and he had a fat lip.

"What took you so long?" he demanded. "Everyone else is waiting for you. This safe house isn't going to guard itself."

The safe house everyone kept talking about was a large cylindrical spacecraft that was buried just below the surface of Crater Park, right under Fred's old Airstream trailer. According to Fred, the ship had crash-landed near the old military base back in the days when Coke still cost a dime and Doritos hadn't even been invented yet. The interior of the spacecraft was accessible through a round metal hatch that stuck up out of the desert sand like a mechanical mushroom. This entrance opened right into the living room of Fred's trailer, a fact he'd always hidden with a fraying throw rug.

Once inside, a spiral staircase led down into the main

corridor, which ran from one end of the ship to the other, about thirty feet in length. Along the way, the passage branched off into a series of smaller cabins. White lights twinkled under the floor and lit up every time you took a step. At one end of the long corridor was an infirmary, in case someone got sick. It hadn't been used in ages, and its collection of bizarre medical instruments gleamed in the light from the bright overhead lamps. A large, round operating table lay draped in white cloth. At the other end of the passage was the cockpit, where a huge dusty windshield looked out over dirt. That's the kind of view you got when you were buried twenty feet underground. Easily the coolest feature of the cockpit was the clunky metal periscope that could be raised above the surface of the sand. Through it, you had a full view of the trailer park, the crater, and the empty desert beyond.

The only area of the ship that Gene was forbidden to enter was a strange room with nothing at all inside it. No chairs or a bed or a sink. It just stood there empty, like an unused phone booth. On the wall next to the doorway was a big button covered by a box of glass. It had a sign that said BREAK GLASS FOR EJECTION.

When Gene, his mother, and Walter moved in, they found a crowd of friends waiting for them. Nearly every cabin of the spacecraft was full. There was Arachnid Boy, Mold Man, Hip-Hop Sasquatch, Fish Foot, the San Diego Dwarf, and a few other Ails that Gene had never met. Even better, three of the cabins at the far end of the ship were occupied by Linus, Matt, and Cathy, a.k.a. Crumble Bun.

When Gene saw his friends, he hurried over and offered welcome high fives. They were hanging out in Matt's cabin, which was the same as all the others—the size of a walk-in closet with a metal sink, a bunk, and a buzzing white light in the ceiling.

"Boy, was I getting worried," said Not-So-Quiet Matt, grinning. "We thought you'd been captured or brain-washed or something." He held hands with Crumble Bun as he talked, her fingers wrapped in the black fabric of her special gloves. "You wouldn't believe what's going on, Gene. This is *huge*."

"I think I have a pretty good idea," said Gene.

Linus smiled. "I'm usually not that glad to see you," she said. "But I am now."

"Um, thanks," said Gene. He poked his head around one of the cabin doorways. "Where's Lucy?" he asked.

His friends looked at each other worriedly, and then they both shrugged. "No Vince either," added Matt.

"Well, we've got to call them," said Gene.

"We've been trying," said Linus.

"Then we have to go get them," said Gene, walking over to the spiral steps leading back to the surface.

Linus frowned. "We can't," she said. "The adults won't let us. The plan is to lie low until Walter and Fred bring the rest of the Ails here to safety. We're just supposed to sit tight."

"Sit tight?" said Gene. "Are they crazy?"

"It's for our own safety," said Crumble Bun.

"Yeah?" said Gene, stuffing his hands into his pockets. "Well, maybe we should stop thinking about ourselves all the time."

Again, Matt and Linus glanced at each other, and then turned to Gene. "Are you sure you haven't been brain-washed?" asked Linus.

Gene rolled his eyes. "Oh, shut up."

Later that night, Gene sat up in his bunk, flipping through a book called *What's With All This Slime? A Young Alien's Time of Change*. As he did, a tentacle explored the room, jamming itself into every nook it could find. So far it had overturned two cans of something labeled ALL-PURPOSE MOLECULAR FEED SOLUTION, set off the spaceship's security system, and gotten caught in what looked a lot like a toaster.

"My life is a nightmare," Gene said to the tentacle. It

suddenly stopped what it was doing and seemed to look at him. It flopped from side to side like a dog tilting its head. "Whatever," Gene added.

Anxious about his friends, he'd searched his room for something to occupy him and had stumbled upon the alien handbook. It started off interesting but grew complicated quickly. By page two he could barely understand it. The chapters had names like, "Aliens Have Feelings Too (Unless They're Robots)" and "Is That Me Glowing?"

After flipping through the table of contents for five minutes, he forced himself to read a few pages. This was a tremendous step, since Gene only read things that could fit on the back of a cereal box. Turning to the chapter titled "The First Week: Get Out the Paper Towels!" he started:

"It isn't out of the ordinary for a young alien to experience a series of electric shocks before turning into a cloud of gas. Don't panic! This is perfectly normal. If you're from Centauri Six and you're worried about suddenly exploding, talk to your parents. If they don't have a fission-powered particle decelerator, they probably know someone who does."

Gene closed the book.

Getting out of his bunk, he left his room and walked down the low bunker hallway to the cramped cabin that had been converted into a bathroom. A small light hummed quietly in the ceiling, casting jagged shadows. He closed the door and locked it. Then he set about getting ready for bed. Every time he moved in the tiny little room, it echoed, as if he were inside a submarine. Regardless, Gene tried to get things done as if it were any other normal night.

It was anything but normal. When Gene tried to brush his teeth, one of the tentacles kept trying to steal the brush and use it to scrub his nose. Then, when he was cleaning his ears, another tentacle snatched a jar of vitamins and tried to jam it down Gene's throat, cap and all. Whenever Gene got upset, a certain tentacle—he was starting to call it Angry—would break something. It started with the plunger and continued on to the mirror, sending shards of glass flying everywhere.

Eventually, Gene lost his battle against the slithering nest of blue coils, and he sat down on the closed toilet seat. "Can you just stop?" he barked, resting his chin on a fist.

And they did.

Finishing up, Gene got ready to walk back to his bed. As he left the bathroom, he heard clanging footsteps at the end of the hall. He found Walter Sparrow leaning against the wall beside the mysterious doorway with the big button. The guidance counselor stared at the box with the BREAK GLASS FOR EJECTION sign on it. It looked as though he was planning on breaking the glass but just couldn't get up the courage to do it.

"Hi," said Gene.

Walter flinched, and then turned around. "Hey, Gene," he said. "What are you doing up and around?"

"I don't know," said Gene. He stuck his head into the weird little chamber to investigate. There wasn't much to it. "What is this room?"

"It's not a room," said Walter. "It's an escape pod."

Gene's jaw dropped. "You're kidding."

"Nope," said Walter.

"How do you know?" asked Gene.

Walter sighed, hands jingling the change in the pocket of his white linen pants. "Because this was my ship," he said.

"Wow," said Gene. "Nice. It's, like, *so* vintage science fiction, really cool." He gestured to the doorway. "So I guess you never needed to escape, then, huh?"

"Well, this escape pod has only one destination," said Walter. "And that's back home."

"The bad place?" asked Gene, remembering all the talk of Walter's big escape.

Walter nodded. "It's just nice to be reminded that I could be back there," he said. "It makes what I've got here on Earth seem that much more special."

Gene left Walter staring into the escape pod, but he couldn't shake what the alien adventurer turned guidance counselor had said. It made him wonder what he had on Earth that was special, if anything.

Walking back down the hall to his bedroom, he collapsed on the bunk, where his laptop sat open. The screensaver drifted with pictures he'd snapped with his phone. All of them were of the aliens he'd written about with his friends. Gene grunted, smiling as he watched a particularly good shot of Calamari Girl float across the screen. She would have been cute if half her body hadn't looked deep-fried.

Then a picture of Vince and Lucy filled the screen.

As Gene watched the photo brighten, linger, and then fade from view, he thought of his two best friends. He'd just seen them the day before, but he already missed them.

Since he couldn't sleep, and since he didn't want to read any more of that stupid book, Gene decided to step outside for some air. He wasn't supposed to, but since that reason had never stopped him from doing things before, he wasn't going to let it start now. Sweatshirt under one arm, he carefully shut the door to his room and tiptoed down the bunker hallway, heading for the spiral staircase that led up, and out, to freedom.

21

ACROSS TOWN ON BERLIN STREET, WHERE THE TOWNS OF
Santa Rosa and Fulton rubbed up against each other, Lucy
Herman sat at her vanity. She was hard at work popping
a zit in the mirror. A breeze blew in through her window,
causing the white cotton curtains to rustle. Shivering, she
got up from her stool and walked to the small balcony
that looked down on the front yard from her second-floor
bedroom.

The world lay still in the lamplight. The streets were
empty of cars. The materials for her father's new garage
sat in the driveway—orange cones, sawhorse, lumber. A
lone dog moaned at the moon. And below, standing in her
mother's prized petunias, was Gene Brennick.

"Lucy!" he shouted, waving his arms.

Gene was tired of being alone. He was not good at
working solo. Some people didn't eat meat. Some people

didn't watch horror movies. Some people didn't wear deodorant. Gene didn't *do* alone.

Stepping out of the flower bed, he ran across the yard and climbed up on Mrs. Herman's expensive brass birdbath to get a better view. Once he reached the top, he stopped waving his arms. It was difficult to stay up there. So he teetered with his arms at his side, balancing like a giant, drowsy pelican.

"Gene!" shouted Lucy. "What are you doing here?"

Gene was about to answer when he felt a cold, slimy wetness on his ankle. Guessing that it was one of his tentacles acting up, he slapped at his foot. Instead of a tentacle, he knocked away a slug. The small blobby creature flew onto the driveway, where it landed with a splat.

"What is it, Gene?" she asked again.

Again, Gene tried to open his mouth, and again he felt a wet slug stuck to his ankle. "Gross!" he shouted.

"What's gross?" asked Lucy, leaning out the window.

"Lucy!" he called. Just then a slug on his shirt dropped onto the patch of skin between his shoe and his trouser leg. It felt like a soggy burrito. With a scream, Gene fell off the birdbath and landed in the grass.

One of his tentacles snapped forward over his shoulder. It scooped up the slug and cradled it in its curved tip.

The gray blob and the blue tentacle looked oddly similar. Then Gene began to understand what was going on. The slugs were chasing him because for some reason they were attracted to the tentacles. "Yuck!" he shouted. He smacked his tentacle, which sent the slug spinning into the yard. "No mating allowed!"

"Lucy!" Gene tried again. "I'm covered in slugs!"

Of course, Lucy couldn't make out what Gene was saying, since he was dancing around her yard as if he were walking on coals.

"You're what?" she shouted back. "Your Communist hugs?"

"I'm covered in slugs," he yelled again.

"Your oven is sludged?" Lucy shouted back.

Shaking his head in frustration, Gene walked over to the driveway. Then he picked up one of the orange cones the construction workers had left behind. Using it like a megaphone, he shouted up to Lucy. *"I'm covered in slugs! And it's nasty, and I hate it!"* He screamed it out as loud as he could, and the sound echoed across the cul-de-sac. *"I hate that Vince punched me in the face, and that my dad was some alien who grew up in Michigan!"* Several front-porch lights flickered on, but Gene kept shouting. *"But most of all, I hate that I have a bunch of tentacles sticking* out of me! One is always trying to feed me stuff, and there's this other one that's always sticking books in my face! If I want to read something, I'll go to a library, thank you very much!"

It was Lucy's turn to wave her arms now as she tried to get him to stop yelling. The entire neighborhood was stirring. People were waking up. Windows were opening. "Be quiet!" Lucy hissed down at him. "Keep your voice down!"

But Gene was tired of keeping his voice down. Being polite was out of the question when you were all alone and no one wanted to listen to you. "I've been doing a lot of thinking!" he shouted, then lowered his voice a bit. "It's just like Vince always said. I should think about what I do before I do it. How does he put it? 'Considering the consequences is awesomeness . . . sss . . .'" He turned away and feverishly shook his head, mumbling. "That is the worst catchphrase *ever.*"

"What are you trying to say, Gene?" asked Lucy.

Gene's face went totally blank. "I came here to say I'm sorry," he said.

Leaning on the railing, Lucy gazed down at where he stood surrounded by broken bricks and power tools. "Is that all you want?" she asked.

Gene always thought he'd have a lot to say to Lucy if the opportunity presented itself. After all, he'd had a crush on her for a long time. Whenever he thought about a girl, whether it was giving one a kiss on the check or asking one for the key to a gas station bathroom, he pictured Lucy. She was what he thought a girl should be—pretty, nice, smart, and funny. Even now, Gene couldn't help smiling when he saw her.

But now that the time had come, he just didn't know how to say any of it. "Kissing you was awesome," he said. "Let's do it again."

"I don't think so, Gene," said Lucy.

"We kissed for like half an hour," said Gene. "It was great."

"We kissed once," said Lucy, "and for like five seconds."

"So?" said Gene. "It was cool, wasn't it?"

Lucy hugged herself, and it looked like she was even thinking about walking back inside. She didn't. "Yes," she said at last.

"Okay," said Gene with a smile. "Good."

Not sure what else to do, he turned to walk away. Before he reached the end of the driveway, something occurred to him, and he stopped. Turning around, he lifted the orange cone back to his mouth.

"Hey!" he shouted. Maybe it was the fact that everything felt turned upside down, backward, the opposite. Maybe he didn't have to be so mixed-up anymore. "I like you a lot," he said at a regular volume. "You're pretty. You're funny. You know how to make my articles look really good on the page. I've always thought you were special, even if I didn't say much about it. And I think you're a great friend, Lucy Herman."

At first she didn't say anything. Then, turning away, she walked inside and shut her balcony door.

Gene hung his head. The tentacles, which had a weird connection to his emotions, drooped. With the darkness of a Santa Rosa morning in front of him, he walked down the road leading to Highway 10, alone.

"Gene." It was Lucy's voice behind him.

The front door of the Herman house opened. Lucy stepped out, dressed in her nightgown, a shawl around her shoulders.

"Thank you," she said.

Gene smiled. "Anytime," he said.

He waited a second to let the moment sink in, and then he added, "Now let's get your bike, because we have to go hide out from the school guidance counselor in Walter Sparrow's old spaceship."

"What?"

Really, that final moment would have been a beautiful one if not for the black SUVs parked along the curb and the lizard men creeping through the bushes carrying ray guns. That kind of thing always spoils a good time.

22

MORE THAN TEN THOUSAND YEARS AGO, THE CREATURE known as Pamela Jinks came into being. Back then, she was simply called Zoxx, Jr., and was made of little more than a black hole and a pair of skinny legs. She never got over the skinny-legs part. During her time at World Eaters Academy, she had to live with a host of nasty nicknames, like Chicken Bones and Flarg Grasper, which was another rude way of saying she had skinny legs.

At the age of one thousand, Zoxx changed. She evolved into her next form, which looked like a cross between a stegosaurus and a jellyfish. This was an extremely unique creature, and one that was very difficult to picture. It's best not to try. Graduating first in her class at the academy, she took a few centuries off to travel. Most of her older brothers and sisters had done this too. It was sort of a family tradition, right up there with the annual holiday party.

But there was another reason she'd always wanted to get away, one that was more important than any of the others. This reason was *him*, her twin brother.

Almost since birth, the two siblings hadn't gotten along. Every time they were together, they argued. Even over the littlest things, like who would get to borrow their mother's turbo rocket sled with power steering. One thing would lead to another and a fight would break out. She would blast him with her eyebeam atomizer, and he would return fire with a storm of flames from his mouth. The battles would rage on and on, more often than not leading nowhere.

However, he had one power that she truly feared. It was called the Proton Vomit. It was an attack that he very rarely performed because it had far-reaching effects. Gravity on the planet Dorfin was still a little wonky from the family reunion disaster nine thousand years ago. That had been the scene of one of the twins' bigger arguments, and they hadn't spoken to each other since.

Zoxx blamed their family problems on her brother's strange obsession with "good." That was what he called *not* wanting to set fire to whole planets: "being good." Whenever the family went on day trips to shrink a sun or to cause an earthquake and destroy a city, he stayed behind. He'd lock himself in his sleep pod and claim that he was tired, the big baby. It drove her crazy. So when the opportunity came for Zoxx to leave home, to see what else was out there, she took it.

She left home alone. She hiked through the Wastes of Asterix Six, and then spent a relaxing year in the mud baths of the Parsum Dimension. It was during her four hundred years on the planet Ion that she met the creature known as Wargash the Consumer, a local warlord and evil tyrant. He was very handsome and very powerful. Every time he crushed someone's skull, a small dimple formed above his right eye. Zoxx thought it was so cute. She fell for him, hard. They were married and prepared to build a life together laying waste to small galaxies and other star systems.

That's when she received the urgent message. She was needed right away back home in her native universe. It was a matter of life and death. Saying farewell to her beloved, Zoxx traveled back to her parents' side. There she received the news that her brother had disappeared.

And guess who their father and uncle chose to find him?

For five thousand years Zoxx followed. In that time, she'd been to planets no other being had ever heard of, much less seen. She dug open mountain ranges and tore apart whole constellations. She followed him to Earth, a small, out-of-the-way planet with nothing special going for it. She burned Rome and dropped the second A-bomb. Century after century, she slogged after him, tracing his trail across the solar system.

And for some reason that her uncle never revealed, Zoxx hadn't been allowed to just boil the Earth's seas and demand that her brother reveal himself. She had been told not to act rashly and do anything too destructive, like shift the tectonic plates and rearrange the continents. Why? No one would tell her. Apparently the small blue and brown planet had significance that even she didn't know about.

Now, five thousand years was a long, long time, even for someone who would probably live forever. But what got her through every day of it was the hope that soon it would be over. Soon she would have him in her clutches.

That morning, Zoxx, who called herself Dr. Jinks, sat in the backseat of an expensive black SUV and drank her morning cup of coffee. Gagging, she choked down the hot brown substance. She gagged every time she tasted Earth coffee. It was absolutely terrible, the galaxy's worst.

"It seems Mr. Haskell was right," she said to the driver.

"What do you mean, mistress?" asked Prak, confused.

"He guessed that Mr. Brennick would return to the girl, this Lucy," she said.

"And it seems he was correct, mistress," said Prak, turning left onto Highway 10. The truck hit a pothole and clanged, causing the coffee to jump in Zoxx's hand.

Steadying her cup, she gazed ahead of them at the oncoming brightness of the sunrise. A flock of birds rose in the shape of a V. Clouds drifted slowly across the shimmering sliver of the sun, as birds sang pleasant songs from the desert trees. The whole thing made her want to vomit. Earth was such a dump. Humans deserved it.

Zoxx settled back in her seat and wrapped an arm around Vince, who was tied up on the cushion. "It seems you were correct, Mr. Haskell," she said with a grin. She stroked his head as if he was her pet. "Well done."

Vince also stared out the windshield at what lay ahead of them. But he was not watching the sunrise or the birds or a bank of clouds. He watched Gene and Lucy pedaling as fast as they could down the sandy road to the old Crater Park trailer park. Their tires kicked up a fan of dust, making a perfect trail to follow.

23

EVER SINCE HE WAS A LITTLE KID, GENE BRENNICK WANTED to be important.

As he coasted up the road to Crater Park that night, Gene felt for the first time that he was part of something bigger than himself. He was helping a group of aliens escape the clutches of an evil villain. *That* was important. Granted, it meant that he was in danger of being eaten by lizard men or set on fire by his guidance counselor. But still, there was something exciting about being part of a bigger purpose. He'd never played the hero before. Usually he just played the kid who sits behind the hero in biology class.

Gene and Lucy pulled up to the Airstream and parked their bikes by the front walk. Almost as soon as they dismounted, the door to the trailer opened and out walked Fred. He pressed an ice pack to his face on one of the big black-and-blue spots where those weird alien agents had socked him. With every step, he winced.

"Where have you been?" he growled, nervously gazing out over Crater Park.

"I had to get Lucy," said Gene. He gestured to his friend, and she waved shyly.

"Hi, Fred," she said.

"Lucy," said Fred, not that interested. Clucking his tongue, he began to pace back and forth on the sand at the base of the steps. "Did you see Walter on your way back?"

"No," said Gene. "Where's Walter?"

"He's not here," said Fred, sitting down in a lawn chair. He began to stroke the red cap of a lawn gnome. "He's still out gathering the rest of the Ails."

"When's he coming back?" asked Gene.

To this, Fred just shrugged and made a noise like *"Pft."* He looked at Lucy again and then began to nod. "It's a good thing you brought her back to the shelter," he said. "If this Dr. Jinks character is using the *Globe* to nab aliens, then none of your friends are safe."

"Someone still has to get Vince," said Gene. Pulling his cell phone from his pocket, he started to dial the number he knew by heart. Before he could, Lucy grabbed his arm.

She pointed far down the trailer park road, past the billboard with the little green spaceman on it. In the distance, a high plume of dust rose up into the early-morning sky. "Is that Walter?" she asked, her voice wavering with fear.

Fred stood up and squinted, placing a flat hand against his forehead to shield his eyes. His clucking grew more excited. "No," he said. That's when he started pushing Gene and Lucy up the steps toward the trailer door. "It's not."

Gene didn't feel so good anymore. *So much for being the hero,* he thought. Instead of helping aliens escape the clutches of an evil villain, he was leading the villain right to them.

With Fred in the lead, the trio rushed up into the Airstream and into the main room. Then, yanking the throw rug aside, he revealed the hatch leading down into the old spacecraft underneath.

"After you," he said to Lucy, who was already halfway down the steps.

They joined the others in the crowded cockpit. Up above a single metal step in the back of the room hung the periscope controls, which consisted of a pair of handlebars and an eyepiece. Fred stood poised at an old control panel, rigid and ready, as if he'd been operating spaceships all his life. This made Gene wonder if maybe Fred had.

With the push of a few buttons, a series of red, blue, and white lights blinked on. The length of the vessel began to shake gently, all thirty feet of it. Fred snapped his fingers and pointed at the periscope. "Gene, if you wouldn't mind," he said. "Give it a look, would you?"

Normally, Gene would have been excited to do this, but not that night. He was afraid to see what was happening out there on the sand. He knew Dr. Jinks had arrived, and that she was looking for them. This was scary enough. But now that Gene was an alien, it meant she was looking for *him*, too.

Stepping up to the handlebars, he tugged them down out of the ceiling and placed his face against the periscope eyepiece. The picture was murky, dark. It zoomed back and forth in a blur. Then suddenly he could make out the purple streaks of the desert dawn and the boxy shapes of the mobile homes set in rows at the base of the dunes.

"What do you see?" asked Fred.

"Not much," said Gene.

Gene turned the periscope in a slow circle around the trailer park and saw the following: a saggy shirtless man walking his dog, a girl staring up at the stars through a telescope in her trailer window, a little boy poking a dead bird with a stick. Then he saw the trail of dust. "Bingo," he murmured. He rotated the view, following the trail of dust down to where the road was being kicked up by the tires of Jinks's black SUVs.

The trucks were still about a hundred feet away from Fred's trailer, but they were coming up fast. Both of them were being driven by alien agents. In the backseat of the first SUV sat Dr. Jinks. Eyes narrowed, she glared straight ahead through the windshield. It was almost as if she were giving Gene the evil eye all the way across Crater Park and down through the twists of the periscope. He shivered.

Continuing to scan, his eye caught something wholly unexpected. The sight stopped his heart, and he had to slowly turn the eyepiece back in the opposite direction to make sure what he'd glimpsed was real.

There, slumped against the backseat of Dr. Jinks's truck lay Vince, his best friend. He was tied up, but other than that, he looked fine. In fact, he was watching a DVD on the in-car video player.

"Uh-oh," whispered Gene.

He didn't know what to do next. Should he act, should he think? Should he run and hide in his cabin with the door locked?

In the end, Gene did none of these things and all of them. Very quickly, and before he could stop himself—or anyone else could either—he jumped off the stool and sprinted out of the control room and down the long, vibrating ship corridor.

"Gene, come back!" Fred yelled after him.

Before Gene could climb too far up the ladder leading outside, Lucy stopped him. "What are you doing?" she demanded. "You can't go out there."

"Vince is with them," said Gene.

"Really?" asked Lucy.

"Stay here," said Gene. "I'm going after him."

She reached up and grabbed his ankle. "Don't, you idiot," she said. "You're going to get blown into Gene-pieces."

"Yes, and I like you too," said Gene, and then, hesitating, he leaned way down and kissed her on the cheek.

"Oh, goodie," said Lucy, sighing.

At about the time that Gene was crawling out of Walter's old spaceship, Dr. Jinks was taking her favorite ray gun out of its long, polished leather case. She twisted the dial and listened to the soft hum of its battery. Then she changed the setting to Fry. She slammed shut the door of the SUV and stepped out into the driveway of Crater Park. The dust settled on the legs of her finely pressed pantsuit.

"Remember," she said. "Get the boy alive, and he will take us to my brother." Her companions nodded their understanding.

Giving a hand signal, she started to walk briskly across the dusty parking lot. Behind her trailed a squad of five Bozon agents. Each of them carried a silver ray gun that was much larger than hers. Some of the biggest guns had tiny guns sticking out of them. There was even one enormous cannon that, instead of laser beams, fired smaller guns that then fired laser beams. The agents moved in formation, glanced around, aiming at anything that moved, including the clouds, which they still mistook for large, puffy birds. They made a beeline for Fred's silver Airstream, which sat lopsided in the clutter of Crater Park like a piece of fallen space junk.

As the group approached, a man in a bathrobe stepped out of one of the other trailers in his pajamas and began dropping bags of garbage into his trash cans. The racket was deafening.

On high alert, Agent Prak spun around, his finger tugging the trigger. With a loud, crackling zap and a metallic shredding sound, the trash cans exploded. Seconds later, the sky began to rain banana peels, used coffee filters, yogurt containers, and junk mail. A half-eaten fish dropped with a splat in the middle of the street, right next to a pothole. The whole trailer park began to reek like garbage that had just been hit with a ray gun set to Explodify.

"Quit messing around!" snapped Dr. Jinks. After hunting for her brother for thousands of years, she was at long last about to catch him. And she wasn't about to let one of her idiot Bozons mess it up. Not this time.

Agent Prak stared at her in confusion. His scaly skin showed through the hole where his nose had been. "The sound of those waste receptacles confused me," he said.

Without so much as a wave good-bye, Dr. Jinks raised her ray gun and blasted him with a bolt of energy. Agent Prak's face melted into a steaming pile of tuna-colored goop. A second later his navy blue suit caught fire.

With a flip of her hair, Dr. Jinks turned to go. "I told you to quit messing around," she said coldly.

The four remaining Bozon agents fell in step behind their mistress. Ray guns at the ready, the group continued on toward the Airstream. They were about fifteen feet from the trailer when Dr. Jinks raised one hand, signaling them to stop.

She sniffed the air, long and hard. Then, in her sweetest voice she called, "Gene." She sang his name like she was calling a dog. "Gene. Talk to me, Gene. I know you're out here. We just want to talk."

"No, we don't," said one agent. "We want to explodify him."

"Quiet!" snapped Dr. Jinks. Then she became pleasant again and cooed, "Gene!"

There was no answer.

"I can help you," said Dr. Jinks. "Walter Sparrow has infected you. That's why you're changing. That's why your life has been turned upside down." She crept up a small dune, at the top of which stood the billboard that said CRATER PARK in large black letters. One of the letters had been painted to resemble a little green man—a Martian—something Dr. Jinks found terribly offensive.

"Tell me where Walter is and I'll take him away," she went on. "You'll be able to get back to your normal life. No!" she interrupted herself. "You will have a *new* life, one of popularity and fame. Isn't that what you want, Gene?"

Reaching the top of the small hill, Dr. Jinks lifted her nose and smelled the air. "Walter has ruined everything," she purred, creeping closer to the billboard. Something was hiding behind it. "How about you take me to him?"

"I don't think so," said a voice in a cool, low tone.

Then a figure stepped out of the crater, casting a long shadow along the sand. He stood tall and straight. His cufflinks glinted on the crisp cuffs of his sport coat. A pair of silver sunglasses rested on the tip of his nose, pulled forward enough to show off his eyes, which flashed a bright red and purple. When Walter Sparrow spoke, a wisp of smoke slipped from his lips.

The cavalry had arrived. Or, at least, a bunch of aliens had, which was better than nothing.

24

IN THE DIM LIGHTS OF THE TRAILER PARK, WALTER LOOKED
just like any other school guidance counselor. Except, that
is, for the way his eyes glowed in the dark. They burned
steadily red and purple and hissed like a couple of ice cubes
on a stovetop. And even though he wasn't raising his voice,
you could hear him all over the place, in every nook and in
every cranny. It sounded like Walter *was* the desert. When
he smiled, he showed unnaturally large teeth, and when he
laughed, the ground shook.

Even Gene shivered at the sound, and he now considered
Walter a friend. He sat behind the billboard, hugging his
knees to his chest.

He watched Dr. Jinks as she tried to stay calm. One of
her high heels had broken, so when she tried to stand up
straight, she wobbled. This did not make her look tough,

especially in comparison to Walter. "You're here," she said, sounding stunned.

"I'm here, Zoxx," said Walter. "Did you really think you'd just come here and take me back? Did you think my friends and I would just come willingly?"

He removed his glasses and tucked them into his shirt pocket. "You've chosen an interesting human form," he said, swaggering toward where she stood with her agents. "It's a lot better looking than your real one. Less pus, I mean." Even though they were nowhere near him, Dr. Jinks's Bozons backed up a step or two. They were carrying their silver ray guns and Walter was unarmed, but still, they were afraid of him. "Hey, boys," said Walter, acknowledging them with a wave.

Gene wasn't entirely sure where the conversation was going, and he didn't particularly care. All he wanted to do was get to the SUV and free Vince.

As Gene tried to think up creative ways to sneak out from behind the billboard, he caught a flicker of movement out of the corner of his eye. He glanced over in time to see three shapes flash past him, behind several of the closest trailers. Crumble Bun led the way, followed by Mold Man and Hip-Hop Sasquatch. The three of them ran single file, and then split off, fanning out behind Dr. Jinks and her agents.

Now the two sides were more evenly matched, with Walter and his three friends advancing on Dr. Jinks and her four agents. It was the best possible time to act. So, gathering his courage, and trying not to wet his pants, Gene bolted for the parking lot. It was the bravest thing he'd ever done, and probably the most important. And he was pretty sure it would be the last thing he ever did too.

After centuries of fleeing across universes and planets and continents, Walter was finally going to make his sister pay. Who did she think she was anyway, with her fancy bangs and her team of Bozon agents?

"You're coming back with me," said Dr. Jinks. "I've spent too long looking for you to return empty-handed."

"You'd better get used to the idea," said Walter, shrugging. "You've never been able to beat me."

"One can pick up a lot of new tricks over five thousand years," said Dr. Jinks.

"But one does not forget his old tricks," said Walter. "The tricks that work."

Summoning all of his strength, Walter was able to focus it into a single stream of energy. When released, this burst of raw power was so incredible, it had once knocked a whole universe off its axis.

Dr. Jinks had never been strong enough to overcome the Proton Vomit. Walter knew how much she hated it. When they were kids, he'd teased her by doing it to her at the dinner table when their parents weren't looking.

"Let's finish this," said Walter, stepping forward. Electricity began to crackle and dance around his head as his mouth opened.

"You're welcome to try," said Dr. Jinks with a knowing smile.

Walter lunged forward, and a bright white light bloomed out from where the two of them stood on the dune. A cascade of sparks shot upward and then rained down into the trailer park like fireworks. This was followed by a loud, hollow boom, which caused the parked cars to tremble.

Right about now was when Walter expected to blast Dr. Jinks back to her home planet or do something else exciting. Unfortunately, that's not what happened. It was Walter himself who said that interstellar travel was a funny thing. That changing forms from a being made of pure energy into a lowly human being wasn't an exact science. He'd even mentioned that, from time to time, powers could be affected by this. They could change or act funny or go away altogether. And that's just what happened.

The Proton Vomit, Walter's most famous of powers, was completely gone.

"Something wrong?" asked Dr. Jinks.

"No," said Walter, backing away.

"Are you sure?" she asked.

"No," he said.

With that, Dr. Jinks blasted Walter Sparrow in the chest with a burst of flame that sent him spinning up toward the clouds. He wasn't laughing anymore.

It took a laser beam blasting a hole in the windshield for Vince to remember how dangerous a situation he was really in.

He wriggled around on the seat, trying to break free of his ropes. Outside in the desert the aliens fought one another madly. Ray guns zapped. Trailers went flying. The whole desert floor seemed to shift constantly, as though he were in the middle of one long, ongoing earthquake. An unpleasant odor, like that of burnt hair, lingered in the air. Every so often it was cut by the sweet smell of powdered sugar.

Over on the roof of a small blue trailer, Crumble Bun fought with one of Dr. Jinks's agents. She had her bare hands wrapped around his neck. Screaming, the man, who actually seemed to be some kind of reptile, melted away into crumbs at her feet. His howl echoed across the dunes before dying away.

On the edge of the crater, Mold Man wrestled with another agent. The two men couldn't seem to get the drop on each other. Mold Man kept creating huge clumps of spores on parts of the man's body to trip him up. But then the agent would lash out with a long pink tongue and wrap it around Mold Man's ankle or wrist, pulling him off his feet. Only when Mold Man covered the agent's head in a giant green glob did the battle start to turn in his favor.

"Take that!" Mold Man shouted, before the agent struck him over the head with his ray gun. There was a crunching sound, and the blue bulb in his helmet broke. Suddenly, Mold Man began to turn green and expand. "Here we go again," he shouted as the agent ran for his life from the growing mold ball.

Surrounded by shouts and booms, Vince flopped around on the floor of the SUV like a turtle turned on its back. Suddenly the door to the SUV flew open, and who was standing there but Gene Brennick.

Vince wasn't speechless, but he was close. "What are you doing here, dude?"

Gene climbed in. He sat there very calmly, his hands in

his lap, blue goop trickling weakly from one ear. "I wanted to say I'm sorry," he said.

Vince couldn't hit his friend with his fists, so he head butted him in the shoulder. "You want to say your sorry *now*?" he said. "We're in the middle of an intergalactic conflict here!"

"My mom always told me that when you have something on your mind, it's best to just say it," said Gene.

"Your mom also told you that it's okay to drink milk after the expiration date," said Vince. "Your mom's a little weird, man."

"It doesn't matter," said Gene. "I've been doing a lot of thinking."

Above them, an above-ground swimming pool spiraled through the air and crashed into a billion splinters on the road. Someone screamed.

"Now's *not* the time!" shouted Vince.

"Then when is the time?" asked Gene.

"When we're not about to die!" shouted Vince.

Gene huffed and ran a hand through his hair. "Well, you can wait for however long you want, you stubborn jerk," he said. "But I just wanted you to know that you're the best friend I ever had. And just because we don't always like the same things or do things the same way doesn't mean we can't be best friends. I'm sorry, Vince. I'm sorry I didn't listen to you all those times."

This seemed to calm Vince down, and he smiled. "I'm sorry I helped write that article about you. It was stupid."

"I deserved it," said Gene. "I was acting like a traitor." Then he leaned over and hugged his friend.

"Um, Gene," said Vince.

"Yeah, man?" said Gene.

"Could you untie me?"

Blinking, Gene looked at his friend, who was still trussed up like a turkey, head to toe in ropes. "Sure, sorry," he said.

It looked as though he was going to say something else. Unfortunately, he never had the chance. From out in the trailer park there came a horrible tearing sound. It was enough to make any fourteen-year-old boy nervous. And in this case, there were two of them.

The horrible tearing that Gene and Vince heard was the sound of Dr. Jinks reaching up and breaking one of the nearby telephone poles in half. Grinning wickedly, the evil alien held the shattered wooden log as if it were a giant baseball bat. Then she reeled back, raised one leg, and swung. *Crack!*

The heavy end of the telephone pole struck the trailer next to Fred's, knocking it up high in the air. It hung there for a second, about fifty feet above the sand, before plummeting silently to the ground again. When it landed on top of Fred's Airstream, the whole mess burst into a spinning fireball.

To everyone within earshot, the explosion sounded like the end of the world. It was a noise often associated with Dr. Jinks, who had leveled numerous cities and been responsible for the destruction of at least one planet. That's probably why she didn't have all that many friends.

A tremendous wind whooshed over the desert, howling, as pieces of torn aluminum shot in every direction. Bolts and screws hailed down into the dunes, leaving steaming black holes where they hit. Furniture began falling, big, flaming hunks of upholstery. Fred's satellite TV dish whistled down from the sky like a Frisbee, spinning over the edge of the crater.

"Wow," whispered Walter as he watched the two hulking trailers burn. He was so distracted by the spectacle that he didn't look up in time to see Dr. Jinks wind up for her second at-bat.

With a thundering rush of air, the telephone pole caught Walter squarely in the chest. *Thud!* He grunted, feet coming up right out of his borrowed loafers. A pain rattled through his chest, and it reminded him of the time just recently when he'd been struck by lightning.

His limp body soared in an arc high above everyone. For the briefest of seconds he was lost in the flickering sun, like a golf ball after a strong drive. Then he appeared again. And he fell. And he fell. And he fell, until he struck the sand with such force that he caved in the ground around him.

Lying on his back in a small crater of his own making, Walter Sparrow was down for the count. Next to him was the metal porthole that led down into the spacecraft that had once brought him to Earth. It was all that was left of Fred's Airstream.

Dr. Jinks stomped toward him. "You dare try to fight me!" she roared. "Me! You know better than that, brother! I *am* going to bring you back, and you won't be able to hide among these weak, ignorant humans any longer. They've turned you into a fragile, scared, mushy little version of the creature you once were." She laughed, a sound like someone struggling for breath underwater. "You came here to be free, but they treat you like some kind of freakish beast. It's almost sad. You know, brother, the one person you can never hide from is yourself. You'll always be different."

Walter lifted his head, and with his remaining breath, he whispered, "These humans like me for who I am." With that, his head hit the sand.

At Dr. Jinks's signal, the two remaining Bozon agents

rushed across the parking lot to finish off Walter as he lay unconscious. Before they could reach him, however, a gruff voice called out. "Step off!"

Hip-Hop Sasquatch leaped out from behind a neighboring trailer in a whirl of fur. Hitting Dr. Jinks in the back, he sent her sprawling into a septic tank, where she banged her head against the rusty side and dropped to the ground, eyes shut. Panicked, the Bozon agents backed away from Walter, their weapons leveled at the hairy alien in the puffy vest. They knew to be ready for anything.

Not only was Hip-Hop Sasquatch hip and stylish but he was also the most dangerous beat-boxer in four nebulas. And as the agents circled him, trying to keep their distance, he began to do his thing. His mouth expanded. It grew so large, it looked completely unnatural on his face. Then, with a deep breath, he began to make a sound. If written down, it would look something like this: *Pffbfhfbfbfbf, puh uhuhhuhuh, chick chick chick ubahubabababababa!*

As most people do when they first hear the Hip-Hop Sasquatch's alien power, the agents began to laugh. They didn't know what else to do. It was a common reaction.

They didn't laugh for long, though. They stopped when they felt their insides wiggle. And what started out as a wiggle became a quiver. Then that quiver became a shake.

As Hip-Hop Sasquatch continued to beat-box, the agents grew more and more uncomfortable. This was because he was shaking them apart molecule by molecule. Not that they could have ever guessed that this was happening to them.

Puhpuhpuhpuhpuh, eek eek hubba, blblblblblblblblb-phbthbtbh!

With shrieks of pain, the agents grabbed their heads, only to have them pop a few seconds later. Their headless bodies dropped to the parking lot, steaming from the neck.

Hip-Hop Sasquatch wound down his song, and then looked around for someone to high-five. He should have been paying more attention. A red laser beam zapped from out of nowhere and hit him with such force that he went flying backward and right through the giant Crater Park billboard. There was a crash, and he plopped spread-eagle to the sand, out cold. Where the little green man had once stood, there was now a giant Sasquatch-shaped hole.

Fortunately for Walter, this battle had provided enough of a distraction for Gene and Vince to open the space-ship hatch and drag his lifeless body inside. They tugged him down the spiral steps, not trying at all to keep his head from bumping every step. With every crack to the skull he made an *ugh* noise, hoping someone would notice. Nobody did.

Vince was last down the steps. Turning around, he tried to pull the hatch down after him, to lock it, but a pair of claws jammed into the open space. They blocked the door before he could close it.

"Going somewhere?" shrieked Dr. Jinks, sticking her face into the gap. Her skin had turned a bright red color, her eyes a bright, crackling white. She snapped angrily at Vince's skull with a set of teeth like steak knives.

Terrified, Vince screamed. Then he tried to get away as fast as possible and ended up tumbling down on top of the others, sending all of them to the floor of the corridor in a pile of arms and legs.

Jumping back to their feet, Gene and Vince pulled Walter's limp body into the nearest cabin, where Lucy was pacing the room.

"Hi," said Lucy, rushing over. "What's going on up there?"

Gene placed a finger to his lips. Lucy shut her mouth.

Together, the three of them pulled Walter into the cabin and laid him on the bunk. He appeared to be breathing, but it was shallow. Gene left his side, and then peered around the doorway, watching as Dr. Jinks climbed down the spiral stairs into the ship. She was alone, and she was back in her human form.

Gene couldn't believe how ordinary she looked. Moments ago she'd resembled something you might find on your plate at Red Lobster, and now she'd changed back to her old pretty guidance counselor self. The only difference was that her expensive dark suit had been almost entirely destroyed in the fire, and now she walked around with nothing but the collar and a single sleeve attached to her body. Underneath she wore a white blouse and boxer shorts with little smiley faces on them. And her busted high-heeled shoes, of course.

Very slowly, Dr. Jinks crept down the cramped little hallway of the ship. "You know something," she said, as she peered into each of the small rooms. "Now that I've found this planet—so small, so helpless, so out-of-the-way—I may just take it for myself. Perhaps I'll make all of you humans slaves. Think about it. I'd have my own empire. Why does everyone else get to have all the fun?"

She spun around to face an open door, and then shot a huge fountain of flame into the room. No one was there. A choking smoke filled the corridor.

"Come on, Walter," said Dr. Jinks. "Come on, Gene. Don't you want to go to the Xenon system? There's a lot of planning still to be done for the party." She slowly made her way toward the far end of the bunker, where Walter's old escape pod sat open and waiting for the day he'd never use it. "It's a straight shot," she went on. "Don't make me go back empty-handed. Uncle Vargon would be very upset to see me without anything to show for myself. Nothing bothers him more than a slacker."

Then it hit Gene like a slap in the face—like one of his tentacles' slaps.

As quietly as possible, he stepped in close to Vince and placed his cupped hand right up to his best friend's ear. He whispered a few words, just enough to get his plan across. It didn't take much. They were best friends, after all.

A minute later, Dr. Jinks was reaching the end of the corridor, when Vince appeared several doors down. He stood in the small empty pod at the farthest end of the spacecraft.

"Hey, doc!" he shouted. "Nice boxer shorts." And he stuck out his tongue.

Dr. Jinks whirled toward him, eyes flashing, her fingers extending to become giant red claws. She snapped them loudly, a sound like a cracking eggshell.

When she didn't follow him right away, Vince did the same little butt dance he'd done for Gene that day outside Dr. Jinks's office window. It wasn't classy, but it got the job done. With a squealing hiss, she rushed at him, claws raised. She left a trail of fire as she ran. It vanished in small, rippling wisps. Speeding over the doorway, she entered the small escape pod, trapping Vince inside.

This, however, was exactly what the boys had been counting on.

"Gene!" screamed Vince.

"Okay!" screamed Gene as he stepped into the corridor.

Whirling like lassos, Gene's tentacles leaped out of his back and flew to several different places at once. Smarty—the one that always seemed to know what it was doing—snapped high over Dr. Jinks's head, causing her to cry out in fear. However, it was not aiming for the guidance counselor but for Vince. The tentacle wrapped around his arm, and with a powerful tug, it lifted him off the floor, over her head, and out of the room. Meanwhile, Angry—the tentacle that liked to hit people—did what it did best, and slammed into Dr. Jinks's chest. This sent her stumbling backward, deeper into the escape pod, and she fell banging against the back wall.

She wasn't down for long and pulled herself back to her feet with one red clawed hand. "All you're doing is making me madder," she said coolly, a ball of fire surrounding her entire body. "You can't keep running."

Gene grinned. "You're right," he said.

There was a loud snapping sound, like the crack of a bullwhip. The tentacle Gene liked to call Tricky shot across the length of the corridor in less than a second, extending to a tentacle span of probably fifteen feet. It clamped its rubbery tip around the handle of the escape pod door, and then yanked. The hatch slammed shut with a satisfying thump. It closed with such force that it knocked Dr. Jinks backward, and she landed on the floor with her high heels sticking up at the ceiling.

"Time for liftoff, Vince," said Gene.

With a small nod, Vince lifted his fist and brought it smashing down on the glass box marked BREAK GLASS FOR EJECTION. He hurriedly cleared the glass away, and then hammered the big button beneath.

A loud siren began to blare, and both Gene and Vince covered their ears. Red lights above the cabin doorways began to spin, moving faster and faster. Dr. Jinks pressed her face to the window of the escape pod, but it didn't stay squished there for long. As she beat at the thick metal door, the screeching siren stopped. Then the spacecraft's gentle hum became a thundering shudder. Chunks of metal fell from the top of the corridor, clanging to the floor. The incredible rumble made the boys forget everything else that was going on, even Dr. Jinks. It felt and sounded as if a volcano were about to erupt underneath their very feet.

Behind its door, the small escape pod started moving. Orange flames sprang up, licking around its base. Then, as if someone had pulled a trigger, the whole room suddenly shot up a long chute leading to the surface. Its jets left blackened streaks along the walls of the long, straight vertical tunnel, and if one really thought about it, they might have thought the streaks looked a bit like claw marks.

As the escape pod rocketed upward through the sand, it blew a hole in the ceiling of the spaceship and out through the desert ground above. And then it—and Dr. Jinks— were gone, lost in the vast blueness of the Santa Rosa sky. She was on her way home empty-handed.

After several minutes, Gene and Vince pulled them- selves up and dusted themselves off. They stood gazing up through that huge gaping hole at the beautiful morning that awaited them.

"Nice job," said Gene.

"Same to you," said Vince.

A moment passed.

Gene bit his lip. "Can I, um, write this story?" he asked.

"It's all yours," said Vince with a smile.

25

FBI SPECIAL AGENT DONALD FAY HAD SEEN A LOT IN forty-four years. He'd seen a man rob a bank wearing nothing but a barrel and clown shoes. He'd seen a woman kidnap an eel. He'd seen a rotating blue circle in the sky that he'd reported as a UFO, only to find out later that it was a side effect of some allergy medicine he was taking.

As head of the government's *actual* department on unexplained events—known as the WUS, or Weird and Unexplained Stuff, department—Agent Fay had seen his fair share of weird and unexplained stuff. But nothing could have prepared him for the sight that greeted him upon driving into the Crater Park trailer residence.

Crater Park was a disaster area. When Agent Fay first set foot inside, he thought a tornado had touched down in the middle of the neighborhood. Six of the ten mobile homes had been lifted off the ground and tossed every which way, and most had burned to a crisp. One trailer even teetered on the edge of the huge crater from which the park got its name. Every inch of sand had been blackened by fire, and most of it had changed into smooth pools of shiny glass. Far across the park from where it belonged, a broken telephone pole stuck up out of the desert like the mast of a sinking ship.

Scattered everywhere were heaping piles of what looked like coffee cake. It smelled like it too. As Agent Fay watched, some of his crime-scene investigators collected crumbs in small plastic bags. He even caught one of them tasting some. He reminded himself to fire that guy later. He'd never liked him much anyway.

Frowning, Agent Fay walked through the wreckage. On the other side waited the police officer in charge of the local investigation. His name was Officer Barnes. He was a plump man with a small black hairpiece that he adjusted whenever he got nervous. Agent Fay didn't like Officer Barnes that much. The man sprayed spit when he talked, and he smelled like cream of mushroom soup.

"Barnes," said Agent Fay as he approached. "What do you have for me?"

Officer Barnes anxiously pushed his patch of fake hair

from the front to the back. It slid around on his white head like a hockey puck on ice. "Not quite sure, sir," he said.

"Is this some kind of natural disaster?" asked Agent Fay.

"It sure looks like it," said Officer Barnes. "But it only happened here; *nowhere* else. Most disasters I know don't stick to a half-mile radius."

"Right," said Agent Fay.

"Hey," said Officer Barnes, interrupting. "What do you think happened? I know you guys out there in Washington are hiding something. Tell me. You think this is the work of aliens? What about vampires? I hear the military has been training a vampire army since the nineteen seventies. Of course, it could be some kind of new robot. I bet robots could do damage like this, with those lasers they got." The chubby man moved his hairpiece in little circles, like he was polishing his bald spot. "Come on, Don, give me the scoop."

But Agent Fay was not interested in talking about aliens, vampires, or robots. All Agent Fay wanted to do was find out the real explanation for the mess at Crater Park and get back to his apartment in Washington, D.C.

"Fine," said Officer Barnes, looking incredibly disappointed. "Follow me."

He led Agent Fay through the wreckage. They walked past a pile of empty black suit coats that were still smoking and up a small dune blanketed with long stringy hair. At the top, sitting on a pair of towels with the words FIRE DEPARTMENT OF SANTA ROSA stenciled across them, sat a small group of people. Two of them were kids, boys. They sat next to each other, close, and at first Agent Fay mistook them for brothers.

They were not brothers, but they were best friends.

Eyes closed, Gene relaxed against Vince, exhausted. If it hadn't been for his friend supporting him, he probably would have fallen over. Then he would have fallen right to sleep.

Gene gazed around at Crater Park. It was hardly recognizable. Dr. Jinks had done quite a job of destroying the place, which was apparently what she did best. Not anymore, though. If what Walter said about the escape pod was true, then Dr. Jinks was gone, at least for a long time. Gene figured that a few centuries would be enough time for him to catch his breath.

He felt a heavy hand on his shoulder. It was Walter. "How are you doing?" asked the guidance counselor.

"I'll live," said Gene with a smile.

"At least until he gets us into some more trouble," grumbled Vince.

The boys smiled at each other.

There were plenty of things they could have said to each other right then, but they didn't feel the need to. Words were good sometimes. And sometimes silence was better.

Suddenly, Walter glanced up. His discolored eyes narrowed. Hurriedly standing up, he began to button up his torn shirt, to try and look presentable. He picked crumbs off his pants, popped on his sunglasses, and shook the last blobs of mold from his loafers. And, since it was Walter Sparrow, he finished off by sweeping a hand through his hair, fixing it into a perfect wave that was far too nice for someone who had just been knocked to a height of three thousand feet and then fallen back to earth.

Two men walked up the dune to where the group sat. Gene recognized one of the men as Officer Barnes from the local police station. The other man, however, was someone he'd never seen before. He looked important, like a mayor, or a businessman in a comic strip. Much of his face was hidden behind a bushy brown mustache, and he wore an expensive suit with a long watch chain looping from a pocket. As they approached, the stranger held up his hand and flashed a fancy badge.

"Hello," said Walter, shaking hands with the policeman, and then with his companion. "My name is Walter Sparrow."

"I'm Agent Fay, WUS," said the stranger. "What happened here, Mr. Sparrow?"

"Fire broke out," said Walter, shrugging. "It was the strangest thing."

Reaching into the pocket of his coat, Agent Fay removed a small pad of paper, on which he scribbled something. "Walter Sparrow, huh?" he said with disgust, as if it were an insult. "I've got all sorts of reports about you." Eyes still on his notes, Agent Fay began to read.

"About a week ago, one Walter Sparrow was revealed in a local newsletter to be related to an extraterrestrial." He cleared his throat. "A day after that there are reports of a man shooting flames from his hands and cars dropping from the sky. These incidents took place at the residence of one Walter Sparrow. Several days before, an entire location of Dippin Donuts mysteriously disappears. Witnesses claim it was turned to crumbs by a strange girl and her two young companions."

Gene, Vince, and Walter looked at one another worriedly.

Finally, Agent Fay ended by stuffing his pad back into

his coat pocket with a crunch of paper. "And finally, we get reports of a light show from down here at the trailer park. People are claiming to have seen all sorts of fireballs and felt earthquakes." He grunted. "They say they saw a rocket ship take flight, zoom right up over the horizon there, if you can believe that."

"Incredible," said Walter.

This did not seem to please Agent Fay. He seemed to think Walter was mocking him. Pointing a lumpy finger in Walter's face, he began to bark angrily, "I'm no dummy, Mr. Sparrow. I know when people are pulling pranks. Fireballs, rocket ships, mold men. I tell you, not once in my career have I ever found a speck of evidence to prove that aliens really exist. And I will not start believing in them now."

"So what are you asking?" said Walter, folding his arms.

"I'm asking you to tell me what you're hoping to get out of this whole hoax of yours," said Agent Fay.

With all eyes on him, Walter thought his answer over very carefully. He scratched his chin, humming, and then glanced at the two boys. Then he turned to the policeman. "Officer Barnes, could I speak with Agent Fay in private, please?" he asked.

Agent Fay nodded his okay, and Officer Barnes left to check on his men investigating the crater.

Walter waited for a few minutes, until he was sure Officer Barnes was gone and that there was no one else within earshot. Once he was satisfied, he stepped forward. Even when he wasn't freaking out in alien form, Walter was an imposing guy. Stepping up to the tiny WUS agent, he towered over him. "Listen, Fay," he said, growing very serious. "I think it's in your best interests to turn around and walk away now."

Agent Fay gave him a curious look. "What do you mean?" he asked.

"You think this is all a big joke," said Walter, and then he smiled. "Well, I promise you it's not." Lifting a hand, he pulled down his silver sunglasses, and his eyes flashed— one red and one purple.

Agent Fay's face changed to the color of tapioca. "I d-don't understand," he stuttered.

"You are going to leave us alone," said Walter. "You're going to make all of those reports you just mentioned go away."

"I am?" asked Agent Fay.

"Yes," said Walter, placing a hand on the man's shoulder.

Then it was Agent Fay's turn to grow bold. Straightening up, he cleared his throat. "I'm not one to be easily rattled, Mr. Sparrow," he said.

"You're not?" asked Walter, surprised.

"No," said Agent Fay. "I was chosen for my position with the agency for one reason and one reason only, and that's because I don't care why something bad happens. My job is just to make sure it doesn't happen again." He wagged his stubby finger at the three of them. "I don't care if Bigfoot came in here and made this mess."

Vince cleared his throat. "Actually, he's more of a sasquatch, sir."

"Pardon me?" snapped Agent Fay. "Did you say something?"

"No, sir," said Vince. "Nothing."

A large crease appeared in Walter's forehead as he tried to understand the situation. "So what are you saying?" he asked.

"What I'm saying," said Agent Fay, "is that if I scratch your back, then you need to scratch mine."

"Are you really going to scratch each other's backs?" asked Gene.

"No," both men said together, glaring down at him.

"Gosh, sorry," said Gene.

Agent Fay put away his badge and rested one hand on his saggy little waist. "If I agree to clean up your little messes, then I'm going to need your help making sure *your* people don't pull another stunt like this."

"I think he means Ails," said Gene.

"Moon Men, Mildred the Martian, Ails, I don't care what you call them," said Agent Fay. "If there're some bad ones out there, then it's a threat to this country." He nodded at Walter, and the two men made eye contact and held it for a few seconds. "If you can help me find them, track them, and stick them somewhere they can't hurt anybody, then maybe we can make ourselves a deal."

"To help you keep humans safe," said Walter, finally understanding.

"To help keep *everyone* safe," said Agent Fay, correcting him. "That's what you want isn't it?"

"Yes," answered Walter, without having to think about it.

Walter turned to the boys. "I'm going to keep talking to Agent Fay," he said. "You guys should go check on the others, and your mom, Gene."

"You sure you want us to go?" asked Vince.

"I've got this," said Walter, giving a thumbs-up.

Side by side, the boys wandered through the wreckage back to the spaceship entrance. A circle of cops stood around the blackened and warped hatch, snapping pictures. Splinters of telephone pole the size of his fist stuck out of the sand like wooden stakes. The trailer park looked like a war zone. That's when it sank in for Gene—he'd barely survived. He'd been lucky, too lucky. And how long could he expect such good luck to hold out?

He wondered, *Is Dr. Jinks really gone?* It was the kind of question he couldn't answer, like, *What is the capital of Algeria?* or *What is the weight of an average human spleen?* Gene had never been very good at answering those sorts of questions. It certainly appeared as if Dr. Jinks had been sent into space for a long journey back to the terrible place she'd come from. He could still hear her angry screams in his head. So maybe she was gone forever. Maybe he'd seen the last of her and her posse of strange thugs.

But while he wasn't the smartest kid in Santa Rosa, he was smart enough to know that no matter what things looked like, there was often more to the story that you couldn't see. It had been that way with the *Globe*. It had been that way with Walter Sparrow. It had even been that way with him. Just when you think you've got it all figured out, there's always another surprise waiting around the corner.

Epilogue

"WHO WANTS ROOT BEER?" CALLED MRS. BRENNICK, walking down the spiral steps. "And there's plenty of tinfoil left, if you're hungry?" She descended the stairs to Walter's old spaceship, which he'd recently renamed the *Aardvark* after the Fulton school mascot. It wasn't the most exciting name for a Class III Intergalactic Stealth Cruiser, but it's the thought that counts.

In the various cabins along the main corridor sat the staff of the *Globe*, all of them hunched over their desks, working hard on the newsletter's next issue. It was a school night, but the staff was in a good mood. That's because Gene had just gotten the first ever interview with Colossal Cal, a giant who lived in the old airplane hangar off Highway 10.

Everyone was there—Gene, Vince, Lucy, Linus, Arachnid Boy, Mold Man, and even Hip-Hop Sasquatch. Only

Loud Matt was missing, and that's because he was on a date with Crumble Bun. They'd gone out for sushi at a restaurant that Fish Foot had recommended. Part of Fish Foot's family worked there, but thankfully not as sushi.

Sixth months had passed since the events involving Dr. Jinks and her short career as the guidance counselor of Santa Rosa Junior High School. Since then, things had not returned to normal but had actually gotten much, much better. Little things that seemed to matter before—like popularity or kisses—mattered less. Big things that really did matter now—like friendship or doing the right thing—mattered more. Or at least they seemed to. When Gene and Vince got up in the morning and went to school, they were excited for what the day might hold, not worried about what their classmates thought about them.

Soon after the battle in Crater Park, the boys had moved the newsletter out of the AV studio in room 113 and into the *Aardvark*, which was now partially uncovered but still a secret to nearly everyone. The old ship had been transformed from a dusty old relic into a bustling newsroom. The cabins were filled with cushy bean bags and aquariums to make them like work cubicles only homier. There was even a Ping-Pong table in the infirmary, on which Vince had conquered Gene in the now famous Brennick Ping-Pong Pounding.

All of these items—as well as the computers, the soft-serve ice cream dispenser, the Coke machine, and just about everything else—were, of course, gifts from the U.S. government.

Mrs. Brennick sat on the edge of Gene's desk, and then offered him some refreshments from the tray. "Snack?" she asked.

"Thanks," he said, snatching some tinfoil from the bowl. One of his tentacles—the one he'd officially named Smarty—continued to bang on the keyboard of his computer, finishing that issue's lead story.

"How are things going?" she asked.

"Awesome," said Gene, nodding. "The aliens of Granger just asked to be put on the subscription list." He shrugged. "There are only about twenty of them, but they don't know anyone outside their town, so they're excited to get the newsletter." Granger was a town about ten miles outside of Santa Rosa. Once upon a time it had been the sandal capital of California. Now it was just another small town in which an alien ran the department of solid waste removal. Like aliens everywhere, those in Granger wanted to find others of their kind.

It was true. With the threat of Dr. Jinks gone, the aliens of the Santa Rosa County area were feeling safer than they had in decades. As a result, they'd begun to pull together, to form a community of their own within the human world. No longer did they need to hide from one another in small groups for fear of being tracked, caught, and sent back to the Xenon system, where Vargon would use their souls to power an evil birthday carousel or turn their skins into party hats. So began a new period of happiness and security for humans and aliens alike.

And surprisingly, there were many more aliens around town than even Gene had expected. People he talked to every day turned out to be from another planet. Like the weird little guy who worked at the burrito buggy, or the woman who went door-to-door selling makeup. Even Mr. Mahoney, Gene and Vince's principal at Santa Rosa High School, admitted that he was a runaway from the all-robot planet of Megavolt. This fact didn't explain why he was such a terrible dresser, but it did explain a lot. Since all these aliens felt safer, they wanted to start enjoying one another's company too. That's where the *Globe* came into play.

What had started as a two-page newsletter stapled together and stuffed into a blue plastic bag had become a hugely popular online blog and social networking site. Aliens from anywhere and everywhere could log on and see what their friends were doing. They could chat, post pictures, and tell their stories. Every week Gene posted a new article, but it wasn't a piece of investigative journalism. Not like the old days. These were human-interest stories. Or in this case, *alien*-interest stories.

"Look who came with me," said Mrs. Brennick with a grin. "Hey, honey, get down here!" She gestured to a man standing at the top of the spiral stairs, only the cuffs of his brown corduroy pants visible.

Nervously running a hand through his hair, Walter Sparrow descended into Bunker 13. He gave a wave to the kids hard at work, and then gazed around. "The place looks good," he said. "A lot better than it looked when I first got here."

Walter walked over to Gene's desk and stood there with his arms crossed. "How's my favorite webmaster?" he asked.

"Good," said Gene. Then he smiled. "How's my favorite secret agent?"

The hint of a smile crept up in the corners of Walter's mouth, but just as soon as it appeared, it was gone. "Can't say," he said. "It's classified."

After Walter's little discussion with the WUS agent, Agent Fay, he'd started working with the government. He still spent three days a week at Santa Rosa Junior High School as their new acting guidance counselor. But when he wasn't helping young people with their problems, Walter was traveling the country with WUS, chasing down aliens that had come to Earth for less than peaceful purposes. He felt it was the best way to give back to the planet that had given him so much. Plus, he got to wear a badge and carry a gun.

Walter spent most of his evenings at the Brennicks' house. He shared dinner with Gene and his mother and often helped the boys with their blog. He enjoyed nothing more than being around his friends. There was even time in his schedule to play racquetball with Fulton Junior High School's Principal Pinkus once a month.

"Hey, Haskell!" called Walter. When he saw that Vince was wearing his earphones, he reached over and peeled them off the boy's head.

"Whoa, hey," said Vince, grabbing around at his head. Confused, he glanced around until he saw Walter. Then he grinned and saluted. "Agent Sparrow, I presume?" he said.

"Where's my pal Fred?" asked Walter.

Vince stretched. "He's up at the big comic convention in San Diego," he said. "We've got a presentation there, for a new spin-off."

"Fabulous," said Walter. "That's just fabulous."

After everything that had happened, Gene's cousin Fred finally decided to stop trying to publish his version of the *Arachnid Boy* comic. Instead, he chose to write something new. It was a graphic novel called *Squid Kid*, and it was the heroic story of a boy who suddenly grows tentacles and is thrown into an adventure in which he must save the world from a power-hungry alien and her army of lizard men.

He had help. Another writer collaborated with him on the project, a young up-and-coming scribe by the name of Vince Haskell.

So far *Squid Kid* had been a huge hit, much larger than anyone had expected. Everyone agreed that it was only a matter of time before both Fred and Vince became famous. Not that Vince cared about that sort of thing. He was fine with just sitting at his desk and creating. Strangely enough, he found that his writer's block went away as soon as he and Gene stopped fighting and became friends again.

"Well, I'm going to go home and get ready for dinner," said Mrs. Brennick, kissing Walter on the cheek. "Will you boys be joining me?"

"I'll go with you now," said Walter. He and Gene exchanged mock salutes, and then the guidance counselor turned government alien hunter headed back upstairs, hand in hand with Mrs. Brennick.

Gene, Vince, Lucy, and Linus kept working as the evening wore on. Like every night, there was some laughter and some insults, some Ping-Pong, and even a few thrown Cheeze Doodles. But it was all in good fun. Even when one of Gene's tentacles tried to feed Linus a moldy nectarine it found behind a bookshelf.

The staff of the *Globe* newsletter had done very well. They were happy. And isn't that all anyone can really ask for?

At the end of the evening, Gene shut down his computer and rubbed his swollen eyes. Whenever he closed them, he saw the vibrating blue square of his monitor. The buzz of his desk's power strip seemed to have settled into his very bones. Yawning, he stood up and collected his backpack, notepads.

Most of the rest of the staff had gone to a movie. Not Lucy. She still relaxed in one corner of the infirmary, hugged on all sides by bean bags. A cooling mug of tea sat next to her on the carpet. It smelled faintly of chamomile.

Gene pulled his sweatshirt from his chair and crossed the infirmary to where she sat. "You're staying late," he said.

"Ever since I started writing articles, I haven't been able to slow down," said Lucy, grinning. "Did you know that Fish Foot can't swim?" She started laughing. "The guy's name is Fish Foot, and he has a fear of water. He can't even stand to be around the lobster tank at the supermarket." She was so tired, she had trouble stopping her laughter. "He cries every time it rains."

"Wow," said Gene. "You learn something new every day."

"I can only imagine some of the weird stuff you and Vince have seen," she said, closing her laptop with a click. "I'm so used to hearing about this stuff from you guys. It's nice to experience it firsthand for a change."

"Well," said Gene, helping her up, "Vince isn't going to be going out on any more stories with me. He wants to stay around here and manage the comic and do a bunch of other stuff that bores me." They walked out into the long passage.

"Really?" asked Lucy. She climbed the spiral steps and unscrewed the hatch. It was a cool night. The moon glowed gray behind clouds.

"Yeah," said Gene, shrugging. When he reached an opening, he paused behind her. "I was wondering if you wanted to be my new partner."

Lucy stared at him for a few seconds, and then blinked. "Are you serious?" she asked.

Gene blushed. He had stared down more than a few aliens, but he was still a little nervous around girls—even girls he'd known for a while, like Lucy. "Only if you want to," he said. "If you don't want to, I'd understand." From out of nowhere, his four tentacles rose up behind him and began to snatch up litter from the ground. One of them straightened his hair for him, something he was thinking about but decided not to lift a hand to actually do. "It's okay if you think it's weird that I'm an alien."

What happened next took Gene completely by surprise. Lucy laughed right in his face. "Are you kidding?" she asked. "I got over the shock. I mean, *you* were as surprised as anyone," she said, gesturing to him.

"That's for sure," said Gene.

Then, flexing up onto her tiptoes, Lucy kissed him on the cheek. "Your being an alien doesn't bother me. Maybe that makes me weird, but I'm fine with it. It's who you are, Gene."

Gene didn't know what to say. So instead of saying anything, he gave her a thumbs-up. As soon as he'd done it, he silently yelled at himself for being the world's biggest dork. Who gives a cute girl a thumbs-up after she kisses you?

"I'll see you tomorrow morning, then," said Lucy with a smile and a flip of her hair.

She walked briskly through Crater Park and was soon lost in the darkness of a fantastic California evening. Gene waited for a full minute—until he was sure he couldn't see her anymore. Then he sat down on the closed hatch and tried to catch his breath. He couldn't wipe the smile off his face no matter how hard he tried. Then, wondering why he even wanted to, he stopped trying. Going back inside, he walked down the spiral stairs. He stood on the lowest step and looked at the corridor with its blinking computer monitors and the smell of ozone, and then turned off the lights.

He grabbed his coat and left the spaceship, hoping to get home in time to have leftovers with Walter.

Back in town, Lucy also felt light and bubbly. She had liked Gene ever since they started working at the *Globe* together. Now the two of them would be doing interviews together every day. It was like a dream come true. She hadn't been this happy in seven hundred years. Not since she'd escaped the Clubfoot Nebula in her solar skiff.

Reaching the end of the block, Lucy gazed up at the stars. There were so many. And each one was a place to wonder about, a story to tell.

Removing her white knit shawl, she carefully folded it under one arm. A pair of large, red feathery wings sprouted from her back and expanded. They stretched once, strongly, sending up a cloud of dust from the sidewalk. Then, with a mighty flap, she rocketed up into the night sky in a perfect arc.

She circled the streetlamp once, like a graceful moth, and then soared high into the night until she was lost among the constellations.